THE SUICIDE OF
SOPHIE RAE

CHERIE FRUEHAN

ESSENTIAL ROCKSTAR, LLC

THE SUICIDE OF SOPHIE RAE
FIRST EDITION , FEBRUARY 2019
Copyright © 2018 by Cherie Fruehan
All rights reserved.

EBook ISBN: 978-0-578-45850-2

Trade Paperback ISBN: 978-0-578-45851-9

Copy Edit: Penni Askew, Word Summit Editing

Cover Photo: Brian Guilliaux

Book Design: Cherie Fruehan

Author Photo: Kathy Walden Photography

For permissions contact author: www.cheriefruehan.com

This book is dedicated to all souls.
That they may find their purpose, their place, their worth.
That they know they are loved and needed.
Kindness matters.

…she signed the letter Love, Sophie…

1

THE SIN

Sophie folded the letter, placed the pages in an envelope, and set it into the small mahogany box. The one she discovered on a forgotten shelf, tucked away in the back corner of the antique shop she used to visit to clear her mind.

She was drawn to that box the instant she saw it, a delicate mother-of-pearl butterfly inlaid into its top, with ethereal wings so finely crafted they were almost transparent. Quite a juxtaposition, a symbol of rebirth, fragile and beautiful, being held so firmly in place in the hard, sturdy wood. Yet it was almost as if, at any moment, those same wings could disengage themselves and flutter away as freely as a warm summer breeze.

She closed her eyes, yearning to feel the imaginary breeze on her face, but allowed herself only a second of daydreaming. For today she had a plan, and it was important she follow through with it. Today, she would die by her own hands. There were only minutes left.

Minutes to sit at her dressing table, once just another abandoned antique in her same favorite shop, hidden away, half shrouded by an old dusty tapestry piled with equally musty books. When she first spied it nestled in its hiding place, she felt a connection to the table. Its warm wood almost disappeared in the dimly lit shop; the way she liked to

disappear when she entered its doors. The shop was a respite from the
noise in her head; a place where no one knew of her secrets.

Sitting in front of the table now, she admired its confident lines
and its mottled mirror. The images it reflected were speckled with
cloudy imperfections as aged mercury splattered and splintered
throughout the glass, creating varying undulating shapes. She liked to
imagine them as the imprints of the souls of those who sat there,
before her. She wondered who they were, the previous owners. Occa-
sionally, if she sat quietly and stared at the mirror's intriguing blemishes, she thought she could see, and hear, their stories being told. Yet,
what she loved most about her dressing table was that—just like her—
it, too, had a secret. A hidden drawer. A place no one else knew
existed.

She ran her finger along the bottom of the table to find the small
wooden button. She pressed the button, jiggled it just right, and the
small drawer popped open. It revealed a place she could hide away
parts of herself, to be protected forever. This sacred vessel contained
the very few and precious treasures from her life. A vintage crystal
rosary, a slim gold wedding band, a faded photograph of her father, and
the piece of torn fabric.

That fabric! She kept it locked away because it could speak, and
boy, the stories it told. As she looked at its brutally torn edges, it was
as if it were trying to scream at her, to tell its tale. Over and over. A
story she'd heard too many times before. Today, she refused to listen to
the screaming. She wanted it out of her mind forever. She wanted to
scream right back at that shrieking fabric. Tell it to shut up.

She quickly tucked her beautiful butterfly box into her drawer of
secret treasures, and closed it so the fabric would just hush. She
thought she heard it whisper "Stop!" as the drawer clicked closed.

She looked into the intriguing old mirror, and wondered if it was
watching her now. Would it remember this moment and imprint it into
faded mercury in order tell her story to someone else in the future?
Would it explain to them why she didn't have the courage to live
anymore? Would it record the fire burning in her eyes, the candle
reflected in them? The type of candle people lit in church when they

wanted to send a quiet prayer up to the heavens. Should she send a prayer right now? Was anyone even listening?

Sophie sighed, strangely peaceful, as a warmth filled her belly. A calm absent for a very long time. No chilling knot tucked inside. No lumps inhabited her throat. No indecision twisted or confused her mind. On this evening she was decided and determined. Her plan was the right thing to do. She reveled in her newfound strength and the power that lay in her hands. Yet, at the same time, she was still as fragile as a butterfly, frozen in wood, hidden in a secret drawer with the screaming fabric.

In the mirror's reflection, she saw herself as much older than thirty-two. Weary from the world. Tarnished and mottled like untouched silver, ignored and abandoned, left on an open shelf to oxidize in the harsh atmosphere. Abused and unloved.

She picked up her antique hairbrush, the one that belonged to her grandmother, and began to brush her long hair. The brush was silver, inlaid with iridescent mother-of-pearl, with a matching comb and hand mirror. She imagined her father's mother lining the trio up neatly on her own dresser. These, and the crystal rosary, were the only things she had that belonged to a family she never really knew. She wondered if her ancestors' souls inhabited the items they left behind.

Spying a white cotton ribbon peeking out of one of the regular drawers of her dressing table, she carefully slid it out without opening the drawer. It still carried the faint smell of vanilla from the bakery box it once encircled.

She gathered her hair into a low ponytail exposing her graceful neck, and methodically wound the ribbon around auburn curls, one, two, three for good travels, and tied the rest into a bow. This will do. She returned the brush to its place on her dressing table just as she had imagined her grandmother must have done.

Lipstick. She ran her finger along the gold tube purchased just for the occasion. It was a lovely package. Expensive. Something unfamiliar to her as she never wore makeup. She never wanted to attract attention. Better to be invisible. However, she always wondered what it would be like to have glamorous cherry lips. The kind fascinating women wore when they went to the Oscars. Women who made a career out of attracting attention, who wanted people to see them. Who, with their matte pouts, blew kisses from the palms of their hands.

She opened the tube and turned the bottom. Slowly, the new stick of red molded wax churned up from its vessel, untouched and perfect —the way she longed to be. Like a warrior going into battle, she stained her lips. She took one last glance at herself in the cloudy mirror of past souls and rose from her seat. She leaned toward her reflection and, with hand to mouth, blew herself a kiss. As she leaned away, she could almost see the mark it left behind as the crimson kiss floated to the glass, becoming yet another mercurial imprint. *Goodbye, Sophie, see you on the other side.*

She blew out the candle, watching the smoke spiral in a dance of curly strands. She picked up the delicate chair, turned away, and walked toward the closet. She pushed open the door to the closet, which switched on the automatic overhead light, illuminating a sparse row of modest but immaculately organized clothing, lined up from lightest to darkest on precisely spaced hangers. Painfully orderly.

Normally, a closet might be a place where one hid their dirty laundry, leaving rumpled piles of clothing tossed on the floor. A place where one could close the door and have no fear anyone would see the mess left behind. Tonight, she would leave her dirty laundry in the closet. She would leave her mess behind.

Sophie placed the small chair in the middle of the closet floor. She walked over to where her two belts—one thin, one thick—were neatly hung. She brushed her hand across the two of them and, if only for a moment, watched them sway in place, swaying along with them, rocking herself to keep the calm. She lifted the thicker belt from its hook and raised it to her nose, inhaling deeply. Her senses heightened, she could smell the earth within the belt. She closed her eyes to concentrate on the almost mossy scent, and for a split second she felt the hairs on the back of her neck stand up. She thought she heard that damned piece of fabric's muffled scream coming from the secret drawer in her dressing table. Her eyes grew wide. *Not now! Stop your screaming! I don't want to hear that story ever again!*

Standing on the seat of the chair, Sophie hurled the buckle end of the belt over the higher bar in the closet. Straining to reach, she slipped the leather end through the buckle and fastened it. It was much more out of her reach than she had imagined it would be, forcing her to stand on tiptoes to slip her head through the loop. She took a deep breath and rested her neck on the earthy leather. Raising up again, she wrapped the loop around her neck one more time. She felt pressure in her neck, something lodged in her throat. She instinctively wanted to swallow, but she couldn't. Was it the rush of adrenaline in her ears, or could she still hear the muffled sounds coming from the secret drawer? *Please stop! I've had enough of that narrative in this lifetime!* Still standing on the tips of her toes, she held onto the noose with both hands, when something unexpected caught her eye.

She caught a glimpse of the scene she was creating reflected in the mirror which hung at the end of the closet. A new, pristine mirror, and unlike the aged mirror of her dressing table, this one did not contain the story of anyone else before her. She was its only owner. This mirror was clear, and the picture was sharp. Sophie blinked hard. It took her a moment to focus. It was surreal. As if she was watching from outside of her body. The reality of what she was doing to herself hit her hard. A gut punch. A moment ago it was a good enough plan. A plan to take her own life. A plan which took months to develop. But now, she desperately wanted to protect the girl in the mirror. She had a change of heart. Maybe there was another solution to make the pain of the past disappear.

However, she was no longer in control. Her fingers felt numb. She had no leverage. The noose tightened. As her throat constricted, she started to choke. She wished she could shout, "Someone help! Help me, please!" A phrase she needed to scream so many times before, but never could. Forget about that now. Who would have heard her anyway, over the screaming of the fabric stuffed away in the secret drawer? Her toes cramped from trying to support her unstable, shaking body. Her calves knotted and burned. The noose tightened further. Her neck was collapsing. Her face felt hot. Her eyes stung with tears. She could push no higher on her toes. Could she shimmy to the back of the chair? Get some leverage? Escape the loop? Her adrenaline raced. The old steel knots returned to her stomach, the familiar lump in her throat, now crushed as the crude noose painfully constricted. Terror gripped her. *Oh God!*

Sophie heard the despair of the fabric in the drawer with the crystal rosary, the delicate butterfly, and the photo of the father she never met. Her eyesight blurred. She lost sight of the girl in the mirror fighting for her life. She clumsily shuffled her feet, making her way to the back of the shaking chair. With one foot on the seat of the chair, she lifted the other foot to the chair back. Her fingers lost all feeling. Was she still holding herself up? Wobbling, but ready to raise her other foot to join the first, she pushed as hard as she could. Onto the chair back, both feet barely planted atop, knees shaking violently.

An obscure blur of horror, as the girl in the mirror shook uncontrollably. The chair flipped out from under her, felling it forward, slamming the door shut, turning off the automatic light in the impeccably ordered closet which now contained someone's dirty laundry.

2

THE REVELATION

There was a stranger standing before her. *Where am I?* Sophie was confused for a moment trying to remember. Her head felt pressurized as if submerged deep under water. What was the last thing she had done? Bits and pieces of what had happened were now coming back to her, flickering like an old film reel. Fragments of scenes clicked through her mind; the box, the mirror, the lipstick, the closet, her reflection, the panic, and then, as the reel turned faster and faster, the whole story began to play out.

"Ahh, what have you done?" asked the man as he stared at her with great concern. She opened her mouth to speak, but the adrenaline buzzing through her body made it hard to form the words. She tried to concentrate, focusing on the stranger's eyes, for they were soft and soothing, the color of dappled moss. He looked unfamiliar to her, yet there was a familiarity about him. She was pretty sure she did not know him, although, given her current confusion, she couldn't be certain. He seemed curious, definitely concerned, bordering on kind and a little bit stern.

"I-I don't know…" she finally blurted out. "I mean, I do know, it-it was an awful plan," she replied, now feeling the embarrassment of her clumsy attempt at suicide.

Had she seen him before, this man with raven hair? She wondered if he lived in the building. He didn't immediately answer her, but he wrote something into the small leather journal he carried.

"This was not the best idea," he said, looking up to the highest bar in the closet, then at her again, writing.

"It was the best idea I had at the time." She felt his judgment. "I just wanted everything to go away. I didn't want to fight anymore," Sophie replied, wondering why she was justifying her actions to the man standing with her in her closet. *Why is he writing?* "I'm...I'm sorry, who are you?" she asked.

He did not answer her, but turned around and walked out of the closet. She followed him, wondering if he lived in the apartment next door, trying to remember if she had called out and it bothered him enough for him to let himself in. Did he help her from her unfortunate circumstance? Was he there taking notes for the complaint he was going to file with the building management? That was not what she needed. She didn't want any trouble, and certainly didn't want anyone to know of her awful, failed plan. She had just recently rented the place; a place where she could run away from her troubles. A place no one in her past knew about. She could not be evicted, because then she would have to go back to the other place. That was not going to happen.

"Excuse me, sir, do you live in the building? I'm so sorry if I caused a commotion, and I'm really embarrassed. If we can just pretend this never happened, I promise I won't be any more trouble."

"You don't have much, do you?" said the stranger, slowly making his way from the once spotless, now tainted, closet into the modest apartment.

"What does that matter?" she replied. Sophie's safe haven was sparse, one open living space connected to a small kitchen. She watched the stranger make his notes, both mentally and physically. She suddenly felt self-conscious watching him take in the bareness of her apartment.

One stool was pushed up to a tiny kitchen counter, there were no dishes in the sink, no pots and pans on the stove. Pretty sparse, save for a dry tea kettle thirsting for someone to fill it, wanting to carry out its purpose of warming someone's soul with a soothing beverage. She wondered if he knew there was no tea for two in this kitchen. There was no couple enjoying a candlelit dinner, no girlfriends giggling over a nice red blend. Clearly, it housed only one lost and lonely soul. She knew what he was thinking, looking at this undisturbed, untouched, unloved space.

"The only companion you must have had here was sorrow," he said as he wrote in his leather book. She was speechless at the insight. She felt a jolt run up her spine, and as Sophie observed him, it was almost as if she knew his private thoughts. His broad shoulders hunched as he scribbled in silence. Sophie felt the man's sadness. Or, was it her own sadness she felt?

She watched as he scanned the rest of the space, noticing the small bed in the corner, meticulously made, with sheets and coverlet tucked perfectly in place. Next to the bed was an end table crafted from an old steamer trunk, atop the trunk sat a small lamp, a white candle in a red glass, and a Catholic Bible. Nearest to the nameless man was the only other piece of furniture in the room—the old dressing table with its hidden secrets, missing its chair. As he walked over to the table, she saw him notice the perfectly aligned comb, brush, and hand mirror, the gold tube of lipstick, another candle, the two visible drawers, and the dingy old mirror.

"Sir?" said Sophie, hoping he would not discover the hidden drawer containing her secrets.

He ignored her. Instead, he leaned down to sniff the candle nestled in the red glass, the twin to the other on her bedside table. Her spine tingled. She felt like a bouncing electrified wire downed in a storm. The man glanced in the mirror saying, "C'mon pull yourself together."

Sophie answered him, "I will, I promise." She wondered just how she was going to be able to keep such a promise to the curious stranger chronicling her safe haven. "Can I see you out?"

Abruptly, and with a sense of purpose, the man turned to walk toward the door. Sophie was glad he finally decided to leave.

"Again, I apologize for any inconvenience I may have caused. I hope we can just forget this hap—"

Before she could finish her sentence, the stranger opened the door and said in an exhale, "C'mon in boys. I'm finished for now, so you can do your job."

Immediately, three additional strangers entered the room. One started photographing what little she owned, while the other two, bogged down with equipment, headed straight into her closet. Sophie called out, "What's going on here? Who are you, and who are these people? Why have you let them into my apartment? I don't understand what the problem is. I could not have caused you that much trouble. Sir. SIR, are you even LISTENING TO ME?"

With that, the man with the sympathetic eyes looked up from his notes and turned to look at Sophie.

"Finally," she said, "Thank you for acknowledging me!"

But the man was not looking at her, he was looking past her, almost through her, to the place of her unspeakable shame and regret: the closet. Frustrated, she turned to look as well, and her heart sank fast and hard. She saw the two men who entered the closet reemerge, wheeling a gurney, and atop the gurney was a lovely young woman with splendid matte red, movie star lips. Lips never softly kissed with love and affection. Lips that would never utter the important words needed to capture the man who made her do this to herself.

3

THE DETECTIVE

Detective Sean McGovern watched as the paramedics wheeled the suicide out the apartment door. *What a damn fucking shame*, he thought as he closed his small leather journal.

He had collected about a hundred of them so far. Leather journals, a brand new one for each case, handsome on the outside but filled with horror stories on the inside. Bound indigo etchings of things he could not unwrite, unsee or unfeel. Stories he pieced together by studying his notes, drawings, and crucial first impressions upon arriving at a scene. It was a bit nostalgic when he received his first journal as a congratulatory gift for being promoted to detective, a title held by his father, his grandfather, and his great-grandfather before him. A job that ran so far up his family tree that, even though he was adopted, he felt it was only right to carry on the tradition. Not out of obligation to his family for adopting him, but because he truly wanted to help people. He wanted to follow the clues in his journals, connect the dots, and find justice for those without a voice. The one good thing, after each case was closed, he could file that particular journal away and never have to look at it again. Sometimes, a case stuck with him. Unlike the other guys in his division, he couldn't turn it off as easily.

It was clear to him the moment this mesmeric girl rolled by on the gurney, this was going to be one of those "sticky" cases, one that would cling to him forever. He began to feel a once-familiar discomfort creeping into his belly. It gnawed deep down into his bones, burrowing into the marrow in order to reach his bloodstream and run through his veins, inhabiting every cell of his being. A perceptivity which, up until this actual moment, he successfully suppressed. Intuition. It was an old friend he openly welcomed as a child, but one hushed and shamed by his devout Catholic mother as ungodly.

As a very young boy, Sean enjoyed the friends only he could see and hear, the signs that warned him of danger or impressed upon him things to come. For as long as he could remember, he had quiet conversations with those who came to visit him, those whom others ignored. This clairvoyant child thought it quite a natural thing to experience. Talking to the dead was something everyone did. He found out it was not when, at the age of ten, he told his mother about his playmates, invisible to everyone else, and how they would come and speak to him at his bedside, follow him to school, play with him on the playground, and whisper in his ear not to step off the curb while the unseen car careened around the corner. Sean recalled with vivid clarity the conversation with his mother, and how her expression grew from amused to curious to concerned, then outright panic. Sensing her distress, he even reassured her they were friendly voices, yet regardless of his own confidence he could see he was not going to persuade her otherwise.

For upon hearing the news of her empathic child, the horrified woman blessed herself with the sign of the cross and quickly whisked him off to the local Catholic church to have the priest pray over him and sprinkle him with holy water in order to prevent his soul from being further possessed by "demons."

"I thought the boy used to talk to himself because he was an only child, Father, but this is frightening. Is he possessed?" his mother pleaded with tears in her eyes.

"Relax, Mary," Father Flaherty reassured her in his Dublin accent. "He's just a growin' boy with a healthy imagination, don't ya think?" Straight off the boat from Ireland, Father Flaherty was loved by everyone. He brought a kind of nostalgia to the church services in this small American town.

"I pray so, Father! The alternative is unnatural, the work of the devil, even!" she replied, gripping her son by the hand a little too hard before whisking him out of the church and down the stairs.

Even as a child, Sean knew his mother was overprotective. Being married to a man on the police force made her fear the living, and he knew she did not want to also fear what she could not see.

She grasped him by the shoulders and shook him so he would look directly into her eyes. The intensity of her grip punctuated her words, "Sean, honey, please, when those evil spirits come to you again, tell them to go away! You just shoo them away with your prayers, okay? You are a good Catholic boy, and we love you and want to protect you!"

"Okay, Mommy." Rattled by how upset she was, and how hard his gentle mother squeezed him, he vowed to keep all future visits and voices a secret, until, at some point, he stopped listening to them altogether.

Determined, this gifted child began to silence his intuition and inner guides. He no longer lived his life serendipitously. He no longer listened to the whispers, or followed the signs, knowing somehow ignoring them took away a bit of his innocence. He kept his wonder, however, and as he grew into a young man, started to question everything, including his Catholic faith. For if he was not allowed to believe in the things he did see and hear, then why would he believe in a God he could not see?

A chill ran through him, snapping him out of his memories and back to the reality of the moment, back to the small, unnaturally tidy apartment, and the memory of the dead girl.

The dead girl. Who was she and why would she do this? More importantly, did she do this?

"All finished up here, Detective. Anything else you need?" asked the forensic photographer.

"Nah, thanks, I got it from here."

McGovern was called in to investigate because something seemed

off to the responding officers. Normally, a person who died by strangu-
lation showed obvious signs of their slow and often painful struggle.
Upon arrival, Sean saw no evidence of this. This girl didn't have a
purple face or bulging eyes. There was no foam coming from her
mouth, no stench from relaxed bowels. To him, her face was flawless,
she was perfect, unaltered by death. His flesh erupted in goosebumps.

Once the photos were developed and evidence gathered he would
be able to start finding answers as to why…and who. Who was she?
Who were her next of kin? Who should he contact? There was no note
left at the scene. Was there foul play involved? Could that be the
answer? There didn't seem to be any signs of outward struggle—
nothing obvious anyway. Her place was neat as a pin. Almost too
clean. Regardless, he would get to the bottom of it at some point—he
always did. He would assemble his puzzle, starting backwards from
this solemn day, methodically and analytically gathering the facts that
would lead him on a journey. But first, something was gnawing at him,
an old familiar ache welling up in his gut. There was one thing he just
had to do, something he had not done in thirty years. He turned toward
the closet, thoughtfully rubbing the scruff on his face.

He felt the urge to inhabit the space just one more time before he
left. He approached, then crossed the threshold. The air seemed haunt-
ingly cold. Was it because her body was no longer there? He wanted to
make sure he took every mental and physical note possible because
those first impressions were crucial. Once inside the tragic space,
standing in the spot directly below where her body had hung, instead of
double checking his notes or writing new ones, he did something that,
until this day, he had never done on an investigation. He listened. He
listened to an intuition he had ignored for far too long. For in the back
of the closet, where the beautiful girl with the auburn hair ended her
days on earth, this reasonable, analytical, faithless detective inhaled
long and deep, closed his eyes, and after a slow cleansing exhale asked,
"Who are you?"

"Sophie," a voice whispered back. His eyes shot open.

4

THE IRISH DOLL

Ailene Aherne hated the label Irish Doll, a pet name given to her by her overbearing, widowed father. He treated her as if she was a doll of the porcelain kind. One that needed to be kept hidden away on the highest shelf so as not to come into contact with, in his words, "any unworthy eejits." She was to be cherished from afar, her thick jet hair never to be cut, her pure white skin never to have a hand laid on it, and her hazel eyes never to hold a long, loving gaze upon anything other than her Bible. She knew her father loved her very much, but after her mother died, he parented out of fear. A fear that one day his precious hummingbird might fly away, not realizing she would never have the strength to do so, for his tight grip was suffocating her in his own palms.

She wasn't allowed any type of social life outside of school. She was only allowed to attend class, learn as much as she could, and head directly home to study. There were no field trips because "there's enough for you to see in this town," there were no school dances because "slow dancing is the devil's work," and there were absolutely no sleepovers, because kids would stay up late and "nothing good ever happens after eleven o'clock."

She could spend countless hours reciting quotes from her father and lamenting that she had no life. She could keep hating the fact he allowed her no freedoms, knowing it stemmed from his own fears. She could also spend all afternoon trying to figure out her next plan of escape through her bedroom window to meet her secret boyfriend while her dad slept. But right now, she needed to spend this very minute figuring out how she was going to tell her overbearing, over-protective, overreactive father that, at sixteen, his precious Irish Doll was pregnant.

Shocked, she peered down at the white plastic stick with the glaring blue plus sign. She had peed on three of them, and they all shared the same message. She was pregnant with Joseph's baby. Even the tears falling from her eyes could not wash away the results. She felt a flush in her cheeks and a knot in her stomach. She had thrown up every morning this week and was yet again struggling to swallow the bile rising in the back of her throat. She wasn't quite sure how it happened. Well, she had an idea, but it was only one time. She thought that if she and Joseph used the condom he kept in his wallet they would be fine. That and the fact that he pulled out was sure to make them safe, wasn't it?

She didn't mean for this to happen! Why didn't she listen to her father? She should have just come straight home after class the way he wanted her to. She did not have to take the position writing for the school newsletter which allowed her to stay after school an extra hour each day. That, in itself, was the initial reason she found the offer attractive, but soon she learned she was a good writer and could earn extra credit in her English class for doing so. She thought it would make her father proud, and once he saw her succeeding at this he would surely give her more freedom in the future. Plus, she desperately craved social interaction. It was fun to get together with the newsletter staff, to present articles and work as a team laying the newsletter out together. If that was her only shot at a social life then she was not going to miss the opportunity.

It was there she met Joseph Anthony Riccio. He was the head of the newsletter staff and its chief editor. He was smart, good at his job, and had an air of power about him. Yet even though she was only a sophomore and he was a senior, he treated her as his equal. He respected her writing and sometimes let her help with the editing. Most importantly, he paid attention to her, and she savored every second spent with him.

As time passed, their working relationship turned into a friendship. She found him funny and charming, and she could talk to him about anything. She liked opening up to him, for he seemed to have all the answers. Their friendship grew stronger until one day it turned into something more. Yes, he was smart and funny and a good listener—it also didn't hurt that he had warm brown eyes and dark wavy hair that fell into his brow when he looked down at her. As far as her father knew, time working for the newsletter grew from one hour a day after school to two hours. Those were the best stolen hours of her life.

Now, looking into the school's dingy bathroom mirror she recognized the child she still was. She washed her hands with the pink soap from the wall dispenser. Its nauseating scent made her throw up in the sink one more time. As Ailene emerged from the bathroom, she saw Joseph heading toward her, wide-eyed.

"Well?" he asked. Even he looked younger to her at this moment.

"I'm…we're…I'm…it's positive…" She couldn't even say it.

"Oh…" the color drained from his olive skin.

His beautiful olive skin, one of the things that drew Ailene to her Joseph, it was something that came natural to a full-blooded Sicilian from New York City, another transplant into this small town. Rumor had it his family was somehow fleeing from or connected to the Mafia. She never believed it. Then again, he never really talked about his family, and she never met them. This was yet another reason her dad was not going to be happy with the news. It would be bad enough, him finding out she was dating a boy, an Italian boy, but the fact that she was also pregnant…

"What am I going to do?" she sobbed.

"We, Ailene. We are going to handle this together. We are going to go to your father and tell him the truth. We are young, and we made a mistake, but we are going to do the right thing." He pulled her close and hugged her tightly as her tiny shoulders silently shook. Ailene knew it would not be as simple as Joseph thought. He did not know her father. How could he? She never dared introduce him before, and now it was going to be a nightmare.

"Plus I'll be graduating in a few months, and I'll get a job and be able to support us while you finish high school."

She looked up at him, still swallowing silent sobs and bile. "Do you love me?"

"Yes." Did he? He kissed her glistening forehead, and she wondered if he'd meant it.

"I love you too, Joseph, but…"

"Then let's get it over with and talk to your dad. Everything's going to be just fine." He grabbed her hand a little too hard, leading her out the door.

But everything was not going to be just fine. Terrified, she could not imagine how she was going to even start this conversation with her father. How was she going to tell him his precious porcelain doll was shattered beyond repair? Joseph had no idea just how strict her father was, and his naivety was nauseating to her. In fact, the whole situation was nauseating—Joseph's naivety, the pink soap, her dad's furious Irish temper, and the shards of porcelain glass she was now treading on, barefoot and pregnant.

INTUITION

T he detective's eyes shot open. Just a moment before, Sophie followed him back into the closet. He stood in the back of the closet, in the very place her feet last touched the mortal earth, and closed his eyes. Did he just ask her who she was? She thought so, but when she replied "Sophie" he did not seem to hear her. Of course he didn't hear her—she was dead! That realization shocked her earlier when she saw her body being wheeled through the doorway on a gurney. That was the epiphany. The crystal clear understanding of what she had done.

She was deceased. It was obvious now, but why was she stuck in this place? Why was she still in the same small apartment she rented just three months before to escape from her hell on earth? Why had she not crossed over? Where was Heaven? Where was her God telling her that even though she committed a mortal sin, He forgave her and welcomed her to eternal paradise with outstretched arms? Where was her salvation?

And why the fuck was she feeling so much? She thought she would escape her emotional pain once her life on earth was over. But now, in this new place, her senses were tenfold what they were while she walked among the living. Her whole essence seemed electrified.

Maybe it was because while she lived she became an expert at being numb? What she felt right now was raw, strong, and intense.

So when the unfamiliar man, who was still in her apartment, entered the closet to ask, to himself, who she was, she stated simply "Sophie." He did not hear her. "SO-phie," she spoke a little louder; still to no response. "SOPHIE!" she yelled. Still nothing from the only person who seemed ready and willing to listen. "SOPHIE! SOPHIE! SOPHIE!" She shouted her name over and over to no avail. "Oh God!" she lamented. Would she be stuck there forever, with no one to hear her cries, no one to help her out of her self-imposed limbo. She broke down into a sobbing heap at the man's feet "Sophie, Sophie, Sophie..." she sobbed as she felt the throbbing pain of heartbreak, knowing no one would ever hear her, let alone see her, again. "Sooophie, Sooophie, Sooophieee!" she cried, like a wounded animal, lost and motherless. Her wailing shifted with one long inhale. Her throat tight and constricted as she tried to draw one slow gasping sob through a windpipe collapsed like a deflated balloon. For a moment there was no noise. But then, the pain of the breath in her throat reached its height, and the sorrow of what she had done to herself coupled with the terror of knowing she would never be heard again. She stood. With every fiber of her being she released the pent up pressure knotting her insides with one guttural scream, "SOOOOPHHHHIEEEE!"

She saw him flinch. He'd heard her! She was sure of it! She was exhausted. It had taken all of her might, but he'd heard her. A slight glimmer of hope. What else could she say? What else would he hear?

Before she could find the answers to those questions she watched him, his eyes wide like saucers, rush out of the closet, leaving his leather journal behind.

THE SCREAMING FABRIC

I can also hear her, from deep within my hiding place. As I sit...waiting. I've been tucked within walls of musty mahogany, walls constructed over two hundred years ago. My current home is a hidden drawer in a dressing table which has served many mistresses and masters, held many secrets. I am now one of those secrets.

Today, I appear to be a worthless, tattered piece of fabric, but I once had royal ties. I once was part of a sacred vestment, fabulous and flaunted, worn by the most powerful, most holy people. I witnessed the birth of kings and the baptism of bishops. Now, I am housed within a sliding wooden box that smells of the forbidden oils and tinctures of the past. Tonics stashed by clandestine poets. Hallucinogenic liquids that, when secretly imbibed, would bring on a creativity far too dangerous for a sober mind. Poppy residue, of the opiate kind, saved by forlorn lovers for when the pain of their broken heart was too much for them to bear.

Today I sit, tucked away by a woman who believed she was power-less. A woman who ran from a truth she was too afraid to speak. A woman who's only just now found her courage and her voice. Sadly, now she is trapped in a world where her voice may never be heard again, for it will take every ounce of her energy to cross through other-worldly dimensions to create even the slightest whisper on the other side of the veil where she used to exist.

She has quite a story to tell, yet now she must tell it from beyond. I can help her, but only if I am discovered. I hold the clues. For I witnessed what she witnessed. I felt what she felt. I was ripped from my original garment the way her soul was ripped from her being. I witnessed her light become darkened by the cruel actions of those she trusted. I bear the stains to prove it.

I am here because she brought me here, because she gave me energy. I have spirit because she transferred spirit to me when she tore me from my original place in the world. I have a voice because she has none. She heard me screaming in her head, or so she thought, but it was actually her own voice she heard.

She was among the living for a reason, just as all souls who come to earth are here for a purpose. But her job is not completed. The cycle was interrupted by her own undoing, and now it must be repaired. She was here to uncover a corrupt being, to catch a criminal. She was here to be the testimony that would save others from being harmed. But since she harmed herself, since she no longer exists on the human plane, she must now touch someone else's life, from the afterlife. She must complete the mission bestowed upon her when she was fortunate enough to be one of the living, using all the energy she can muster to break through to the other side.

But who is the chosen one? Who will hear her voice as she struggles to project it from beyond? Who will feel her presence and notice the signs when it takes all of her might just to make the fragile breeze of a butterfly's wing? Will he hear her? The man standing in the place where she took her last breath? The analytical man who as a boy once spoke with spirits? The faithless man who now denies his childhood gifts? Will he allow himself to become who he once was? Is he going to allow himself to realize the slight change of electricity in his hands and not mistake it for his own adrenaline flowing through his veins? Will he acknowledge the faint scent of her presence in the air? Will he deny his head and follow his heart?

He will need to be an open conduit to hear her story. I will help if I can, but I can't help if he can't free me from the confines of this secret hiding place, nestled between a crystal rosary and a golden wedding band. He cannot find me without her. What a complicated choreography we must all learn to dance together. It excites me to my very fibers!

She must get through to him, for if she does not, she will be forever suspended in her own personal limbo. Her place between heaven and earth. A place of overwhelming emotions and profound frustration. She needs to be her own guide, to find her voice and make sure someone hears it loud and clear. Once she does, I am here to help her. I am waiting and willing to talk.

TELLING PAPA

T rying to focus through her tears, Ailene watched Joseph's silhouette disappear from view as her father drove her away. Just minutes before she had pleaded with her father.

"Please…listen to me, Papa!"

Joseph was wrong, just as Ailene knew he would be. Her father had not taken the news of her pregnancy well. He was irate. She and Joseph tried to make him understand they were ready to do the right thing by accepting responsibility and raising the baby together. He was having none of it.

"No! I will NOT listen to anything you have to say, girl! You have sinned and brought shame to this house!"

"But we love each other, Papa, and we will take care of this baby. Joseph will graduate in a month and find a job to support us while I finish school." Ailene attempted to convince herself as well.

"Yes, sir, I…uh…love your daughter, and I will do right by her…" Joseph shouldn't have opened his mouth at all.

Ailene watched in horror as her father grabbed Joseph by the collar and pulled him inches away from his own face, almost lifting him off of the ground.

"Don't ya speak to me ya stupid wop!" Her enraged father spat his words into Joseph's face. "You're lucky I don't kill ya right here and now! What do ya know about love? Th'only one you'll ever love is your damned self. I can feel it in ma' bones. You…are pure evil!"

Ailene saw the madness in her father's eyes, and it was terrifying, but she wanted Joseph to fight back, to stand up to her father, to prove his love for her. She wanted him to plead with all his might to ask her father to let them be together.

But Joseph did nothing of the sort. Still being held by her father, Joseph's shoulders drooped in surrender, his eyes locked to the floor. Her heart sank. He was not going to fight for her. She knew right then and there he was going to give up on her and their baby.

"Joseph?" she asked as her father pushed the boy away, causing him to stumble backwards.

"I'm sorry, Ailene." Joseph could not look her in the eyes as he made the decision to save himself.

"Ya see? He doesn't love ya, not even one…little…bit." Her father poked the boy's chest hard, causing Joseph to stumble again. "Get out of my house boy and don't ever think of coming back here. You'll never see my daughter again." With that, he pushed the boy out the front door and down the porch stairs.

"No, Papa!" Ailene pulled on her father's shoulder, trying to stop him from pushing away the first and only boy she would ever love.

Her father turned and jerked her by the arm, walking her over to the waiting car in the driveway. He opened the back door and pushed her into the seat, then slammed the door shut.

"Don't ya move!" His pointed hand trembled with fury.

She watched Joseph as he just stood there, watching her father hop into the driver's seat. She watched Joseph as he just stood there, watching her father turn on the car and back out of the driveway. With her heart breaking, she watched Joseph just stand there, doing nothing, as her father drove her to the convent where she would be locked away, pregnant and alone, to repent her sins for the rest of her days.

8

FORGETFULNESS

"Dammit!" Sean said out loud as he rummaged through the pockets of his overcoat, carelessly strewn over the chair. "I must have left my journal in Jane Doe's closet." Dripping wet with soapy hair and a hastily wrapped towel, he tracked wet footprints across the hardwood floor. While replaying the events of the previous day in his mind, mid-shower he remembered he had not unpacked his leather journal of notes when he returned home.

A few minutes later he was back in the bathroom having a conversation with his reflection in the steamy mirror as he shaved. "Get your shit together, man! Don't start getting sloppy now." As he daydreamed, he nicked his Adam's apple. "Fuck."

It wasn't that the case had caught him off guard—he had investigated many crime scenes before, including suicides. He learned over the years how to separate his emotions from his work by behaving more as a spectator than one of the cast of characters, ensuring his emotions would not cloud his process. After all, a good detective was analytical, not emotional. Unfortunately, he did remember being taken aback when he first arrived on the scene and entered the closet, only to see the striking woman hanging there in front of him. He may have even remembered catching his breath when he first saw her. She seemed to be sleeping, not dead. He had seen his fair share of corpses. They were bodies, cadavers, mere shells that used to house the souls of the people they once were. But she was perfect, as if she could wake up at any moment. It appeared that she was dead but not gone.

He certainly knew there was more to the story than what was swaying in front of him. He knew the statistics. It was less likely for a woman to take her own life by hanging than a man. Was there foul play involved? Who was this woman? What was her story? A lovely face may catch him off guard at first, but it certainly was not something to jar his equilibrium.

It was what happened later, when he returned to the closet, that startled him. When he heard the name Sophie, the delicate breath, so faintly whispered into his ear, it was a shock to his system, like being plunged into an ice bath. His own breath sucked in by the biting chill. It rocked him to the core and threw him off balance, not unlike his bad golf swing. He was not expecting an answer to his question. Yet, he willingly toyed with the idea of letting himself go there. It touched something dormant.

It had been years since he trained himself to ignore the voices that spoke to him so readily as a child. He worked hard at pushing that shit down, turning his back on the gift he was born with. He had convinced himself all this time that it would just play with his judgment. Why now, in one instance, was he so willing to let it all come bubbling up?

As he applied tiny pieces of toilet tissue to his nicks, he decided he wasn't. He wasn't going to let it all come back. He had done just fine as a detective up until now, and he wasn't going to start making stupid, emotional mistakes.

He threw on his clothes and decided to grab a coffee on the way into town, since his coffee maker was still packed within the pile of boxes stacked atop each other in his newly purchased brownstone. He'd been inhabiting the space for a few months and realized the only two rooms he had unpacked and been living in were his bedroom and his bathroom. Well, if he could call it living. *Seems all I do is shit, shave, and sleep.* He was logging so many hours lately it was all he had time for. His phone buzzed on the counter.

"McGovern," he answered

"Hey, Detective, it's Joann from the station. I've got your file started from yesterday's Jane Doe, but it seems your usual impeccable chicken scratch notes are missing and you know how much I love transcribing them for you!"

"Hey smartass! How many years have we worked together now, and every time you call me you announce who you are and that you're calling me from the station. I'm a fucking detective. If you called me from an unknown number and disguised your voice I'd know it was you!"

"Yeah well, old habits die hard. You just turned the big four-oh. It seems to me you're getting to be an old habit!" she joked. Her sassy tone made him chuckle.

"Ha! You should do stand up in your spare time. Oh yeah, that's right, if you stood up no one would see you, you're so damned short!"

He heard her laugh-snort on the other end. Joann was one of his favorite people. She was the department secretary, a jolly fireplug of a woman with a quick wit, who, he assumed, was working well past retirement age, though he didn't dare ask her age for fear of being slapped. She was a widow, married to their former captain who was killed a few years back in a mob bust gone awry. They never had any children of their own, so the station became her home. She thought of the officers as her family and they thought the same of her. Sean assumed she would work there until her dying day. He had no problem with that. She was good at her job, thorough and sharp, which brought him back to the reason for her call.

"Well, one thing is right—I must be getting old. I left my notes on the scene yesterday." He wasn't ready to admit it was more likely he'd left in a panic after he'd heard the voice. "Can you call building management and let 'em know I'm coming? I'll swing by and pick 'em up on the way into the station. Then you can enjoy the thoughtful prose by which they are writ."

She snorted again, "Will do! Sweet Jesus, I'd better shine up my readers. I'll be waiting with bells on! Safe travels, honey." And with that she hung up.

Sean grabbed his gun, badge, and keys on his way out the door and, as he caught his shin on the corner of one of the larger moving boxes, made a silent vow to himself to unpack the rest of his place over the next few days. The weekend was coming and he could probably find some time then.

Right now, he needed to head on over to grab his forgotten journal. He wasn't sure if his eagerness was in retrieving the notes he'd made or in visiting the scene once again to see if anything else arose. But first…coffee.

AN INVISIBLE FOG OF WARM, wet, arabica air enveloped Sean as he entered the small coffee house situated on a corner just a few blocks away from his townhouse. He preferred the tiny shop over the big brand names any day of the week. He liked that it wasn't bustling with enterprising starter businessmen making slightly loud phone calls, or yoga-clad moms on the go, planning their PTA agendas while whispering the latest gossip in between line items A and B. It was just a little hole-in-the-wall that catered to schleps like him, running in and out, usually on a time crunch and looking for a caffeine fix to help substitute for the sleep lost the night before.

"One coffee, and I'll have a bagel too, plain," he said to the perky barista behind the counter. She must have been new—he didn't recognize her, an added bonus to his favorite little spot. She smiled at him, her eyes lingering on him for an extra second.

Hmmm…is she staring at me? He looked over his left shoulder to see if someone was standing behind him. Nobody was there. *She is kind of cute. A little too young for my taste, though.* She handed him his coffee and bagel with a giggle and a glance.

There it is again. His ego fluffed a bit. *I think she finds me attractive. Maybe I'll have to come back here tomorrow. I did order one coffee. A single coffee, for a single man.* He never really made the time for a serious relationship. He'd had a few flings in the past, but they always ended up one of two ways: with the woman finally realizing she could never marry a man on the force or with him not being able to put the quality hours in.

"See you tomorrow," he said with a wink. *I can't believe I just fucking winked.* "Keep the change," and left with an extra skip in his step even before the first sip of caffeine entered his system.

One coffee, he thought, sipping as he drove. The steam from the cup fogged his sunglasses as his mind wandered back to the woman in the closet. *She probably ordered only one coffee.* Even though she was beautiful, something told him she had no handsome barista making eyes at her; her apartment seemed so lonely, sad, sparse. *She must have been so low.* Then again, he wasn't sure she actually died in the way it appeared. He'd have to wait for the results to return from the lab.

Pulling up to the curb, he saw the building manager was already waiting outside, scruffy beard, slept-in clothes, keys in hand.

"Detective, it's nice to see ya. Silas Martin in case ya forgot. I called the police about the dead lady. I let you guys in yesterday." He reached to shake the detective's hand.

"Yes, Mr. Martin, I remember," he said shaking the man's sweaty palm. *I'm a fucking detective, it's my job to remember.* He marveled at how people continually forgot what a detective's job was. Still shaking hands, Silas Martin stared at the detective's face for a beat too long. It started to get uncomfortable, and Sean pulled his hand away.

Realizing what just happened the man said, "Oh! Sorry detective, it's just that ya have…uh…pieces of…uh…ya got shit all over ya face!"

Sean raised his hand to his face and realized he had forgotten to take off all of the bloodied pieces of toilet paper he'd let adhere to his shaving mishaps. Embarrassed by how he must look and now realizing why the barista must have chuckled—she wasn't flirting with him, she was laughing at him.

"Ugh, I'm never going back to that coffee shop!"

"What?" asked the confused man.

"Never mind, Mr. Martin. Can you just let me into the apartment? I left something in there yesterday."

"Sure, Detective, happy to help ya." The two men entered the old, musty building. Silas Martin lead the way as they stepped into the humid elevator. It smelled like Chinese takeout. "If there's anythin' else I can do…"

The detective watched the man's finger, dirt under his nail, press three. "Mr. Martin, can you repeat what you told me yesterday about the woman who lived here? Is there anything more you can add that maybe you remembered last night or this morning?"

"Well…uhm…I don't really got nothin' more about her. Like I said, pretty lady. Came by about three months ago askin' about an apartment. Showed her the place. Gave her a price. She paid for the first months in cash. Not much of a talker. Ya know what I mean? Didn't wanna shake hands. Seemed shy."

"Do you know anything about a family? Has anybody been here looking for her?" Sean asked. He noticed the man had crumbs and oily marks, most likely from his last meal, resting on the shelf created by his protruding belly.

"Nah…like I said yesterday, she didn't say much. Didn't see her leave the place much either. Maybe just to go to the market? She would sometimes have a small grocery bag. Once in a while I would see her hurry in. She never had no visitors that I noticed. Always wore black. Such a gloomy color. It's a shame. A pretty young lady bein' a shut-in like that."

"Still no idea what she did for a living? Where she may have worked?"

"Not really. Didn't have no mail or work papers discarded in her recycling bin. Just junk papers. Ya know? Takeout menus, an occasional church program, newspaper. Nothin' of value in her gar…" The man realized what he had just said and looked down at his scuffed work boots, fidgeting. Sean took mental notes. Nervous, nosy building manager who rummages through his tenant's trash, single woman, recluse, paranoid (of her nosy, creepy building manager perhaps), church programs. He recalled the candles on her dressing table and end table, and how they initially reminded him of church. He would write this down in his journal. He would make a point to stop by the church, where maybe someone there would have a clue.

"Here we are, third floor," said Silas as the elevator doors creaked open and the two stepped out into the equally warm hallway.

"Mr. Martin, I'm going to need you to get me any paperwork, contracts, leases that you may have for Jane Doe so we can try to find out who she is and contact her next of kin."

"Uh, we don't got nothin' like that for cash leases…uh, you know, the uh bookkeepin' in this place ain't all that great. It ain't quite the Ritz here…ha, ha…" Tiny beads of sweat began to form on the man's forehead as he laughed nervously.

"So you don't have any documentation on who this woman was? No name? Previous address? Phone number? A utility bill, perhaps, with her information?"

"The tenants only pay rent and a common area fee. We take care of water and electricity. It's too expensive to split the meterin'. So she ain't gonna have no bills of that sort."

"Didn't you keep any information on her just in case she trashed the place?"

"Eh, never got around to it, I didn't think she was the type to cause no damage to the place, bein' she was so meek and all. Plus, I got a security deposit up front too."

"How can I get in contact with the landlord?"

"Uh, I am the landlord," replied the man.

"You are her landlord as well? I thought you were the building manager?"

"Landlord, buildin' manager, plumber, handyman I do it all. Good people are hard to come by, Detective."

So they are, Sean thought, now noticing how unkempt the property was. He made more mental notes. Nosy slumlord, lazy, sloppy with addition of greedy.

"Well, I'm sure the IRS will be interested in who this woman is, since she had a bunch of cash on hand to pay you. I may have to point them in your direction. To ask you some questions."

"Uh, er, uh…maybe I gotta paper somewheres with her name on it," the now-perspiring man stuttered as he fumbled the key into the lock. It was the wrong key. He flipped through the ring to another, "I think her name was Sally or Suzie or somethin' like that." The key did not fit. On to another. It fit, with a jiggle. The man continued to rattle the key and the doorknob, "or Sonya or So-" The man started to press his squishy shoulder against the door, leaning on it while rapidly turning the knob and key, "Sophie!" The door swung open, banging into the wall behind it, "That's it! Her name was Sophie," the man proudly proclaimed as he wiped off the sweat running down his face.

The detective felt a familiar chill run up his spine as he stepped over the threshold, past the yellow police tape now hanging from the door jamb. He thought it odd the tape had been removed on one side.

"Do you have a last name for her, Mr. Martin?" he said, trying to counteract the slight trembling he started to feel in his body. *Who turned on the air conditioning?*

"Nah, don't remember no last name. There are a lot of tenants livin' in this buildin'. But I'll do my darndest to dig it up for ya, Detective. Eh...can we just wait on the IRS thing until I try and find out?"

The overwhelming chill Sean felt distracted him from the shady man. "Yes, Mr. Martin, just get me what you can, and get it quickly."

"OK, Detective, if there is nothin' more I can do, I gotta leave ya here so ya can finish your work. I gotta go run and check on the AC units, it's so freakin' hot in this buildin'," said the man, whose shirt now grew moist under the armpits.

"Yeah, that's fine, I'll let myself out," said the detective, shivering, while staring at the sweaty man. As the landlord turned away from him, Sean asked, "Uh. Mr Martin, one last thing."

"Yeah?" Martin's shoulders hunched.

"How was it you came about her body?"

"I, uh, I just stopped by cause I hadn't seen her around, and I uh, knocked—a few times—and no one answered so I let myself in. I didn't know if maybe she split or somethin'." There was a long silence as the detective stared at Silas Martins back, the man did not turn around, but asked "Anything else, Detective?"

"No. You can go."

Silas Martin hurried out the door and shut it, leaving the detective alone in the chilly air, where he stood still for a beat, taking in his surroundings.

"Here we are again," he said out loud, scanning the modest apartment and recognizing things he saw on his first visit.

He walked the squeaky wooden floor lining the open space, which housed in no particular order, one stool, a thirsty teapot, a meticulously made bed, an old dressing table with an equally old mirror, a red glass candle, its mate sitting atop a trunk used as end table. As his eyes fell on each item, he knew his initial impressions were most important, but also revisiting the scene would tell him more of the story, maybe something he overlooked the first time. Of course it would tell him more, if he would only allow himself to tap into the thing he denied for years.

Then there was the closet. The door was still open, the automatic light still on, illuminating the setting of the scene where he'd first met his Jane Doe. The fateful place where he'd gone to do his work just like he'd done countless times before, yet this place was different. This place, this case, touched a part of him he'd kept hidden away, and he wasn't sure why.

One thing he did know—his journal was in there. Dropped and forgotten when he darted out of the closet, startled by nothing more than a whisper of a name even the lazy landlord had a hard time recalling. Yet it was spoken so clearly to Sean. It was an answer he did not expect, one that shook him a bit. He was a brave man, but this rattled him because it touched on something different. This brought back memories he had learned to forget as a boy. Sean McGovern, the analytical detective who, up until the previous day, silenced his inner voice, was now being led through this investigation by his inner child.

As he walked toward the closet through the chilly air in the hot apartment, it brought back a memory of being a boy and the spirits that would come to visit him. The ones his mother told him were evil. He remembered when they were near, the air would feel just like this. It could be high noon on a hot summer day, and he would feel chilly in the presence of the dead only he could see. As he walked toward the closet, his heart started to beat a little faster. He could feel it in his chest, gently tapping at a quickened pace. *Shit, there's no need to be nervous.*

Feeling unsettled about returning to the scene just didn't make sense to him. He approached the closet door and felt a rush of adrenaline as a cool wave of energy moved up his arms and into his face, stinging his cheeks. His hands felt cold and he pumped his fists to try to get his blood circulating. He could hear the hum of the closet light, beckoning him to enter. It was time to step in and settle his unease. Yesterday he was caught off guard; today, he was ready to confront the unknown.

He took a deep breath, ran his fingers through his rumpled raven hair, and entered. His passage into the closet proved most uneventful. The air was chilly but hung quietly. What did he expect? Did he think he would hear something, or see something other than a sad lonely space where a woman ended her life? There was nothing there waiting for him. Nothing was touched, other than the makeshift noose was gone, most likely taken by the forensics team as evidence. The chair that once belonged to the old dressing table sat in the middle of the floor, brought in by the woman and tipped over by her struggle. It was now upright, dusty with the residue of fingerprint powder, looking as if it was asking for someone to put it back in its rightful place. On the floor next to the chair he spotted his journal, in the exact place he dropped it. He leaned down to pick it up, disappointed in the stillness of it all. Maybe he was expecting to hear her again. Was it even she he'd heard in the first place? Why was this so important to him? As he reached to grab his journal, a static electric shock snapped at his fingers, startling him. He let go and jumped back.

"Fuck!" He held his hand to his chest and then chuckled at the thought of how high a little rogue electricity made him jump. "What's going on in this place? Thank God none of the guys are here," he said to his audience of orphaned clothing. "I'm turning into such a pussy, they'd never let me live this down."

He reached down again to retrieve his journal, this time without incident. He also gently took the chair and brought it back to its rightful resting place in front of the dressing table. He placed the chair and sat down to address the flawed old mirror. He did not look at his own reflection. Instead, he noticed all of the lines and clouds in the mirror itself, a product of the mercury aging and releasing over the years.

"I bet you have all the answers," he said to the old mirror. "I wish you could tell me what happened here. Was there foul play, or did she do it? Why would Jane Doe take her life? What'd she see in her reflection she hated so much? I know you can't tell me. I'll piece it all together, and maybe someday I'll tell you the story." He opened his notebook, and next to Jane Doe he scribbled the name *Sophie* and circled it.

With that, the detective got up and started to look for clues he may have missed the first time, anything that would give him information. He pulled out his cell phone, and along with making notes in his journal, he took photographs, studying her whole living space. He captured everything the small space had to offer. The meticulously hung clothes in her closet, mostly black and bland, with sensible shoes. He got close enough to detect a sweet, woody aroma emanating from the fabric. There were no fancy dresses or high heels. She obviously had no social life, which was confirmed by the little amount of information he got from the landlord. He photographed the space where she had hung herself and approached the mirror at the end of the closet. He felt bad for that mirror and the scene it had to capture within its pristine reflection. As he stood, facing the mirror, his phone flashed, his camera capturing an accidental selfie.

He photographed her kitchen drawers, also neatly arranged, which contained only the essentials needed for living: mismatched forks, knives, and spoons; salt and pepper; a nameless and faceless matchbook, not one from a fancy restaurant or bar. There was no wine bottle opener. She was probably not a drinker or smoker.

On the counter under a fresh layer of dust was a pen, a pencil, and some writing paper. Her doorless cupboards were almost bare save for a partial loaf of bread, some boxes of crackers, cans of tuna, and tea bags. There was water and cream and an old piece of chocolate cake in her refrigerator. In her bathroom medicine cabinet there was soap, toothpaste, and powder, but no perfumes or makeup, except for the one pristine tube of red lipstick he had seen on her dressing table on his first visit. He remembered her beautiful red lips as she was wheeled away from the scene and how they drew him in when he first saw her. This thought pulled him back toward her dressing table to collect the golden tube, which also gave him a small static shock before he placed it into his pocket.

The chill in the air caused everything to be electrically charged. It was not police protocol to remove personal items from the scene, especially without wearing gloves or slipping them into a plastic bag. Removing such an item was actually not allowed at all. But surely this one item wouldn't be missed.

There were two drawers in her dressing table; one contained a pen and another faceless matchbook, the other was filled what looked to be used ribbons and string.

In her trash can there was a rotting banana peel, a takeout container with the remnants of pasta sauce in it, and a wadded piece of colored paper. The detective uncrumpled the paper. It was a flyer for a spaghetti dinner held at St. Catherine's Cathedral. He smoothed out the wrinkles, folded it in half, and tucked the flier into his leather journal.

There were no family photographs on display, no cards or letters to be found; the only book was the Holy Bible. He opened the cover and flipped through the first few pages to see if there was a signed bookplate. There was no identification, nothing personal at all. Not in the book, not in the whole living space. It seemed too antiseptic to be her home.

Sean could not help but feel bad for this sad, lonely, scarlet-lipped woman. He wanted to help her, even though she was already gone. Something gnawed at him. He felt there was so much more to the story, and intuitively knew the less shown to him with physical evidence, the more answers lurked behind the scenes. It was too clean to be innocent, too vague to be ignored.

He was not going to allow her to disappear without respect. Surely her family missed her. He needed to get to the station and start piecing things together with the little evidence he had. He needed to do her the honor of finding her loved ones so they could put her to rest. He walked toward the entry.

"Ok Sophie, you told me your name, now you need to tell me your story." And with that he grabbed the door knob, shocking himself one last time, before he left the cold apartment and stepped into the stifling hallway.

9

WHAT'S IN A NAME

S ophie heard the jiggling of the doorknob as muffled voices conversed on the other side. She had been pacing all night, but it seemed like years. The whole while she looked for ways to get out of what now appeared to be her eternal prison, a hopeless limbo.

What did she do to herself? She had paced and cried, frantically trying to open doors and unlatch windows to no avail. No matter how hard she tried, nothing responded to her efforts. No knobs turned in her hapless hands. No latches gave way. She didn't know what to do. She couldn't imagine being stuck there forever, feeling and reeling in her own private hell. Before she died, she was able to sneak away, to find a bit of respite from her other life, the awful other life that forced her to leave the living. But this experience, beyond life, was even worse. At least when she was alive she had choices and options. She could come and go as she pleased. Here, she could not. It was painfully clear. She made the wrong decision.

As the door opened, she saw the man again. The one with the kind hazel eyes, soft matted moss on unmoved bedrock. The one who was there the first time she awakened, who left his journal on her closet floor in a startled rush. He entered her apartment and shut the door. She saw he was shivering. Was he cold? She could not feel the temperature of the room. She couldn't feel anything except her own electrified anxiety pulsing through her body. She had a million nerve endings buzzing all over her.

"Here we are again," he said.

What? Did he know that she was there with him?

"Hello? Can you see me?" she said. No response from the man. "Ugh…I'm here! You've got to know I'm here!"

The man did not flinch, but began to walk toward the closet. Sophie had not re-entered that dreaded place since the last time she was there, when she screamed her name and scared the stranger away.

She stood in front of the closet door hoping he would get a glimpse of her. Surely if she were standing right in front of him…he kept walking toward her. She held her arms straight out to stop him from entering.

Suddenly, she felt a whoosh of energy burst through her as her existence in limbo scattered apart. Not unlike a swarm of summer gnats giving way to a jogger, only to come back together again in perfect formation of their choreographed dance. Her entire soul reverberated. She saw stars in her eyes, and when her vision cleared, the stranger was no longer in front of her but behind her. He walked right through her!

She turned, stunned, and followed him into the closet. She saw him stand there as if he was waiting for something to happen. She also stood, waiting. Nothing. Seeing his journal was still on the ground, she reached down to try to grab it. He reached at the same time, and for a moment they touched hands. Again she felt a tingling in her body, and he jerked his hand away as if shocked by something.

"Fuck!" She heard him say as she watched him grab his chest. She could see he was startled. "What is going on in this place? Thank God none of the guys are here," he said out loud. "I'm turning into such a pussy, they'd never let me live this down."

Who was he talking to? It was clear to her he could not see her or hear her. He seemed to be conversing with no one. However, she didn't mind. She liked the company, for she knew at some point he would go away, leaving her alone in this abhorrent place. She watched as he once again reached to grab his journal, this time on his own and without incident. The chair that failed her sat innocently in the center of her closet. She watched him pick it up…useless piece of wood.

She observed him exit the closet with chair in hand only to place it in front of her dressing table and sit. And sit he did, for quite a long time. He stared into her favorite mirror. It seemed like a lifetime. She noticed something about his gaze—he, too, looked deep into the mirror, not at it, the way she had done countless times before. Did he see the cloudy, storied imperfections the way she did? Did he see secrets revealed in the smoky shadows of mercury blooming behind the glass?

She started when she heard him proclaim, "I bet you have all the answers." She had often thought the same thing looking into the old, beautifully flawed mirror.

"I wish you could tell me what happened here. Did she do it? Why would Jane Doe take her life?"

"My name is Sophie," she said to him.

He continued his questions. "What did she see in her reflection that she hated so much?"

"If only you knew what happened to me. What horrible awful things were done to me."

She hated how tarnished she had become. All she wanted to do was live a righteous life and help others. She tried her hardest to stay pure and true, but she was violated by a monster.

"I know you can't tell me. I'll piece it all together, and maybe someday I will tell you the story."

Would he? Could he? Was there a chance he could actually learn and begin to understand who she was and what she had been through? Would he tell the story to the wise old mirror? How would this be possible?

She was a nobody. A ghost of a woman, in more ways than one. She left no breadcrumbs behind for him to follow. He was a mere mortal, curious, but in another realm. He couldn't see her or hear her. For God's sake, he walked right through her! As he opened his notebook, she drew closer to him as he scribbled the name *Sophie* and circled it. Her name! Did he actually hear her? If so, why couldn't he now? Why couldn't he see her when she was standing right in front of him, arms outstretched? Why couldn't he see her when she was now standing right beside him? She waved her hands in front of his face. Nothing.

"Hello!? Can you hear me?" Nothing.

Her eyes followed him as he stood up from the delicate chair to walk past her, and she reached out her hand to graze his shoulder. Tingles. He scratched his broad shoulder with the back of his pen and brushed it off as he wrote more notes. She noted his methodology as he once again entered the closet, this time paying attention to the hanging clothes, huddled close together, squeezed tight, as if protecting themselves from the trauma they witnessed. She was intrigued by his process as he moved about, noticing everything, photographing everything, breathing in the energy that hung in the air, then jotting down a word or two. She stood behind him as they both gazed at the mirror in her closet, the one that witnessed her undoing. A flash startled them both.

Once in her kitchen, he open her refrigerator and drawers. He hovered over them, seemingly deep in thought about the contents within them, snapping more photos. He moved toward the space that was her bedroom. He lifted the sheets, he got down on his knees and looked under the bed. She knew he would find nothing there. He lifted the Bible from her makeshift end table. She wanted him to fan the pages to the end, to see it was not whole, to take it with him. But he only opened the first few and placed it right back on the table in the same condition he had found it.

He entered her bathroom, studying the space. As he eyed her medicine cabinet, she wondered if he felt disappointment in the blandness of its contents. There was nothing inspirational there, nothing feminine and beautiful to be found. It reminded her of her lovely tube of lipstick. It was the only indulgence she did buy for herself. Her war paint for that fateful night. She turned to look at it, still on her dressing table. Nearing the shining tube, she reached for it, yearning to trace its lovely lines once again. She knew she wasn't going to be able to feel it. Not with her newly anesthetized touch. At that moment the man's hand brushed past hers and scooped up the tube, slipping it into his coat pocket.

"Hey! Why are you taking that?" Sophie reprimanded him, frustrated he was pocketing the one thing she cherished. "That is not going to help you."

Her words were falling on deaf ears. The golden tube filled with crimson wax was not going to give the man the answers he sought. She was beginning to think nothing he could see in this whole terrible awful prison would help him. He opened the small wooden drawers to her dressing table, and it dawned on her there was something of use to him other than the Bible he refused to examine. In fact, there were many things that would help him understand who she was and why she made the worst decision of her now-wasted life. But the items he needed to discover were out of view. Hidden by Sophie, poetically stashed in the secret drawer. She was the only one on earth who knew they were there.

As the man started to walk toward the door, panic washed over her. He was going to leave and never come back! She would be stranded, and she couldn't bear the thought of it. She'd be driven mad in a place from which even death could not remover her.

"Wait!" she cried as he walked toward the door. "Please!" she yelled. "You need to come back, you need to look over here!" She tried to pound on the dressing table to make some noise, but with every attempt, her fists would pass right through its surface. "NO! Don't leave! Please don't leave me here!" she pleaded. "You didn't find what you need!"

How could she make him hear her? She needed him to turn around and do his job. How to make him realize that within a perfectly hidden drawer there were clues to be found? She rushed over to the door, and as he reached to turn the knob she tried to grab his hand "WAIT!" she screamed.

He jolted his hand back, recoiling from the electric shock. "Dammit!" he shouted. Sophie was startled too. Not because her arm was still buzzing, but because now it became clear she had control over something. Even though she wasn't sure what that something was. Distracted by her thoughts, she missed the man reaching once again for the doorknob, first lightly tapping it with his fingertips. He turned the knob and opened the door.

She tried to follow him out, to trail behind, but was frozen at the threshold, the slab of wood shutting right through her. Standing nose to door, she prayed the man would return. She was beginning to formulate a plan

10

THE CONVENT

Ailene lay on the bed in her little room at the Immaculate Conception Convent, captivated by the way the shimmering dust specks danced in the rays of light streaming through the stained glass window.

Smooth, white alabaster walls were the perfect canvas for the colorful prisms projected onto them. Tiny masterpieces, created by the intricate patterns of colored glass. This was the only time of day there was anything of interest to look at in her humble room. The pristine walls were bare, save for the ebony crucifix hung above her bed. A simple quilt clothed the single mattress tucked within the arched alcove of her room. She had one wooden chair, a table, and a chest of drawers. Atop the Spanish tile floor lay a small rug she had made by hand on a loom in the textile weaving class she was offered at the convent.

She had not spoken one word to her father since he brought her there that fateful day eight and a half months ago. It was the day she pleaded with him to let her and Joseph stay together. He didn't.

In the car, she begged her father to change his mind. She promised him she would never, ever disobey him again. She would do whatever she was told. She just wanted to go home. But he would not listen to her. He would not change his stubborn mind. He drove her, stone-faced, weaving through traffic, ignoring her tearful pleas. His angry hands gripping the steering wheel, forcing all of the blood to drain out of his bitter white knuckles. The same hands that were clamped to her upper arm as he ushered her up the convent stairs. She couldn't remember feeling her feet even touch the treads of the stairs, not until he planted her firmly in the vestibule. The musky scent of incense tingled in her nostrils as she pleaded with him to take her home. He ignored her. He had no words for her. He left her standing there as he turned his back on her to walk steadfastly to his car and drive off. She had nothing, no one, only the clothes on her back and the baby in her belly.

Not much had changed during her stay at the convent, except her perfectly round stomach. She cradled her belly, and as it moved it was a tiny comfort, reminding her she was not alone.

Her father tried to visit her on occasion, tried to talk to her, telling her to repent for her sins and pray for forgiveness. He believed a group of nuns would do a much better job raising her since he had obviously failed her as a father. She didn't care what he had to say. She grew to hate the sound of his voice. His droning, unkind, judgmental voice. On the odd days he did come to visit, she would stare off into space, focusing on anything else but him; a bird singing in a distant tree, the number of cracks on a painted windowsill, the scent of cherry blossoms in the air. Anything to help her block out his overbearing presence and protect her from the painful memories. She would let her imagination wander to far-off places, happy places…numb places. It was the movement deep in her tummy that brought her back into the moment.

On his visits, when her father was finished babbling, she would just get up and turn away from him without a word, allowing him to watch her leave. Hoping he felt the same amount of pain she felt when he took her away from her Joseph and abandoned her. Eventually, she refused to see him at all. She cried herself to sleep every night and willed her heart to become harder and harder in order to keep it from shattering into a million porcelain shards.

She had not seen or heard from Joseph, nor was she expecting to.

She knew on that horrible day when her father drove her away, Joseph wasn't going to fight for her. She didn't blame him. She was certain he knew her father would kill him, and she would much rather him stay alive so one day he could be reunited with her and their baby. At some point, she would plan their escape. She would get word to Joseph as to where she was, and their little family would live happily together forever.

Ailene loved her little baby bump. It was the only thing in her life that gave her any sense of hope for the future. It was her link to Joseph, her link to love. She would lie in her bed and sing sweet lullabies to her tummy. She read passages from the small Bible, a gift from the nuns. It was the only thing she was allowed to read when she was alone in her room. Sometimes the baby bump responded to certain passages. This day was no exception.

She was rereading Genesis, Chapter One about the creation of heaven and earth, and her little bump was more restless than usual. It was then, when she got to the part where God said, "Let there be light!" she noticed the dancing dust particles in the sunbeam shining through her window. Entranced, she laid the Bible on her tummy and watched the playful flecks floating and sparkling in the air. Her little baby bump was really kicking, enough to make the Bible shift.

Ailene tried to imagine herself as one of the soothing, drifting specks floating in the light, in order to calm her tummy down. She could not get comfortable. She lifted the Bible from her stomach, placed it on the floor next to her bedside, and turned onto her side to see if that would help the restlessness. But changing positions did not seem to help either. She took some soothing breaths and started to feel a dull pain in her back. It lingered and then radiated to the front of her stomach. Sweat beaded at her temple as she was unable to escape the uncomfortable pain.

She felt as if she had to go to the bathroom so she stood up from her bed, and when she did, she felt a rush of water pour down her legs onto the floor, soaking the Bible. She bent over to pick up the book and the next pain came like a bolt of lightning in her abdomen. She shot up, screamed in pain just as the door to her room opened. Everything went black.

Ailene woke up in a different bed, this one in the small infirmary on the same campus as the convent. The scent in the air was heavy and musky, hay-like and damp. She opened her eyes to see what looked like a man and two nuns standing over her.

"Hello, dear," said the man. "I am Doctor Hebron. How are you feeling?"

"I'm okay, I guess." She could see her tiny reflection in the doctor's thick glasses. Her jet-black hair was sweaty and matted—her face flushed—she looked even younger than her seventeen years. "Where am I?" she said, trying to understand her surroundings.

"You are in the hospital. You fainted and had quite a fall."

Ailene was confused for a moment, then remembered the pain she felt before everything went black. Instinctively she reached down to make sure her baby bump was alright, but it felt different. It did not feel round and hard the way it had felt earlier that day. It felt soft and sore and—empty! She began to panic.

"My baby! Where is my baby?"

The doctor took Ailene's hand as the two nuns looked at each other. Still holding her hand, the doctor said, "You won't be able to see the baby, dear."

Ailene was confused. She jerked her hand away from the doctor's grip and tried to sit up, but a pain in her gut sent her reeling back down.

"Ouch!" she cried. "Where is my baby?" She frantically scanned the room, trying once again to rise from the bed.

"The baby is not here," the doctor sternly said, reaching for the syringe on the table next to the bed. The nuns looked nervous, one wringing her hands and the other biting her lip. He brought the syringe closer.

"What do you mean the baby isn't here?" Her voice was hoarse and her throat dry. "Please, I want to see my baby!" Her heart raced in her chest, the shock of adrenaline pulsing through her entire being. She was weak and lightheaded.

The doctor looked at the nuns, and they nodded at him. Your baby is dead," he said flatly as he inserted the syringe into the IV in Ailene's hand.

She opened her mouth to speak, but nothing came out. Through the hot tears in her eyes she watched the guilty doctor and the nervous nuns as they faded out of view. She then had a vision of herself as a porcelain doll, falling, falling, down, down, down and shattering into a million shards never to be mended again.

11

JOSEPH

As Ailene's father drove her away, she did not know it took every ounce of Joseph's willpower to not run after the car. She did not know her tearstained face was the only thing Joseph could focus on. She did not see his nails cut into the palms of his shaking fists. She was unaware that his blood was boiling, anger from the poke still burning in the center of his chest, a hateful fire, ignited by her father's ignorant finger.

If Ailene could hear his thoughts, she would know Joseph planned to show her dad just how strong the ties of a "wop" could be. If she could hear his thoughts, she would know he wanted to chase the car down and drag her father out to beat him to a pulp. But she did not know any of this, and Joseph resisted because he knew the more trouble he made and the harder he fought, the more impossible it would be for him and Ailene to be together. More importantly, he did not want to do anything to make it difficult for him to be near his baby. He was going to have an heir, an extension of his bloodline. Scenes flicked through his mind faster than he could comprehend. Scenes of Ailene, her asshole of a father, a developing child, and Joseph himself. His future flashed before his eyes.

Joseph knew her father's type, and he knew just how to deal with them. If only Ailene knew Joseph only pretended to accede to her father's wishes. In time, he would find her and their baby, and they would escape together, far far away from the controlling ways of the overbearing bastard.

Through his family connections, it took only a few months to find out her father had hidden her away in the deep recesses of the Immaculate Conception Convent. Joseph chuckled at the thought, mostly at how fitting it was the old man wanted to cut her off, not only from him, but from all of humanity. Joseph thought the man insane at this point, but it was of no worry to him. He knew where she was hidden, and he was going to sneak his way in—or at least get word to her that he was coming for her.

Ailene never saw this side of her Joseph, for if she had, she would see he was the type of person who needed to win at any cost.

Alas, the convent was a bit more of an impenetrable fortress than Joseph imagined. He was refused at the door, his calls went unreturned, and every letter he sent to her was mailed right back to him, all unopened with a big red stamp shouting RETURN TO SENDER. This angered Joseph. Apparently, they did not know who he was, or who his family was. They were unaware of who they were trifling with. He was through playing by their rules. He was formulating a few of his own, and little did the convent know they were no match for Joseph Riccio and his family ties.

His family had been deeply entrenched in the mafia since its inception, with his great-grandfather being Don, a title also earned by his Grandfather. His own father did not live long enough to carry the torch, but Joseph, one of the last two Riccio men, still had his family connections. Once you were connected, you were connected for life. Ailene did not know Joseph had an uncle, Salvatore, his father's brother, who also happened to be his baptized godfather. Salvatore was a priest at Holy Heart Seminary on the monastic campus which, coincidentally, housed the Immaculate Conception Convent.

If Joseph was ever going to see Ailene and his baby again, if there was ever a chance to add to the Riccio family, then he was going to have to enlist the help of a higher power, someone with authority over the nuns. Joseph set out to visit his uncle Salvatore.

12

THE DECISION

When Spring arrived to thaw the earth, Ailene's heart remained frozen. She never saw nor spoke to her father again, and Immaculate Conception Convent became her forever home. The nuns, having taken pity on her, allowed her to stay at the convent. How could they turn away an orphan with a dead baby?

It had been months since that awful day in the hospital, and even though she could have used sympathetic shoulders to cry on, few were offered to her. The nuns were matter-of-fact about their daily rituals, and even though they were generous in nature, they kept their distance. Ailene didn't try to make any friends either. There was no point in becoming close to anyone. No point in taking the chance of losing another person she loved. Instead, she remained an island, isolated from others both mentally and physically.

When she found herself with time to spare, she spent it alone, sitting on a bench in the courtyard, underneath the cherry blossoms, watching their delicate flowers combust into a flurry of petals blown apart in the chilly wind. Lovely scented confetti only nature could provide. But no matter how hard they swirled and whirled, trying to garner her attention, their beauty was lost on her, for she was determined to never allow anything to warm her heart again.

On her bench of solitude, underneath the invisible cherry blossoms, she watched all of the future nuns and seminary students coming and going between Immaculate Conception Convent and Holy Heart Seminary. They rushed to their classes, deep in thoughts and prayers pertaining to their coursework and spiritual activities.

Right there, she had a small revelation. How simple a life this must be, never having to worry about a broken heart, since you only gave yourself to God and no other. At that moment, she wondered what it would be like to go through the process of discernment to become a nun. Could she give herself to God? Since she could not see God, nor touch God, she would, in essence, be giving herself to no one and that would be just fine with her. At that point, it didn't really matter. Nothing mattered. She was alone. She would always be alone.

She was always thinking about Joseph. She hadn't heard a word from him, and she certainly didn't have the strength to try to find him. She wondered if he would be devastated or relieved their baby died. Feeling a chill, she zipped her light jacket and raised the hood over her head. She closed her eyes to fend off the tears trying to form. Success. She had become an expert at stifling her emotions. She continually tried to push him out of her mind's eye, for she did not want to remember the lines of his face. She tried to dull her senses, for she did not want to smell his familiar scent. On this day, she wished the birds would just stop singing, because she did not want to hear the tone of his voice embedded in their song. For some reason, she could not shut out all the memories she wished she could erase. For some reason, today they were stronger than ever.

Hearing footsteps approaching, she closed her eyes tighter and pulled her hood further over her head, hiding her face, pretending to be deep in prayer, hoping whoever was approaching would walk on by. She hated small talk with strangers, and she knew it would ultimately ensue. She did not want to be told she was a child of God, that she was loved, that she was not alone. Once in a while, the nuns in the convent would try to speak to her, but she did not want to hear their sage advice. The kinder they were to her the more she hated them. The footsteps drew nearer and nearer and, for a moment, seemed to hesitate.

Please keep walking! She wished she had the power to make herself disappear. She willed the stranger away in her lonely mind. Luckily, it was as if they read her thoughts, for she heard them pick up their pace again and continue their journey. She felt the breeze left in their wake as they walked past her, and instead of feeling relief, the hairs on her arms rose as if a magnet pulled them, summoning them to follow. Not able to deny this instinct she opened her eyes to watch the back of the man walking away from where she sat on her bench, away from her and up the Seminary stairs. She could only see his back, but his confident gait, the lines of his body, the way his raven hair waved, was everything she worked so hard to forget. With a small gasp of air shot like an arrow straight into her hardened heart, she whispered, "Joseph?"

13

SEMINARY

J oseph walked through the crisp ambrosial air only an early spring day could produce. As he trudged with determined strides, his chilly hands found refuge in the pockets of his peacoat.

Soon, Immaculate Conception Convent appeared to his right. It was a large limestone building with wide cement stairs leading up to a looming Gothic entryway. The historic building's only ornamentation was its beautiful stained glass windows, hand cut and placed into intricate patterns by the skilled artisans of the past. A mass of trailing ivy crept and traveled the span of the building's facade, driving its tendrils deep into the mortar as if to hold the stones of the old girl together. Soft pads of moss formed between the cracks in the pavement, making it look romantic and eerie at the same time. It was surely an intimidating place for a young girl to have been left on her own—a refuge and a prison all at once.

As he passed the convent, he spied an infirmary and next to that a tiny chapel, all built of the same gray stone, assembled piece by piece in the 1800s. Beyond the chapel stood a library, and finally the structure he was looking for—Holy Heart Seminary. The seminary building was much larger than the convent, yet it was somehow less looming.

Its proud stone architecture was accented by humble wood-paned windows, giving it a more stately appearance.

Hidden in the center of all this hardscape was a lush and beautiful courtyard known for its meditative, serpentine, cobblestone paths, famously lined with cherry blossom trees. As Joseph made his way along the winding walkway, he could smell the sweet scent of their bouquet, wafting through the air and into his nostrils. Heavenly sweetness, swirling and dancing, tempting him like the seductive pheromones of a beautiful woman. Something he had been no stranger to in his young lifetime.

The bittersweet perfume brought back memories of the like, memories he did not share with Ailene. Yes, he was a young man, but he grew up much too fast in a family connected to crimes of the organized kind. Without a mother to guide him and a father who was too often preoccupied with business, Joseph was reared amongst a group of men who were ill prepared to raise a boy. There was money and booze. There were drugs and guns. And there were also women, older women, who taught him how to be a man when he was merely a child.

There were many things he should have told Ailene about his life, about his family, but he did not want to ruin the image she carried of him in her mind. Her perfect Joseph. He wanted to keep it that way. Her image of him as heroic and strong, intelligent and protective, all reflected back at him from deep within her big doe eyes. It was rich, her father thinking him not good enough. Joseph knew how tainted his life was, being the bastard child of a family riddled with criminal activity. But when he was with Ailene, it was as if his past did not exist. He knew she looked up to him, that she adored him, and he liked the sense of power he felt being with someone who was in awe of him.

She was not a woman, she was just a girl, and he didn't want to ruin her naive outlook on love. For if he did, it would mar the reflection he saw of himself, perfectly powerful, and he liked it that way. When he met her, she was innocent and fresh, and he could tell she was sheltered. It didn't take him long to start up a conversation with the shy girl in class, and he knew she was a conquest he could win. He almost felt bad taking her virginity. Almost. He knew better. He should have let her save it for when she was mature enough to handle it, but he liked the feeling of being the first. He liked the power of being able to snatch something no one else would ever be able to attain. The deed was done, and now there was going to be a child. His child. Something he could possess and mold and raise the right way, unlike himself.

Most importantly, he was going to keep his family name alive. He would claim his child, no matter what it took. Which was why he found himself on a path leading toward the seminary, to find his uncle Salvatore, a priest. Every crime family had one, buried deep within the church. Ailene's father thought he hid her away, but Joseph's family ties would lead him right to her and his child. His mind wandered, and he paused for a moment to glance at his final destination. As he stood there, he knew his life was about to change. He picked up his pace once again, and the building grew closer. As he passed a hooded stranger seated on a bench, praying under the cherry blossom trees, he started thinking of all the ways to reach Ailene and his baby.

14

THE STATION

Detective Sean McGovern ascended the cement stairs of the 51st precinct like he'd done hundreds of times before. Only today, he took the stairs two at a time. Gray concrete under foot, bounding pair by pair, until he reached the arched entrance into the building. Something about this case gave him a sense of urgency. Something told him this was not going to be a routine investigation. Yes, it appeared to be a suicide, everything except the appearance of her face, which is why he was called in by the first responders. Her face was untouched by trauma, unchanged—her skin remained perfect. There were no broken capillaries, there was no bloating, no discoloration. He needed to delve a little deeper. Find out who this woman was.

He was lost in thought as he entered the old building. Paying no mind to the way its massive leaded glass windows let in fractured beams of light from the outside, illuminating the crackling frescoes on its tall plaster walls. Now a police station, in another lifetime, over a hundred years ago, it had been a handsome stone estate built in the center of town by a wealthy banker. The beauty of the building, which resembled a small castle, was lost on Sean. He worked there every day and had become accustomed to its architecture. He was immune to its splendor, spending more time there than in his own home. Unlike visitors, who would enter in awe and marvel at the dichotomy between the historic architectural grandeur set as a backdrop to the bustling workings of a police station. But not Sean. Every day he stepped out of his car from the same parking spot and bound up the familiar gray stairs with his head down. He entered the same front doors, immune to the smell of old plaster and burnt coffee, clip-clopped on the same marble floor, greeted the same damned people typing, talking, and scribbling at their desks, and entered the same old office. Only to sit down in his squeaky chair and start listing the facts of whatever case he was working on.

Had he not been blinded from familiarity, he would have been enamored with the exterior of the magnificent structure. Its facade, punctuated by a soaring arched entryway, was assembled completely out of stone, concrete, and marble, chiseled and hand stacked, portraying both elegance and strength. Two wing walls flanked each side of the entry and, perched atop, were two menacing gargoyles. Attached to the back of the old building was a glass and copper solarium, verdigris with age, which now acted as a cafeteria. The building's copper rain gutters, also weathered green from the passing of time, gave the structure a romantic air. Upon the roof sat more gargoyles keeping a watch over those below. Just as they had watched Sean enter a moment ago.

Breezing in and peering down at his leather notebook, he heard a familiar voice. "Hey hot stuff, what's the rush?"

Looking up he saw Joann "from the station" studying him over the top of her leopard-print readers. Her brown, wavy hair was teased and pulled up into a frizzy bun on top of her head. Baby-fine tendrils were whipped and swirled into a fluffy mound of pouf. Smacking her gum and smiling through lipstick-smudged teeth, she looked more like a chicken ranch madam than a police station secretary.

"Were you just gonna walk by me without saying hello, honey?" She tried to be stern but was really as sweet as a grandmother. Well, a grandmother who was savvy enough to run a whore house.

"Good morning, Joann. My! Aren't you looking spectacular

today?" Sean said, rubbing his two front teeth with his index finger, signaling her lipstick smudge. His own embarrassment of ordering a coffee with toilet paper shards all over his face was still fresh.

"Thanks, honey," she said, holding up her compact mirror and wiping her teeth. "I've been working all day with these hoodlums, and not a one of them had the guts to tell me. Well, if that's the only thing that gets stuck to my teeth today, it's a good day!" She then laugh-snorted for a good ten seconds. "How's the move coming? Do you have yourself all unpacked yet in that new fancy brownstone?"

"Yep, things are great, coming right along," Sean lied.

"Uhm-hm," she said, analyzing him over her thrift store frames, not believing a single word. "Do you have any notes for me to update the file on yesterday's Jane Doe?"

"I will in a minute. Just need to go to my office and jot down a few things, and then I'll get them right to you. Did you get photos and report back from forensics?"

"Not yet. Seems like everyone's dragging their feet. Let's not take too long with that chicken scratch because I've got files piling up a mile high, and I'd like to have them done before I retire."

"Yes ma'am!" Sean promised with a wink and a salute, knowing Joann would never retire from her job. He knew that for her, working at the station was more like spending time with family; there were memories of her late husband in the old walls. Every day she came to work was a day she could be with her dearly departed Mickey, the captain who was like a father to them all.

Sean entered his office, placed his sport coat on the back of his chair, and sat down at his desk. He laid his journal out in front of him, staring at it for a moment. Gingerly, he reached for it, tapping it lightly with his middle finger, drawing his hand quickly away to see if he could get it to shock him again. He thought back to being in Sophie's apartment and how certain things he touched gave him a good zap. Still eyeballing the closed journal, he took a deep breath and let out a long exhale. He hovered his hands over his journal and closed his eyes, as if to try to get some type of feeling, some type of message. He tried to recreate the energy he felt in Sophie's apartment. Eyes still closed and concentrating deeply, Sean slowly breathed in…exhaled out….breathed in…then exhaled…concentrated…BUZZZZZZZZ!

"Fuck!" He nearly jumped out of his chair when the intercom on his desk rang.

"No napping on the job! I need those files ASAP! Snort!" Click. He could see Joann peering at him through his office door from behind her desk, hanging up the phone, her shoulders shaking with silent laughter. Embarrassed, he gave a half smile and a wave as if to say okay, all the while thinking himself an idiot for his unsuccessful attempt at journal whispering.

"What is wrong with me?" he scolded himself under his breath.

He opened the book and began to review his notes, editing them in his head, *female… Jane Doe…Sophie…lovely…suicide by hanging… appearance atypical…closet…humble surroundings…no identification…St. Catherine's Cathedral?…creeper landlord…Silas Martin… foul play?…* Picking up his phone, he dialed the landlord's number. After quite a few rings…

"Yeah…" said the uninterested voice on the other line

"Silas Martin?"

"Yeah…who wants to know?"

"Mr. Martin, Detective McGovern."

"Oh! Uh, uhm, yeah, hey, Detective." The man went from blasé to flustered, once again reinforcing the detective's suspicions about him.

"Mr. Martin, have you looked into your files? I was hoping you would be able to give me some more information on your tenant Sophie. Do you have a last name for me or any other information so we might be able to identify and contact her next of kin?"

"Uh, no Detective, I don't got any other information for ya…at this time." Sean could hear the rustling of papers, certain Silas Martin was just pretending to create the noise of someone actually looking for something.

"Would you like me to come to your office and help you look, Mr. Martin?"

"Uhh, NO! No, Detective that ain't necessary. I'll get to it," he stuttered, shuffling papers even louder and closer to the phone receiver.

"OK, Mr. Martin. If you think of, or hear of, anything, or if anyone comes around asking for her, feel free to call me, anytime. If I don't hear from you, I will be calling you!"

"Will do," replied the nervous man.

Sean hung up the phone and picked the receiver right back up, dialing Joann's desk.

"Hello? Joann here."

"Jo," said Sean.

"Those files ready?"

"Almost. Can you do me a favor? Can you run a quick credit history on a Silas A Martin, Glen Lake Apartments, Beechbaum Street, driver's license 99-652-149 and get some background information on him? Pull any files you can."

"Sure. Is he connected to your Jane Doe?"

"As of now, he's just her sleazy slumlord, but he leaves me with more questions than answers, and her name is Sophie."

"I'm on it. Anything else? I hope not, because this work is piling up."

"Yeah, actually. Do you know anything about St. Catherine's Cathedral?"

"Sure I do! I go there. It's beautiful. Biggest Catholic church this side of the Susquehanna. But you should know that. Doesn't your family belong to that church?"

"No, we went to St. Judes. My mom used to drag me there kicking and screaming when I was a kid. I stopped going when I was a teenager."

Sean remembered exactly when he quit going to church. He was sixteen. He would borrow his parents' car and tell them he was going to Saturday evening mass and instead pick up his friends. They would drive to the railroad tracks and smoke cigarettes under the trestle bridge while waiting for the trains to flatten the coins they'd placed on the tracks. He thought himself smart back then, but he should have known better. He should have known his mother, who had a direct line to Father Flaherty, would find out he wasn't going to church.

She would drag him to a few Sunday masses and definitely holi-

days until he was seventeen, but then came college and the police acad-
emy, and he just never made the time to go after that. His mother was
disappointed, but he just didn't see the sense in it.

Sean was able to sneak out of going to church as a teen, but not as a
child. His mother was religious to a fault and, at one point, was
parenting out of fear. Mrs. McGovern was convinced his intuitive gifts
were pure evil. She brought him to church more times than was healthy
for the average kid. She wanted him to be washed of his ungodliness.
He was certain she would try anything short of an exorcism.

One summer—he had just turned eleven—his mother brought him
to church almost every day. The only problem was, when Sean was in
church his visions became even more clear. They were, after all, a gift
from God. He could see the souls of those who were departed. They
did not haunt him, they spoke to him kindly and gently. They told the
stories no one else could hear. Whispers in his ear. They were
desperate to speak, to get word to their loved ones. The departed
wanted their living relatives to find peace, to know they were alright.
But he was too young to understand, or even know how to explain it to
his mother. She scared him into thinking his intuition was the work of
the devil, and the devil was terrifying to a child. So while in church,
when the visions would come, and the voices would whisper, little
Sean would try to push them away, to drown them out. His mother
would be reciting prayers into his right ear, and a recently departed
would whisper into his left. He would cover his ears and shut his eyes.
He got so worked up trying to appease his mom's wishes, trying to
drown out the signs from beyond, his palms became clammy and his
heart raced, making it hard for him to catch his breath. He would feel
cold, nauseous and nervous, and have a full blown panic attack. This
happened every time. Eventually, he associated being in church with
feelings of stress and strife. Why then, would he ever want to spend
any time in one?

Thinking back on his life, he felt a little melancholy how it was
then and how it was now. He had grown into such an analytical man; a
factual, no nonsense, non-intuitive man. He used to be so different.
Time on the job had changed him. Seeing people at their worst,

harboring hateful intentions, he found it harder to relax. Sean followed the facts, connected the dots.

Looking back, he realized he had a gift. A wasted gift. Now that he was an adult, would he handle things differently? Could he be a conduit of strong intuition when he was able to trust his gut…well, more than just his gut? Maybe. Maybe that's why this case felt so important to him. It felt as if it was bringing something back he had suppressed for too long. Joann's voice woke him from his daydream.

"Well, it wouldn't hurt you to get back in there, honey. It's not just church, it's community. And once a month they host an amazing spaghetti dinner in the church basement. I think they do it to grow their male congregation because the way to a man's heart is, well…you know! Plus, you might meet yourself a nice young lady! Ha!" Snort.

"The spaghetti dinner," Sean mumbled, remembering the crumpled paper he found in the waste basket at Sophie's apartment. He pulled out the flier he had tucked inside his journal. "Thanks Jo, gotta go!"

"Alrighty, don't forget to give me those fi—" he could hear her trailing off as he hung up the receiver. Sean looked down at the red piece of paper in his hands and read:

Join Us

at

St. Catherine's Cathedral

1612 Main Street

for our

Third Sunday Spaghetti Dinner

(the third Sunday of every month)

6:00 PM

All are welcome!

HE READ IT AGAIN. That was all it said. He turned the paper over, looking for, hoping for, clues. A scribble of anything that would lead him to information about Sophie. Unfortunately, there were no pen marks, no phone numbers, no names, not even a takeout order. Nothing. He'd hoped to find some kind of hint as to who this girl was, who she knew, why or if she killed herself. But there was nothing of the sort. Sean knew he had to do what he did best—his job. And the place he was going to start was St. Catherine's.

"Hey, Gov!" a head popped into the doorway, followed by a sizable body.

"Hey, Joey! Come on in," Sean said with a smile.

Sean watched, amused, as Officer Joseph Caputo walked into his office eating donuts out of a bag.

"You going to O'Doyle's later to watch the game?" he said, lisping snowflakes of powdered sugar onto his uniform as he spoke.

Joseph Caputo was known to his friends as Joey-Bag-a-Doughnuts, as he perpetuated the urban legend that all police officers loved and ate the sweet confections. He was six feet six inches tall and three hundred fifty pounds, intimidating to anyone who did not know him, especially to those who broke the law. However, those in the precinct, his family, knew that inside the gargantuan man, he was as sweet as his favorite food.

"Yeah, I'm planning on it, but I've got a new case and I need to run over to St. Catherine's to ask some questions," Sean answered.

"Ooohhh St. Catherine's," Joey's eyes lit up, and as if on cue, "They have warm Krispy Kreme donuts after every Sunday morning mass! Those things are sooo light and sooo fluffyyyy."

Officer Caputo hummed melodiously, closing his eyes and eating the rest of the donut he held. Savoring it, all the while making moaning noises and kissing the tips of his fingers on his right hand, like a French chef after a good tasting.

Sean knew his own mouth was hanging open in awe of what he knew he could not unsee. He was speechless for a moment, and as Joey opened his eyes he saw Sean's incredulity.

"Uh… They also have a good spaghetti dinner once a month," said Joey, embarrassed and trying to take the attention away from his sweet-eating ecstasy.

"So I've heard," said Sean, rising from his chair, grabbing his jacket, journal and papers, "I've got to get these notes to Joann," then walking toward the door. "You missed some," he said to Joey, pointing up at the large doughnut crumb clinging to the officer's shirt. "I guess I'll see you tonight," patting him on the arm as he walked out.

"OK, Detective."

Joey Bag-a-Doughnuts looked down at the large crumb on his shirt, picked it up, smiled at it, and popped it into his mouth.

15

ST. CATHERINE'S

Early afternoon felt balmy as Sean walked toward St. Catherine's Cathedral. The sun pulsed through an opaque sky caused by the burn off of the morning's dew. His senses were heightened as he cut through suspended moisture in the air, feeling it evaporate from his skin just as quickly as it was dampened.

The light reflecting off the church's stained glass windows acted like a beacon leading him to his destination. As he drew closer, the colorful glare gave way to abstract patterns of glass and lead which then became more prominent shapes, until they were the familiar figures of saints and angels depicting stories from the Bible.

He walked up the vast expanse of stairs to the large doors of the cathedral and pulled on the iron handles. The doors into the building were locked. It was curious to him as he thought the church was always open to the public during the day. Placing his hands on either side of his eyes, like blinders on a racehorse, he peered through one of the portholes in the door.

"Can I help you?" he heard a friendly but curious voice coming from behind him. He turned around to see a diminutive nun, dressed in blue, standing at the bottom of the stairs, an overwhelming stack of books in hand and a welcoming smile on her face. He deduced she couldn't be any more than twenty-two years old, probably a student.

"Hello, and yes," he said, walking down the stairs to meet her. "I thought the church was always open during the day."

"It usually is," she replied excitedly, "but they're working on the inside, getting it ready for the ordination of our new bishop in just over a week!" She seemed very excited about the prospect.

"What kind of work are they doing in there?"

"Just touching up. A little bit of painting here and there. Changing light bulbs in the chandeliers. Cleaning mostly. There's a heck of a lot of marble in there to polish! All of those statues and the altar. I'm glad it's not my job! They're trying to get it done in a few hours here and there every day, a little bit of work in between masses. Were you looking to get in?" She spoke quickly and matter-of-factly, shuffling her books from one hip to the other.

"Actually, I am looking for some information on someone who may have been a parishioner at St. Catherine's," Sean said, pulling out his card and handing it to her. "Detective Sean McGovern…and you are?"

"Oh!" said the girl, sounding even more excited. She transferred her books once again and reached her hand out to try to shake his. "I'm Sister Mary Teresa. I'm a student here. We have a lot of parishioners here, Detective."

"Well, I am looking for one in particular, maybe someone who may have recently attended one of your spaghetti dinners. Someone possibly named Sophie?"

"Hmmm…" said the girl, with a determined look on her face. He could sense she was going to be an eager-beaver junior detective, deep in thought already. "I am on my way to the rectory, detective. It's the church office," she replied. Sean knew all too well what a rectory was, having spent too much time in one during his youth. "I volunteer there in between my studies, doing some clerical duties. If you'd like to walk with me, maybe I can help you? I can look at the computer to see if your Sophie pops up in our database." A tiny white butterfly flitted past, landing on the detective's shoulder causing the small nun to giggle. Sean brushed it off.

"That would be ideal, Sister Mary Teresa. You lead and I'll follow. Would you like me to help you with your books?"

"Nope! I'm ok. It's good exercise to carry these while I walk." She rearranged the stack one last time to gain her footing.

A few shorts steps later they were on the front porch of the rectory. It looked more like a large private residence with its white wooden siding, black shutters, and expansive front porch, complete with a hanging swing on one side and rocking chairs on the other.

"If you'd like to try the door, it should be open," she said. Sean reached for the handle and opened the door.

"After you," he said, and watched as the sister entered, plopping her large stack of books on the console table in the entryway.

"Come on in," she said.

To him, it smelled like an old person's home as the scent of moth balls and afternoon cooking welcomed them in. From where they stood, Sean could assess two large rooms, one to their right and one to their left, divided by a wide staircase ascending to a second floor. Next to the staircase, on the ground floor, was a hallway leading to what he supposed were a kitchen and dining room. The room to the left of them was a formal, but inviting, sitting room with a mohair sofa, two large wingback chairs, and a brick fireplace. He could imagine the visitors who came to sit in this room. Possibly a young couple meeting with a priest about officiating their upcoming nuptials, or an old widow discussing the readings he would say at her dearly departed's funeral. Or even a boy who had visions of the dead, dragged there by his panicked mother to have his demons exorcised. This room was all about deep emotions, about hope and consolation. The room to the right, however, told a different story. It was a large front office with a mahogany desk and leather chair. On the desk stood a green banker-style lamp, some neatly ordered papers, and a large computer.

"That's kind of a dinosaur, don't you think?" Sean said, gesturing at the oversized computer.

"Haha, yes, it is," said the chuckling nun. "That's why I'm here. To help them convert their operating systems and bring them confidently into the twenty-first century! Everything is a bit antiquated in here, and that is fine for the furniture, but not for the computer systems. Come on in and have a seat." She gestured to the hunter-green leather chair in front of the desk as she took a seat in the large rolling chair behind it. Sitting in the chair made her look even smaller than before.

"Where is everyone?" he asked. The place seemed deserted to him.

"I guess the sister before me had to leave. I am a little late for my shift, but not by much."

"I hope it's not my fault that you're late."

"Don't worry about it. Besides, someone is always here even if you don't see them, which is why the door is usually unlocked. When there is no mass, the fathers are upstairs in the residence resting if they're not out on a call. So tell me again who we're looking for?"

"Well, the only thing I have to go on is her first name, Sophie."

"Let me see." His eager junior detective clicked away.

She looked as if she were an eight-year-old playing office as she typed on the antiquated keyboard behind the monolith of a desk. Wisps of blond hair peeked from underneath her coif, pointing to her furrowed brow, animating the determined look on her face.

"When I search the name Sophie, nothing comes up. I have everything from Sarah to Soraya, but no Sophie. Do you have a last name? Because maybe she's not registered as a parishioner, but her family could be."

"No, unfortunately I have nothing more than that right now. I do know she may have attended one of your spaghetti dinners."

"Oh." She chewed on the inside of her lip. It was the first time her face changed from eager to concerned. "If that's the case, it may be a lot harder to find your girl. We don't really keep track of the people who attend the spaghetti dinners. Our youth groups do sell tickets, but there is no record tied to them. A lot of the transactions are cash, and we feed many transient people who attend. We don't ask for money from those who are without. It's really a big endeavor."

"So you have no digital record of who attends?"

"No, I'm sorry," she looked disappointed, as if she'd failed her first task. All of a sudden, she seemed excited again. "But I know someone who can maybe help you! Sister Mary Vincenza is the one you want to talk to when it comes to the spaghetti dinners. She does wonderful work with the homeless. She is such an amazing person."

"How can I get in touch with this Sister Mary Vincenza?" he said, taking out his journal and scribbling her name. His answer came not from the diminutive nun, but from behind him.

"Sister Mary Vincenza is away on religious retreat. Who is asking?" said a stern voice out of nowhere.

He saw his once chipper helper stand to her feet and look flustered, smoothing the front of her jumper as a blush washed over her face, her eyes flitting over his head toward where the voice emanated.

"Uh…oh…hello Mother Superior!" The flustered nun barely eked out the words while clumsily trying to bow her head. Keeping her eyes down, not making eye contact, the way a submissive dog would behave when the alpha entered the room.

The detective stood and turned to see an imposing nun, dressed all in black, the kind of nun he remembered from his youth. The ones that used to scare him when he was a boy. He had heard stories of them wielding rulers, ready to crack any knuckles on a left hand that defiantly dared to write.

"Hello, Mother Superior," he said, reaching his hand out to shake hers.

She kept hers clasped in front of herself, not returning the gesture. She furrowed her brow, accenting her piercing hazel eyes, which were intently scanning the detective's face. The lines etched into her expression told him she was not going to be as helpful as his eager assistant. He then reached into his pocket, removed one of his business cards, and held it out toward her.

"My name is Detective Sean McGovern, and I am trying to garner information about someone who may have been a parishioner at your church."

"Our parishioners' records are private, Detective," the nun said, glaring over his shoulder at her subordinate, whose face grew even redder, eyes still cast downward. "That will be all, Sister."

The tiny nun hurriedly walked out from behind the desk, past the two of them, then out the front door, not even looking to say goodbye, abandoning her pile of books still stacked on the hallway table.

"I'm sorry, Mother...er Sister," he said, suddenly self-conscious, not knowing what to call her. "I'm investigating a case, and we have no positive ID on the woman, other than her first name is Sophie. She is deceased, and we want to be able to find her next of kin so they can be notified."

The stern nun's face grew a tiny bit softer as she reached out to take the card from the detective. "Why are you looking for Sister Mary Vincenza, Detective?" Her voice did not soften.

"I believe Sophie may have attended one of your spaghetti dinners. I found a flier in her apartment and also a container with remnants of food," he said, not wanting to let on his junior detective already told him Sophie was not a registered parishioner. "Sister Mary Teresa, who was just about to help me, mentioned that Sister Mary Vincenza was involved in organizing the spaghetti dinners."

"Well, I am very sorry to hear about the deceased, Detective. God bless her soul. We will pray for her and do what we can to help you identify her. As I said, Sister Mary Vincenza is on religious retreat, and she is sequestered. There is usually no contact in or out of the campus, but let me see what I can do. I will be your point of contact here at St. Catherine's from here on out."

"Of course," he said, knowing there would be no other option. "I would appreciate that. When will you know anything?"

"I don't know, but I will contact you as soon as I can. Is this number on your card the best way to get in touch with you?"

"Yes, yes it is."

"Very well, you will hear from me then," she said, matter-of-fact. "Now let me see you out."

16

UNCLE SALVATORE

J oseph sat in front of his uncle, Father Salvatore Riccio, in the priest's office at Holy Heart Seminary, recounting to his elder the events of the past year. Most importantly, Joseph's fathering of a child, only to have the mother swept away by her overbearing Irish father and turned over to the nuns at Immaculate Conception Convent.

He told his uncle how he had spent much of his time trying to get in touch with Ailene and that he wanted their child, but the nuns had been an impenetrable force. He asked his uncle for help. The priest listened until Joseph was finished with his narrative, not addressing anything the young man had to say.

"It's good to see you, Nephew. It has been too long." He spoke to the boy from behind his ornate mahogany desk, his glacial blue eyes intent on sizing up his late brother's child. He was an old man, but looked distinguished in his black accoutrement, his white clerical collar matching his snowy hair.

"Yes, Uncle. Sorry. It's been too long and I've been rambling. How rude of me. How have you been?" He noticed his uncle giving him the once over.

"Ah, not bad for an old holy man. My ticker has its issues, but through God's graces, all is well in the world. You're looking well, my son. Strong." The cleric pressed his glasses to his nose to get a better look at his nephew. "The spitting image of my late brother." He paused. "What are you going to be doing with yourself now that you've graduated?"

"Uhm." Joseph scrunched his face as he thought about the question, slightly annoyed at his uncle for not addressing any of the issues he had just expressed. "I'm not sure yet."

"Do you have employment?"

"I work at Sal's Pizza on the nights and weekends, making deliveries."

Looking down his nose at his nephew, "Does it pay you well?"

"Psssh." Joseph rolled his eyes. "Not really."

"How do you intend to raise a child if you don't make enough money?"

Finally, he did hear me. He answered his uncle, "Well, I hadn't thought about it," suddenly feeling foolish. He had spent so much time plotting to get to Ailene and his child, fantasizing how he would finally defeat her father, he had not considered the next steps. Thinking on his feet, he said, "I enjoyed working on the school newsletter, I was thinking of applying at *The Times*."

"Hmmm…" the priest purred. "An inside man on the newspaper staff. Not a bad idea. However, I have a better idea." His uncle removed his glasses and stood from his chair, approaching Joseph. "And it will be beneficial for the both of us. Beneficial for the whole family. Come. Walk with me."

Joseph and his uncle entered the private gardens behind the seminary. Their shoes crunched along the gravel paths as crooked trees bowed in respect. Lazy branches, encouraged by the breeze, tapped their melody on the wrought iron fences enclosing the property. While they walked, Father Salvatore Riccio explained his plan.

"I don't feel it would be a good idea for you to go to speak to the girl right away, Nephew."

Are you fucking kidding me? "Why not, Uncle?"

"It's too soon. It would cause too much chaos."

What the hell are you talking about, old man? "Chaos?"

"The nuns are very protective; they wouldn't let you near her. You see the way you have been treated so far, don't you?"

"Yes, Uncle." *That's why I have come to you. Have you not been listening?*

His uncle continued, "She is under their watch until she is at least eighteen years of age."

Joseph, distressed, stopped to face his uncle. "But, Uncle, that's a year from now! That's way too long! My baby won't know who I am."

Father Riccio cupped the young man's elbow with a wrinkled hand, bent and crooked with time, nudging him to keep walking. "I understand that, Nephew. I'm not saying you won't be able to be reunited with your family. What I am suggesting is that you stay out of sight, and I will speak to your girl…what is her name?"

"Ailene Aherne."

"I will speak to Ailene myself and let her know that you are here. I am an old fixture on this campus. No one will be the wiser." The priest clasped his hands behind his back as they walked. His long black cassock rustled with each step.

"What should I do until then, Uncle?"

"I'm glad you asked, my son. It's time you start working for the family. Do some jobs."

"What kind of jobs?"

His uncle became annoyed at the question, "Do you need my help or not?" His chilly eyes pierced Joseph, causing a small jolt in the young man's adrenaline.

Joseph felt like a reprimanded child.

"Of course. I'm sorry, I didn't mean to offend," he said, resenting having to apologize.

"Small jobs. Pick up where your father left off. You can report to me."

Joseph agreed, knowing he didn't have a choice.

17

O'DOYLE'S

Tendrils of smoke drifted above the dimly lit bar, creating mystic halos around swaying light bulbs and buzzing neon letters while nicotine-tinted photographs hung on the walls, narrating stories of past visitors to O'Doyle's.

It was this neighborhood bar, bathed in nostalgia, handed down from generation to generation through the O'Doyle family, that was the setting for many a celebratory gathering, but in the most modest way. A familiar staple in the neighborhood, it was the go-to place for locals, especially those who worked on the force, since it was just a block away from the station. On any night of the week, one could find a familiar face—belly at the bar, contemplating a long, hard day over a drink, while catching the latest game. This night was not unlike any other.

As Sean made his way through the crowd and approached the bar, he could hear familiar voices. His territorial coworkers monopolized the left corner of the bar, the one with the best view of both the mounted television and the front door. Officers never sat with their backs to the door. Joann sat on the barstool, her short legs dangling as she yelled at the television screen, while Joey-Bag-a-Doughnuts reached into an oversized jar for a pickled egg.

"Come on guys, ya need to get your eyes checked! Is someone going to dispute that? That was clearly a home run! Let's see that on the instant replay," Joann armchair officiated, yelling at the old television set above the bar.

Then, as if on cue, the announcer called, *We will cut to a word from our sponsor as the officials cue up the instant replay. We will be back right after this short message.*

"Well, look at this motley crew!" Sean said with feigned disgust as he reached out to hug Joann. She smelled like old roses and new whiskey.

"Hiya, honey! Thank God you're here—you'll be a nice distraction from this circus." She hugged him with one arm and gestured at the TV with the other.

"Why, what's going on here?" he asked, winking up at Joey, who was popping the whole egg into his mouth.

"Isn't there some sort of standard that needs to be followed when hiring these officials?" she complained. "Don't these boys need an optical check before every season? I mean, seriously! Instead of being sponsored by Miller Lite they should be getting free eye exams at Ross Optical!"

"Ha," Sean chuckled, "I'm sure they do, but no one'll ever live up to your eagle eyes, my dear. Hey, Joey Bags!" he said, slapping his friend on the back. "How are those pickled eggs treating you?"

"Hey, Gov, I've only had one so far, but so far so good!" he mumbled, mouth full of egg.

Joann lightly kicked Sean on the shin, denoting Joey may be fibbing as to the quantity of eggs he'd ingested to this point.

"What'll ya have, Sean?" asked the bartender.

"Hey, Jimmy, gimme a Jack and Coke"

"Coming right up!"

Sean looked to find an open barstool next to his friends, but there were none. It was a busy night in the hazy bar—the game always drew a crowd on a Friday night. The announcer came back on the television, *And after a short review, the play is noted as a home run. The Sox are now ahead by one!* The fans in the stands and bar patrons alike erupted.

"I told you so!" squealed Joann, with a clap of her hands. "Here, honey, take my stool," she said to Sean. "I can't sit here all night and watch these blind bats officiate. Plus, I've got to be at the office early tomorrow. I'm working a little overtime to keep you boys on track!" Then looking up at Joey with a pointed finger, "And no more eggs for you, young man! Eat a vegetable once in a while or your cholesterol is gonna be off the charts!"

"Yes, ma'am," Joey replied sheepishly. "See you later, Joann."

"Hey, Jimmy, be a gentleman and walk me to my car—these boys need to catch up," she called out to the bartender.

"Sure thing, Aunt Jo," he said as he placed Sean's drink in front of him. "Be right back, guys, keep an eye out." Jimmy came around the end of the bar to help his aunt hop off the bar stool, and Sean took her place, taking a sip of his drink as Joey helped himself to another pickled egg.

"How'd it go today, Bags?" he asked Joey.

"Not too bad. Some minor traffic violations. One domestic call, over at the projects. Some crazy old white guy in a wife beater. Had wiry gray hair, looked like cats had been sucking on it, sticking out all over his crazy-ass head. Was wielding a crowbar and screaming at his neighbor, this big old Hispanic woman, in some kind of flowery muumuu and fuzzy slippers. Rollers in her hair. Upsetting the whole damned neighborhood. Screaming at each other like feral animals. And all over a grocery cart!"

"A grocery cart?"

"A damned grocery cart! Like whose damned turn it was to roll that damned cart back over to the damned Walmart, fill it up with freakin' groceries, and roll it right back again so they wouldn't have to carry their damned bags."

"Sheesh!" Sean took another sip.

"But that's not even the worst part," said Joey, grabbing another egg and popping it into his mouth—obviously eating to calm his stress. "Duh mold madies moobs," he mumbled, mouth full and dry with yolk. Sean looked confused. Joey held his finger up and grabbed his mug of beer, trying to wash down the egg that garbled his words. "Sorry," he said swallowing hard. "The old lady's boobs!"

"What in the fuck?" Laughing, the detective grabbed a handful of bar nuts, threw his head back and dropped them in.

"She was old, Gov, and she had these reeeaaally big boobs!" he said, holding his hands out from his body, "And no bra, so they were dangling reeeaaally low." He moved his suspended hands down to his waist.

Sean had to stop himself from choking on the nuts as Jimmy, who had returned, listened, mouth agape, mid bar wipe.

"And they were just swaying everywhere and making those big tacky flowers on her muumuu move! Like big flowery waves! And the more she yelled and waved her arms at the old guy, they more they flopped around!" said the man-child. "They were like ginormous water balloons! I couldn't focus, Gov, and I wasn't distracted in a good way. They were hypnotizing me! Making me seasick. I was trying to break the two of them apart."

"The tits?" asked Sean jokingly. Jimmy laughed.

"No, the people!" said the officer, too entrenched in telling the story to get the joke. "The old guy and the lady! But I was afraid to step in between them and put out my hands for fear that I would slap one of those big swaying flowery bags!"

"So what'd ya do?" asked Sean, laughing.

"I pulled out my baton. I needed something. I wasn't going to let my hands touch anything! But I think the old guy started to get hypnotized by those fleshy pendulums, cuz all of a sudden he lets go of the cart, drops the crowbar, and just walks off babbling and yelling at himself."

Joey was a gentle giant who was unaware of his intimidation factor over others, but Sean knew his six-foot, six-inch frame, wielding a baton, would make any public disturbance become orderly very quickly.

"My stomach hurts just thinking about it," said the distressed officer.

"Could be the eggs," said Sean.

"Yeah," said Joey, letting out a heavy sigh. "Jimmy? Can I have a ginger ale?"

"Sure thing, Joe," said Jimmy, chuckling, filling a fresh glass with amber sparkling liquid and sliding it over to Joey, who was rubbing his stomach. Finally conceding, "Well…at least no one was injured or died, so I'd say it was a good day."

"Cheers to that," said Sean, lifting his drink.

"Salud," said Joey, meeting Sean's glass with a clink of his ginger ale. Both men sipped.

"So how was your day, Gov? Anything interesting to report?"

"More on the suicide from yesterday," Sean said, matter-of-fact, not wanting to get into the details, then trailing a bit, "Beautiful woman."

"Aw, really?" said Joey sympathetically, casting his eyes downward. "Sorry to hear that."

They both sat quietly for a moment, staring at their ice cubes, until Joey broke the silence.

"How'd she do it? If you don't mind me asking?"

"She hung herself," said Sean, taking a beat to remember her scarlet lips and unaffected face, and how his heart dropped when he saw the woman hanging there. "Well, at least that's what it looks like." It was never easy to witness tragedies. This one haunted him.

"Ugh…what makes people do things like that?"

"I have no idea, my friend."

"Did she leave a note?"

"No," replied Sean, frustrated. "Couldn't find one. Not one damned word. Don't even know if she has a family. She's basically a damned Jane Doe as far as I am concerned. Landlord only has a first name, Sophie. And boy, is he a shithead!" He paused. "Something's not right about this, Joey."

"Not right? In what way?"

"I dunno yet. There's so little evidence, but I'm not talking just evidence. I mean, it's most likely a suicide, right? But there's no note, no explanation, right? Why wouldn't she leave a note for somebody?"

"Not everybody leaves a note, Gov."

"Yeah, I know. But here's the weird thing, Bags."

"What's that?"

"She was beautiful."

"Yeah, you said that."

"No, I mean…" Sean struggled to find the words. "She was perfect. Untouched. Almost ethereal."

"Hmmm, those are some fancy words, Gov." The large officer nodded—he had no idea what ethereal meant.

"Yeah. All I know, it's got my stomach in knots, Bags. I am going to try to get to the bottom of it." They both nodded.

"Well, let me know if you need any help."

The bartender topped off Joey's ginger ale. "Would you like another drink, Sean?"

"Sure, Jimmy, I'll have one more, but then that's it for me. I've got a house to unpack in the morning."

"How is the new place?" asked Jimmy.

"It's got good bones, Jimmy. But I've been walking through a maze of boxes for months and that shit's driving me crazy." He slapped Joey on the back. "Actually, my friend, I do need your help. What are you doing tomorrow?"

"Nothing, I'm not on shift until Monday."

"Would you mind driving your truck over to my place tomorrow and helping me unpack and load up all the empty boxes? We can bring them to the recycling center."

"Sure! I can do that!"

"Great! And would you do me a favor?"

"What's that?"

"Could you bring your uniform?"

"Uh…my blues?"

"Yes…I want to swing by Sophie's apartment building. It's on the way back. On Beechbaum. We need to have a chat with her landlord, see if the guy can give us any more information on her. Didn't have much for me the first time. With you towering by my side, let's see if we can jog Silas Martin's memory."

18

REMOVING CONENTS

Sophie heard the jingle of a key ring rattling near her door. Metal slid into the lock, a jiggle, no entry, a slide of metal pulling out, only to be replaced by a cacophony of what she imagined were different shaped keys, one after another, attempting to pop the lock. A determined visitor on the other side.

In another time on earth, she would walk right over to the door, peep through the hole, and then turn the knob to let the visitor in if she chose. Of course she wouldn't have, but at least then she had free will. Not now. Not in her current state. Here she had no power over anything. She could not turn a knob, slide a lock, or open a window. As a matter of fact, in this place where time stood still, it took a moment for her to be able to even place her hands on anything she'd left in the physical world. Her body buzzed with energy, but it was energy she could not harness in a useful fashion. She felt as if atoms bounced frantically within her, from her fingertips to her toes, electrified and unruly.

She was going to have to learn to will herself, invisible to all but her, to touch, push, pull or even sit. Like a child learning to walk, training its brain to make its legs work, she had to train her new self, a toddler in her own way, to do the things that once came easy to her when she was among the living.

In the beginning of her new state, anything she reached out to touch passed right through her hands, as though she were made of fog. She wondered if that was what it felt like to be a cloud. The thick billowy kind one could see up close from an airplane. The kind that, upon approach, looked as if it were made of mountains of white cotton candy, touchable and pull-able. The kind that, if the plane were to come in contact with it, it would catch on the wings and be dragged along the sky in a white fluffy mass. But alas, clouds were deceptive. They were figments of the viewer's own romantic imagination. For when met with the wing of a plane, clouds dissipated, twirling and swirling into tiny droplets of mist allowing the metal to pass right through.

Sophie wanted to escape her lonely prison. Using all of her energy to focus her concentration, she would reach out and grab for the door knob, but instead of feeling the cold metal in her palm, she would feel only a buzzing in her body, its vibrations numbing her touch. If she could not feel its physical sensation in her touch, how could she grasp it to turn it? Over and over she fumbled for a grip; nothing. She would try to press her hands and forehead against a window, attempting to peer out at the world she had left behind. Nothing. *I am not a cloud nor fog, I am a failure of a ghost, who can't even muster up the energy to walk through walls.* She yearned to be a cliché.

She was a figment of her own mind's eye, doomed to this existence by her own hand. Now stuck in the place where she first ran to find solace. A private place, far enough away from everything she both loved and hated. Far away from both the angels and the demons in her life. Unfortunately, now she could inhabit her space but she could not touch its contents. She could not leave a fingerprint if she tried. Nor could she leave.

Over time—it seemed a very long time—with a lot of concentration, her sense of touch intensified, but not like in the physical world. Now, when reaching out, the buzzing she was used to feeling gave way to a shock of energy that would pass right through her as the things she touched evaded her grasp. It was devastating to her. How was she ever going to escape? How was she going to move on from this companion-less place to where she knew she deserved to be? Where was the heaven preached about in church? Where was her all-forgiving God? She was a good person while she was among the living. She gave to others, she said her prayers, she lived a modest life. Surely her mistakes would not condemn her soul to exist in limbo forever, would they?

She wasn't quite sure about the passage of time, or how long she had been trapped in her alternate universe, but she was sure it felt like a hundred years. She tried to call for help. She called for someone, anyone, to take her away from her self-imposed oblivion. She tried her best to scream and shout. She cried and sobbed. She fought to claw her way out, but to no avail. Or was it? Who was this intruder on the other side of the door attempting to gain entrance? Had someone finally heard her? Would she have to warn them? Maybe they would become stuck there, too. She heard the key click in the lock and watched as the door slowly swung open.

Oh... It's just him. Was she expecting someone else?

The visitor's large jingling keyring slipped from his grasp, snapped back by retractable cord to its resting place on his hip, concealing itself under his protruding belly. He walked through the door awkwardly trying to balance a stack of large empty boxes haphazardly piled upon the dolly he wheeled in.

"What's this?" she said aloud.

Silas Martin unstacked the empty boxes and placed them on the floor of her small apartment.

"What are you doing?" She knew he could not hear her, but still she walked over to him and got right in front of his face, almost nose to nose. "Hello! What are all the boxes for?"

He rubbed the tickle from his nose and then looked right through her, scanning the room to assess the treasure that lay beyond. She backed away, knowing he did not see her. She wondered if she would ever get used to this. The landlord then proceeded to walk right through her. She felt a shock of static electricity rush through her body, as if she had been struck by lightning. He seemed unscathed by it all. He moved with purpose as he began to nose around her apartment. He perused the place, opening the closet, looking to see what he could take. He took stock of the contents in her kitchen cabinets and drawers. Once he seemed satisfied he had looked into every nook and cranny, he grabbed a box and started to pack away the few items she had left behind in a world she no longer belonged to.

"Hey, stop that! Those are my things! They do not belong to you!" She protested, knowing the landlord did not hear a word she said.

The greedy intruder looked disappointed with his modest findings as he rummaged through her kitchen drawers, removing what little she had stored away, pouring out their contents one by one. Transforming boxes from empty to full, he took her toaster from the counter and her thirsty teapot and even pulled the clock from the wall. It was still ticking, painfully reminding her with every click that time would keep on going, even though her own life had ended.

"Why are you taking my things?" She was annoyed, even though she knew she would never be able to use any of her belongings ever again. "Ewww..." she said as she saw him open her refrigerator and sniff the slice of old chocolate cake, gobbling up the stale crumbling piece in one gulp. Chocolate icing remained on his fat, unshaven face.

Silas Martin made his way over to her modest bedroom. There was not much there for him to remove. He took the small lamp from her makeshift end table, the red glass with its candle, and the Bible that lay next to it. As he lifted the holy book to place onto the heap of her other stolen belongings, a small page fluttered out of it. Like an autumn leaf, it drifted and floated without a care, lodging itself partway under her bed. Silas then plopped himself down at the foot of the bed.

"Psshhh," he hissed like a leaking tire. "I ain't gonna make shit from this pile of nothin'," he complained, wiping the chocolate icing from his mouth onto his sleeve.

"If you are going to take my belongings, you should be donating them to the less fortunate, not keeping them for yourself or making a greedy profit on them," Sophie scolded the oblivious intruder.

The man huffed as he scanned the rest of her barren apartment. His eyes lit up as he spotted her dressing table. Atop the table sat the mother-of-pearl comb, brush, and hand mirror set, and another candle.

"Oh, whadda we have here?" he squealed in greedy delight, jumping up from his spot at the foot of the bed. "Finally, somethin' of value!"

Sophie's heart dropped—her dressing table held all of her secrets. In the hidden compartment were not only the few treasures she owned, but also answers to the questions her death would initiate. She did not want this rapacious man to be the one to have them. She intuitively knew he had a dark soul. She could feel it. If he were to gain access to the things she had so carefully hidden away, he would use them for evil, not good. There was only one person she knew who could be trusted with the precious contents hidden deep within the secret drawer, but she also knew she would likely never see him again, especially if her apartment had nothing left in it. She knew she must keep the landlord from taking her belongings— and most importantly, from taking the dressing table.

As Silas Martin reached for the brush set, Sophie tried to grab his wrist, but it was a failed attempt as his arm evaded her invisible grasp.

"Ahhh…these'll fetch a pret-ty pen-ny," he purred as he proceeded to put items into one of the boxes.

He also took the other candle; its burnt wick taunted Sophie, its blackness reminded her of how easily she snuffed out both its warm glowing flame and her own existence with one fateful breath. One careless decision. Its reflection in her own eyes, the spark of life now extinguished in both. The landlord closed all the boxes and hoisted them onto the dolly, rolling them out of Sophie's apartment as she was still entranced by her unfortunate memory. A moment later he re-entered, keeping the door wide open, and she knew he was coming back for the table.

Jolted back into the moment and angered at her own carelessness, Sophie turned to confront the man. She tried to step in front of him to stop him, but again, he walked right through her, leaving her buzzing in his wake. The buzzing left her feeling the most intense emotions. Existing in this space, she was agitated so much more than she ever was when she was among the living. As a matter of fact, all of her emotions were much stronger in this place of limbo. She angrily turned to see the obese man pushing the table toward her and the door.

"NO!" she yelled as she tried hard to push back against the table.

The ceiling lights in the apartment flickered. This time, the table did not pass through her as if she were made of fog and mist. This time her hands pressed and stayed against the old mahogany wood. She pushed back hard with all of her might against the man who was stealing her treasures and secrets. Silas Martin stopped for a bit and looked up at the dimming lights, then he looked down at the floor, checking to see if one of the table's legs was stuck on an old hardwood board. He did not see anything and started to push again. Sophie pushed back hard as the man grunted.

"Urggh! This damn thing is heavier than it looks," he said aloud, unaware someone else was listening.

Beads of sweat formed on his twisted brow as he shoved even harder, his key ring jingling as a hairy sliver of belly peeked out from underneath his stained, ill-fitting shirt.

"NO, you CANNOT take this," she cried as she tried her hardest to push against his growing efforts.

The palms of her hands began to sink into the wood. She imagined all of her treasures being hauled off by this greedy, greasy man and could not bear the thought of him discovering what she had so carefully hidden away. The letter, the rosary, the wedding band, along with the fabric! Oh what a story that fabric could tell, but only to the right person. She knew if Silas Martin were to find her treasures he would discard the fabric, thinking it worthless, and then no justice would be served for the injustices done to her. *If only I hadn't been so stupid!*

The lights flickered again, causing a loud buzzing noise. Her feet slid back across the floor as the now-perspiring landlord crouched down and wedged his shoulder against the side of the table, shoving it with all his might. Sophie lay her whole body over the top of the table in one last attempt to try to give weight to her cause. One last attempt to save her secrets.

"NOOOO…." she wailed, but unfortunately her resistance became futile, and once again she was as light as air.

The table gave way as Silas Martin pushed. He was stronger than this ghost of a woman. As he shoved with all his might, the dressing table crossed the threshold and slid right through the doorway and out of the apartment, leaving nothing behind but the buzzing light.

19

GHOST IN THE WOOD

I am no longer alone in my special hiding place. I am a shard of fabric, burdened with secrets, no longer living a solitary existence, nestled deep within these mahogany chambers. For now she is here with me.

My company is a ghost in the wood. She inhabits the space as easily as the natural grain running through it. She has turned it now and forever into a haunted piece to be marveled at by the ordinary and to be discovered by the one who has the intuition to know.

She tried her best to protect me and the rest of her treasures. I've got to admire her for that. Her undertaking was mighty. All that ranting and raving to prevent that greedy fat bastard from taking her beloved belongings, removing us from our resting place. All that anger turned her into pure energy. That energy now haunts the very thing she did not want to let go of. She grasped so tightly to her beloved dressing table, it caused her very existence to seep deep into its pores and become enwrapped in its essence.

She doesn't know quite what she is. She is still becoming conscious of her state of being. She's got so much to learn, which has put her here in the first place, and here she will stay, with me and the rest of her secrets until she can reach the other side. But it's going to take some doing.

You see, she can leave any time she wants; however, she is unaware and will remain unaware until her spirit is recognized. She will stay, encapsulated, until her story is heard by a gifted one. An empath who walks among the living. Not everyone has the vision. It is a gift given to few, and of those few, only some realize they have it. An even smaller amount of those who realize they have it will dare admit it to the world they live in.

However, I need her to become aware. I need her to be seen, or I am doomed to remain here, locked away within this musty confine. I certainly cannot accept that fate, for I have a job to do. I have a duty. A very special assignment. The weight rests on my gilded shoulders to tell her story, to do her bidding. Something she was unable to do. She should have used her voice when she was among the living. It was her destiny to do so, to bring justice. To bring light to evil. To bring a black soul to an end. But she panicked. She did not see her strength, and she succumbed to fear instead. She believes she has sinned and has not forgiven herself, and that is why she is stuck. We are stuck.

But if she can just harness her power, tell her story, forgive herself. If she can just project herself out of this chiffonier and draw attention. If she can make someone look deep enough, then all will be well in the world, for I will be discovered, the truth will be told, and she will be set free.

20

SIDEWALK SALE

S ean attempted to sip hot coffee from the tiny hole in the takeout cup as Joey's truck caught one of the many potholes along their drive.

"Fuck!" he yelled, his lip scalded from the steaming liquid.

"Sorry, Gov," the officer apologized.

"Ahhh…don't worry about it, Bags, it's not your fault. If they are going to brew this shit so hot, they should serve it in a fucking sippy cup."

"Haha! Yeah, plus these roads are a damned mess. There's a damned pothole every half mile," said Joey.

"Ain't that the truth! Isn't there someone we can arrest for that?" They both pondered the thought.

Sean and Joey had just spent the morning unpacking the detective's belongings, breaking down the moving boxes and hauling them off to the recycling center. Sophie's apartment was on the way back to his place, so Sean decided they would check on Silas Martin to see if he had unearthed any other information about the girl. Joey had changed into his uniform after helping the detective unpack. Sean knew by bringing Officer Caputo along it would add to the intimidation factor, and maybe he could scare the information out of the shady landlord.

"Turn right here, Joey—it'll be a block up on the left."

The officer made the turn down the tree-lined street. There were cars parked bumper to bumper all along the curb as a small crowd of people buzzed about.

"What's going on here? It's pretty crowded," said the detective. "There's the building, right there. Park wherever you can."

Unfortunately, there was nowhere for the large vehicle to find a place to nestle into. Joey eyed a handicapped spot right in front of the building and pulled his truck into the space. He reached over into the glove compartment and pulled out a handicapped parking permit to hang onto his rear view mirror. Sean looked at him sideways.

"What? I don't want to get a ticket."

Sean shook his head as he opened the door of the truck and got out. There was a small crowd gathered at the front of Sophie's apartment building, and as the officers made their way closer, they could see what appeared to be a sidewalk sale. A man walked by with a lamp, another with a toaster, one woman had an open cardboard box and in it was an antique mother-of-pearl brush set complete with comb, hand mirror, and red glass with candle.

"Hey, wait a minute," Sean said to the woman, who stopped, startled at the detective's command, "Where'd you get those?"

"I just bought them," said the woman, pointing "From that guy. He's selling a bunch of things."

Sean turned in the direction she pointed and saw none other than Silas Martin standing among a bevy of items and boxes all filled with what looked like the result of years of dumpster diving. There were old chairs and ottomans, lamps and toasters, clocks and sofas—mostly junk. What did catch his eye was one grand piece of furniture that stood out from all the rest with its graceful lines, majestic wood, and imperfect mirror. He knew that piece of furniture well. It was burned into his memory. For he'd sat at that table, looking long, hard, and deep into its soul, asking it questions it did not have the answers for. He turned back to the woman, "I'm sorry, ma'am, those items are not for sale."

"What do you mean they're not for sale? I just bought them," she was clearly annoyed.

Sean produced his badge, "They are police evidence taken from a crime scene."

"But I just paid fifteen dollars for them."

Sean reached deep into his pants pocket pulling out a twenty dollar bill, "Here's twenty. I'm sorry, ma'am."

The woman hesitantly took the twenty dollars Sean offered and handed him the box of items. He then turned to his friend, "C'mon Joey, it's time for a shakedown."

The two officers walked over to where Silas Martin stood, his back to the men, counting his fist full of newly earned cash.

"So, what's the going rate on the street these days for a dead woman's dressing table?" asked the detective.

Silas Martin turned to confront the voice behind him. "OH…huh, huh, hi, Detective," the nervous man stuttered, quickly shoving his cash into his pants pocket.

"Mr. Martin, what the hell do you think you're doing here? You were not to remove anything from that apartment!"

"Uh…I uh." A few people started to gather.

"Mr. Martin, this is Officer Joseph Caputo. He's helping me on this case. We came to ask you if you had any more information on Sophie. However, I can see you're busy selling off her property and our police evidence."

Officer Caputo stepped forward and Silas Martin was met face to belly button with the lawman. Joey was big to begin with, but compared to Silas Martin he was a giant. Silas Martin was a roly-poly, short man, and for what he lacked in height, he made up for in girth.

"Uhm…er…" the greedy man stuttered, "I…uh…I didn't think that anyone was gonna miss this stuff bein' as she was alone and didn't have any family members to speak of."

"And how the fuck do you know that?" Sean was getting angrier with each lie that poured out of Silas Martin's mouth. "Is there some-thing you know that you haven't told us, Mr. Martin?"

"Uh, I told you everything I know detective. She came to me one day lookin' for a place, kinda frantic, like she needed it right away. I told her how much and she paid me in cash."

"Do you have any written records, Mr. Martin? A lease with her name on it? Anything that'll give us one fucking clue to who she was?"

"Well, I got it on a paper somewheres in my office. I was lookin', but I couldn't find nothin'. I was gonna get to filin' my paperwork, but time flies. I gotta lotta shit to do. She was only here for about three months, and I already told ya, she paid me up front."

"In cash, Mr. Martin."

"Er, uh, yeah," admitted the man looking down at his feet.

"Yep. IRS will definitely be interested in that as well, and also this little side business you've got, selling off your dead tenant's belongings. And what about the rest of this stuff? Who does all of this belong to?"

"Look, Detective! I don't want no trouble here. I am tryin' to make a livin' the best way I know how. Sometimes people just abandon these apartments. What am I supposta do with the stuff? Listen, how can I make it up to ya? Here, pick out anything that ya want and ya can have it for free!"

Sean lunged toward the rotund man and grabbed him by the shirt collar with his right hand while still holding the box with Sophie's grooming set in his left. At that point Joey stepped in to pull Sean away from the man. He had never seen his friend lose his cool so quickly before. The small crowd of shoppers dispersed, and other onlookers gathered to watch.

"Are you trying to bribe an officer of the law?" said Officer Caputo as he eased his friend back and started to remove his handcuffs from his own waist belt. "Would you like me to arrest him now, Detective?"

Silas Martin squirmed, and his ruddy face broke out into a sweat.

"Nah," Sean said pulling himself together, wondering what had come over him and why he was feeling so irate around this particular sleaze ball.

Officer Caputo shooed away the small crowd that had formed. "Alright people, break it up, ain't nothing to see here. Sale's over."

Disappointed shoppers went back to their lives as Sean assessed his own mood. He had dealt with many a slumlord before, but was not sure why Silas Martin rubbed him the wrong way. He let out a deep breath and scanned what was left of the stolen inventory.

"I've got a better idea," Sean tried speaking in a slower, calmer manner, the kind of calm that simmered beneath the vibrating lid of a pressure cooker. "I am assuming this is all that's left of Sophie's belongings?" he asked.

"Yeah." answered the nervous man. "The dressin' table, that box you got right there, and this Bible." Silas Martin picked up the Bible stacked atop a pile of old books.

The detective grabbed the Bible from the landlord's hand and put it in the box he was holding, he then handed the box to Officer Caputo. "Where's the steamer trunk?"

"Uh, er, I left it at the top of the stairs, in the hallway outside her door. There's nothin' in it."

"I want to go have a look at it," announced Sean. He held out his hand, "Key."

"Key to the apartment?" asked the landlord, "But there is nothin' in—"

Sean did not let him finish. "Yes, I want the fucking key to the apartment. Don't push me, Mr. Martin!"

Silas Martin quickly grabbed the key ring hanging below his paunch and pulled it up toward his face. The retractable cord created an indent in his fat belly. Sean and Joey looked at each other as the land-lord clumsily fumbled with the multitude of keys.

"NOW, Mr. Martin!"

The sweat dripped from Silas Martin's face and he tried to wipe it off with the back of his hand as keys slipped through his grasp. His shirt was soaked under his armpits as well as under his man breasts.

"HERE," he squawked. "Here it is!" He twisted the key off of the keyring and handed it to the detective.

The key was wet from sweat and Sean abstained from punching the man in the face. He turned to Officer Caputo and handed him the box of Sophie's belongings.

"You and Mr. Martin are gonna take this box of stuff and the dressing table, and load it into the back of your truck. We're taking it with us. I'm gonna go upstairs to inspect the steamer trunk and take one last walk through the apartment to see if there's anything else in there." He turned to enter the building.

"Detective?" Silas Martin tried to speak, but Sean paid no attention to him.

"Not one more word from you, Mr. Martin," said a stern Officer Caputo, "or we will haul your ass off to jail for removing evidence from a crime scene and obstructing an active police investigation. Here's twenty bucks for the lot of it! Now let's get this stuff loaded."

As Sean entered the building, he knew he didn't really care at all about the steamer trunk. What he did care about was being back in her apartment. He wanted to revisit the space to see if there was anything else he could gather in a moment of hushed silence.

Not physical evidence, intuition. He wanted confirmation that maybe he could trust himself on this one. It seemed this was the only way he was going to be able to figure out exactly what was eating at him.

It had been a very long time since he listened to the voices in his head, trusted the knowing in his gut, and getting a taste of that old intuition made him realize he missed that part of himself. His authentic self. Once upon a time he was a child with vision and he wanted to become reacquainted to that vision once more.

21

NOTHING

S ean opted to take the stairs to the fourth floor instead of hopping in the old elevator. He needed to blow off some nervous energy. He was not sure why being around Silas Martin made him so angry. He was used to dealing with that particular type of jackass, but for some reason the closer he got to the man, the more intense his emotions became.

He ascended the squeaky wooden treads with his usual stride, two by two, as he thought about the dead girl. He was eager to enter her apartment and revisit the space. He wanted to feel the energy he felt the last time he was there.

When he reached the fourth floor landing, he saw the steamer trunk placed outside of the door to her apartment. He raised its lid to see if there was anything inside. There was nothing; it was as empty as the cavity inside Silas Martin's chest.

He let the lid fall and turned to face her door, where he was greeted by the number 403 right below the peephole. Four-oh-three. How many other lost souls may have inhabited the place? He noticed the peephole in her door. Why hadn't he noticed it before? It was then that he remembered this apartment building used to be a hotel in its former life.

He recalled stories from the older officers on the force, tales of an era during the 1950s when the place was frequented by members of the mob and their mistresses. It was the usual scene of Italian food and jazz crooners distracting the crowd from backroom gambling and illegal hooch. Men wore their finest three-piece suits and two-toned shoes while women dripped in silk and diamonds. But as drugs and crime crept into town, the luxurious guests were driven out, having to find other, more plush and safe establishments to stay. Thus leaving the hotel to die a slow death, a skeletal shell to be devalued and then bought for a steal by a lineage of slumlords in order to be turned into low-income apartments.

"Why—of all places—did you pick this tenement?" he said out loud as he placed the key into the lock.

Even though he didn't know the woman, he couldn't imagine why she would live in such a place. He took a deep breath and then exhaled as he turned the key and opened the door, entering the apartment.

The open space was completely empty save for the mattress on the floor in the area that used to be her bedroom. There was nothing left on the walls, and what little furniture she did have was gone. Most of all, it was quiet. Ordinarily and un-interestingly quiet. Dusty beams of light shone in through the undressed windows, illuminating the grain of the old hardwood floors; even the scuffed planks were stagnant. What was he expecting? Hoping for? Obviously something more.

He walked over to her closet, his footsteps echoing in the empty room. The sound bounced from wall to wall as he stepped inside. It, too, was stripped of its contents, void of everything that had set the stage for the tragedy. Only a few mangled wire hangers clung to the rods. He reached up to touch the metal rod. He was sure he would feel a jolt from the static electricity in the same way he was shocked once before. Nothing. The rod held no charge, the closet held no life, and the apartment held no energy. There was no sign of the soul that ever so lightly brushed his intuition, waking it from its dormancy.

In a way, he was devastated. He felt empty inside, and he did not like it. He wanted to be excited. He wanted to be intrigued. He wanted to feel the sensation of receiving a message from someone he wasn't quite expecting. But there was nothing.

With disappointment in hand, the intuition-less detective exited the closet. His hollow steps trudged their way back to the front door. He took one last look into the barren space and knew that he would not be back again.

22

A NEW HOME

Itt was nine o'clock on Sunday evening, and Sean sat on his sofa, white noise emanating from his snowy television set. He had been living in a brownstone that, up until this moment, had been staged as if he had moved in just days before.

As the screen hissed at him, it reminded him he had no time to watch TV, let alone set up a day to have the equipment installed. Plus, he hated that scheduling an appointment with the cable company meant "reserving a window of time." It was complete bullshit that he had to schedule a spot between 8:00 A.M. and 2:00 P.M. or between 2:00 P.M. and 8:00 P.M. just to sit around and wait for some pimply technician to show up at the very last second, upsell him on a sports package, and then hand him a remote he had no idea how to use. He'd wait a little bit longer before he'd wage that battle. Plus, the blizzard on the screen was somewhat comforting to him.

Yesterday, Joey helped him unpack the clutter of boxes that had sat there for days on end, filled with the belongings he obviously didn't need in his day-to-day routine. The bare necessities were all he was using as he meandered his way through a maze of cardboard. All he needed were sheets, towels and clothes; a toothbrush, toothpaste and some deodorant and of course a razor. One that was so old, it bit him every time he ran it up his cheeks. He was amazed at how simply he had lived with just a few essentials. He liked not having an overabundance of possessions. Except, on this day, he inherited a few new things. Among them, the antique dressing table from Sophie's apartment. He could not stomach that sleazy douchebag Silas Martin trying to profit off the few items she had left behind. How many other people had the slumlord stolen from? He shook a scowl from his face at the mere thought of the man. He sipped on a cold beer as he stared at the dressing table, situated directly across the room from him. He had been sitting for hours, just staring at it, when his cell rang.

"Yeah, McGovern here."

"Hello, Detective," said the voice on the other line. "This is Reverend Mother Mary Runa. I apologize for calling you so late."

"I'm sorry. Reverend Mary who?" he said, confused for a moment.

"Reverend Mother Mary Runa, Detective, it's Mother Superior, we met in the church rectory at St. Catherine's."

"Oh yes, Mother...er Sister...I'm sorry," he said, grabbing his journal and scribbling the name *Runa*, an equal sign, and *Mother Sup*.

"It's not a problem, Detective, I don't expect you to keep up with all of our holy names."

"You are certainly a lot of Marys," he said, trying to make light. There was no laughter on the other end. "How can I help you, Mother...er...how can I help you?" he said, feeling like an idiot for his awful attempt at a joke and for stammering over his own words in addressing her.

"Well, I was wondering if you could stop by to see me tomorrow? My office is at Immaculate Conception Convent. I have some news on Sister Mary Vincenza."

"Great! Did you talk to her, do you know if she knows anything about a person in your congregation that would fit our Sophie?"

"No, I am sorry, I did not speak with her. As I previously told you, she is taking part in a special religious retreat being held in honor of the upcoming ordination of our new bishop. The sisters on retreat are all sequestered. They do not have access to a phone."

"But this is important. A week is a long time when dealing with an investigation. Can't you just make them aware of the situation?"

"Yes, Detective, I realize that, and I am sorry, but I can't get word to anyone right now. However, I can possibly give you some guidance tomorrow on how you can speak to her yourself. Will you be able to stop by?"

"Of course. I'll be by first thing, if that's okay with you?"

"See you then, and God bless you, son."

"Thank you, Mother...ugh." He hung up, feeling odd at calling another woman "mother."

It had been almost a year since his own mother had passed away, and even though she was his adoptive mother, he had loved her with his whole heart and soul. He was devastated, yet relieved at the same time, when the cancer that racked her body had finally taken her. He had hated to see her suffer in the end. Sean was content in the fact that she was probably in a better place, along with his dad, living a happily ever afterlife. He was not afraid of death. For as a child, having had the ability to communicate with those who had crossed, he intuitively knew it was not the end. Something would live on. It was ironic to him, however, that his religious mother had urged him to suppress his gift. If he had not, would he be able to speak to her right now? His dad? He wished he could speak to them once again. Maybe one day he would, but as of now, neither she nor his dad had shown up. As a matter of fact, he had suppressed so much of his intuition that no one had shown up since those days long ago, when his mother dragged him to the priest to be blessed and then to all those masses. Those angst-ridden, panicky masses that gave him stomachaches as a kid. It was no wonder he was successful in stuffing down all communications—he would have made himself sick had he not.

His chosen profession definitely helped to keep him analytical, as he was forced to rely solely on facts and not hunches. So far, he had been a very successful detective, following the facts and breaking cases. He had also been very successful at keeping his inner voice quiet...until now. Maybe that's why he wanted to find out more about Sophie. For as he sat staring at her dressing table, he had a small revelation. Up to this point, his life had been just okay. He'd been going through the motions, but now he wanted more. He needed more, and his mother wasn't there to persuade him otherwise.

Would his biological mother have encouraged his gift? Was she still living? If so, where? And if she was, what would she have told him to do had she raised him? In the end, it didn't really matter to him —the only tie to her was DNA. His adoptive parents had given him all that he had needed in life, and now, his coworkers were his family. That was the one thing he loved most about being a detective on the force—they took care of each other, just as his friend Joey did earlier by helping him unpack his place.

So, as he found himself reminiscing on the sofa, in his now-organized apartment, still facing the rescued dressing table, he made a silent vow. He vowed to keep listening to his inner voice and perfect it. He felt a need to take care of the unknown girl. He took one last swig of his now room temperature beer and rose to turn off the snowy television. The screen went black. He walked over to the old dressing table and glanced into the mirror to take a look at his own tired eyes. He ran a hand through his disheveled hair.

"That's enough for now. Tomorrow is a brand new day."

23

WHITE NOISE

Sophie was panicked in the dark place as the smell of old mahogany enveloped her. Its deep, rich odor seemed to permeate all the cells of her being, making her feel musky and dusty all at once. She was confused as to her whereabouts, but knew her limbo was infinitesimal when compared with what it had been before.

The last thing she remembered was pushing with all her might against the efforts of her awful landlord who was trying to steal her secrets. She remembered shoving back at her beloved dressing table against the efforts of the rapacious man, feeling an overwhelming sense of anger, electricity, and madness all at once. Then, everything went black.

The blackness gave way to a profound murkiness. She now found herself confined within a shadow world, as if she had been placed into a heavy-handed, charcoal drawing, where everything was an even darker shade of obsidian. She blinked her eyes, trying to peer through the denseness, and felt the boundaries of her surroundings press in on her. She could not move an inch as she imagined mahogany walls compressing her, restricting her existence. She was trapped and isolated. Her breath, already restricted by building anxiety, was being squeezed from her lungs by the very nature of her confines. She needed to pull herself together. How, without body, did she still feel her body? She guessed it was much like an amputee still feeling their legs even though they were no longer there.

Squinting harder, she tried to make out the images before her. She could see nothing. She squirmed and turned to try to gain a new perspective, and that was when she saw the familiar thing before her. She was able to make out shadows and shapes. Her eyes traced the outlines and curves. There was something familiar about what was reflected there, the mottled markings and the stories being told by their placement. She knew them well—they were like an old friend, retelling their adventures, only on a much deeper level. For now, she knew she wasn't just listening to their tales of adventure, she was presently one of them.

In an instant, she realized this was her old beloved mirror, the one connected to her dressing table of secrets. This mirror, the one she had peered into so many times before, no longer stood in front of her. She was not looking at her own reflection. She was not looking at the mirror at all. She was encapsulated within it!

Once Sophie realized she had willed herself into becoming a part of the very thing she loved and tried to protect, she saw her darkened world with a clearer perspective, both literally and figuratively. She felt a lightness in her body, as if everything was able to expand just a little bit more. She was able to breathe again. She had become a mercurial imperfection within the mirror's glass, all on her own. Embedded into a sea of others, all ingrained one by one with each life event it had witnessed. The common saying was "if only walls could talk." But what if a mirror could speak? Oh, the stories it would tell. For, unlike walls, people engage in mirrors with direct intent. They look straight into them and expose themselves in the most honest way. Mirrors see people's vulnerabilities—and their confidences. Mirrors see the raw truth in a bare face and the made-up fantasies in a painted one. They suck in all the images they are given, and that knowledge remains forever imprinted into their very fiber.

But what was she going to do within this new prison? Certainly, she was not destined to stay there forever, was she? All of a sudden, something caught her eye. She noticed a slight movement, but where was it coming from? She realized it was far beyond the mirror. From within her mirror she could see into another world, an outside world where she could make out a figure. She squinted past all the veined markings and smudges that obstructed her view, into the unfamiliar space beyond. Sophie realized she and her mirror, along with her dressing table, were no longer housed in her apartment. They were no longer in her safe haven, sheltered away from the cruel world and its harsh realities. Was there another dimension from beyond her self-imposed limbo? Was this the bridge from her old tortured world that would cross her over into heaven? A figure drew near. Was this her God? Was he coming closer to remove her from the place she unwittingly elected to inhabit?

As the figure closed in, she started to make out details beyond an overall shape, then a face...looking right at her!

"You," she whispered aloud. The face grew nearer, peering deep into the mirror. "Do you see me?" The tired eyes looked for another beat. "HEY!" she raised her voice, "I'M RIGHT HERE!"

"That's enough for now. Tomorrow is a brand new day," the man replied, turning to walk away.

"WAIT! NO!" Sophie pleaded, unsuccessfully banging against the glass with her fists. "YOU DON'T EVEN KNOW IF THERE WILL BE A TOMORROW! HELP ME!"

No response. The man disappeared into a room, only to close the door behind him. Sophie knew if there was any chance at all she was to be set free, this was the person who was going to do it.

"PLEASE! COME BACK! SEE ME!" she banged and banged against the air but no one came to rescue her. The room was silent. Except for the TV that had turned on by itself, the snowy screen hissing at her, seemingly to shush her quiet.

24

MOTHER SUPERIOR

Sean groggily sat at the edge of his bed as his alarm buzzed. He had just closed his eyes, only to find morning rushing in ahead of schedule. He'd barely slept. He tossed and turned all night, knowing he had a big day ahead of him. He was eager to see what Mother Superior had for him. This case was important to him, igniting what he had suppressed for so long. It took the small pilot light that had burned so quietly inside of him and turned it up to maximum capacity.

He showered quickly and got dressed, yawning as he pulled his sweater over still-damp hair. He felt a chill in the air. He had a hard time remembering the dreams that shuttled through his subconscious, but knew they were plentiful. They kept him on the edge of wakefulness all night.

Pushing the bagel into the toaster slot, he inhaled the satisfying aroma of the freshly brewed coffee, made in his own kitchen with his newly unboxed coffee pot, all the while saying a silent thank you to his friend Officer Joseph Caputo for helping him to unpack. It was nice to finally have everything in its place.

His surroundings started to have a new energy. It started to feel like home. He poured the steaming liquid into a mug and took a satisfying sip. He heard something coming from the other room and entered to find the television set still on, still broadcasting its blizzard from the previous evening. *Sheesh! I thought I turned this off last night. I really must have been in a daze!* He turned off the television and took another gulp of coffee as the pop of the toaster summoned him back into the kitchen to enjoy his small breakfast. When he was finished, he grabbed his gun, badge, journal, and keys. He opened the door and had just about stepped over his threshold when his cell phone rang.

"McGovern," he answered, closing the door as he left.

"Hiya, honey! It's Joann from the station."

"Hi, Joann," he smiled every time she announced her byline. "How are you doing this morning?"

"Well, my bunions are aching, and my Spanx feel tighter than usual. It must be going to rain tomorrow. But other than that I'm swell! Are you coming in first thing?" she asked.

"I've got to head over to Immaculate Conception Convent, to talk to someone, but then I'll be in. What's up? And what's a Spanx?"

"Aww, honey, it keeps me from having to tuck my boobs into my waistband! Snort!" Joann laughed at her own joke, while Sean shuddered at the visual. She continued, not missing a beat. "Joey left an old Bible at my desk. He said to give it to you, said it was left in his truck. Said it was part of the inventory you collected this past weekend?" she said.

"Oh, yeah! Could you be a sweetheart and put it on my desk? I'll get it when I come in."

"Sure honey, it'll be here waiting for you. What are you two boys up to, working on your days off?"

"We're up to no good. You know that," he said jokingly, trying to evade her question. He did not want to admit he was delving deeper into a case, fueled by a name spoken to him out of nowhere.

"That's for sure!" she agreed, "Maybe you'll want to read a few verses from this Bible when you get back here."

"Oh yeah?" Sean chuckled, "Do you think it'll help?"

"Well, it's a start," she answered, "But you'll have to look hard to find the right prayer— a lot of the pages are missing from this book!"

"Hmmm…noted. You don't miss a trick, do you?"

"Honey, I've been in this game so long, it's hard for anything to slip by me."

"Amen to that!" he said.

"Ya see? We've got you praying already!" And with that she hung up.

Sean slipped his phone into his jacket pocket, took out his journal, and penciled in *Bible* and *pages missing*. He hopped in his car to head over to the convent.

SEAN'S first impression of the grounds of Immaculate Conception Convent was one of awe and wonder. He could not believe how beautiful the campus was. Its winding paths, lined with cherry blossom trees, seductively meandered their way between stone buildings that stood pristine and proud. The sidewalks were clean and the hedges were impeccably trimmed. Even the birds singing in the trees were perfect, welcoming visitors in, enticing them with their sweet lullabies. To any person, this would seem like paradise—Walt Disney himself could not have created a more spectacular view. As he walked up the stone stairs of the convent and into the vestibule, he was immediately greeted by a matter-of-fact, yet polite, nun and before he even opened his mouth to speak, the nun addressed him.

"Hello, Detective McGovern, welcome to Immaculate Conception, the Reverend Mother is waiting for you. Let me show you to her office."

With that she turned around and he followed, not saying a word. As he trailed behind her, her long, black habit seemed to hover above the floor, billowing just enough, creating a shushing sound along the patterned hallway rug. An aroma of incense, burning candles and mothballs lingered in the air, and it was very quiet within the building. While traversing the hallway, they passed rooms of which some doors were closed and others were open. Through one door he could see a small group of women, not all dressed in habits, a few in more casual clothing, sitting on varying chairs and sofas in a makeshift circle, quietly reciting their morning prayers.

The furniture in the convent seemed antiquated and of good quality, yet mismatched— almost as if everything was donated or bought from varying local thrift stores. There were crucifixes and portraits of bishops and saints hanging on the plaster walls, and the woodwork was polished and dark. Tapestry-like curtains hung from the tall, leaded glass windows, and the lighting was dim.

They approached another open door, and Sean could hear what sounded like babies crying. He peered into the room and saw cribs lined along the walls, with a few babies in them, being attended by nannies in habits. As he paused a moment to get a better look, one of the nuns inside the room approached and quietly closed the door.

"Do you have a daycare here at Immaculate Conception?" he asked his guide.

"Actually, some of those babies are getting ready to go to their adoptive families," and before he could ask another question, she said, "Here we are." She opened the door in front of them, letting him in but not entering herself.

"Thank you," he said.

She bowed her head, closed the door, and left him there. He took off the sweater he had donned earlier in his chilly apartment. He was in a small but handsome office with the same dark woodwork he saw while traveling down the hallway behind the floating nun. There were floor to ceiling bookshelves filled with books, some philosophical, some medical, and some looked to be different versions of antique Bibles. There was a modest wooden desk with a small lamp, a chair behind and two in front. A large oil painting of Jesus hung on the wall behind the chair, and an oversized rosary sat on the desk, along with pens and pencils, writing paper, and a name plate that read *Rev. Mother Mary Runa*. He also noticed there was another door, and, as if on cue, the door creaked open and in walked Reverend Mother Mary Runa, better known as Mother Superior. This time, she seemed a little more approachable than at their first meeting in the rectory. This time, her gaze was a little bit softer.

"Hello, Detective, it's nice to see you again," she said as she entered.

"It's nice to see you as well, Sister…er…Mother," he rolled his eyes at, once again, his own incompetence in addressing her.

"It's okay, Detective, you can call me Reverend Mother or Mother Superior."

"Yes, Reverend Mother, thank you, and thanks for meeting with me."

"It's my pleasure. I am here to help you in any way that I can. Have a seat," she said matter-of-factly, and gestured at the chair in front of her desk.

Sean obeyed. He felt her intent gaze on him as took his seat in one of the two chairs in front of the desk, placing his sweater over the arm of the chair. She then walked behind and sat at hers. Mother Superior was a tall woman and appeared to be in her late fifties. She was dressed head to toe in a black habit, which hid every inch of her, including her hairline and neck. She wore a large cross around her neck. Everything else was tucked inside the layers of fabric. The only thing visible was her creamy white face, framed from forehead to chin, void of makeup and etched with lines that furrowed her brow. Sean wondered if she had lived a happy life, for there were no crow's feet spidering from the corners of her hazel eyes to signify she had experienced a life of joy and laughter.

"You look familiar, Detective. Do you belong to St. Catherine's?" she asked.

"No, ma'am, my family went to St. Jude's when I was a kid, but they are all gone now."

"Oh, I'm sorry, " she said looking down at her desk, quickly changing the subject. "I have some information I think would help you in furthering your investigation. I know you are looking to identify a specific person and I know when you visited St. Catherine's you were not given confirmation, am I correct?"

"Yes," he answered. "I came to see if you have any record of a woman by the name of Sophie. Maybe she was a parishioner registered with your church."

"I'm sorry we could not help you then, and I'm afraid that I don't have a definite answer for you right now. However, that being said, a few times per week our own Sister Mary Vincenza leaves the campus to minister to individuals. They are usually shut-ins, poverty-stricken, or the elderly who have a hard time getting out and about. As you already know, she is in charge of our monthly spaghetti dinners. We usually have food left over, so on the following day she also takes all the leftover rations and delivers it to the homeless shelters. I am assuming she would bring food to her roster of people that she ministered as well."

"So, these are people who may not necessarily be registered as parishioners?" asked the detective.

"Correct," replied the nun.

"Is there a list of names for those she visited?" He knew finding confirmation for Sophie would not be as easy as that, but he had to ask.

"Unfortunately, no. There are no names as far as church records, since they are not regular parishioners. You will have to speak to Sister yourself if you want names. What I do have, however, is a list of addresses she has visited in the past, shelters and apartment buildings that are part of our usual rounds, mostly in more underprivileged neighborhoods. A lot of the tenants are transient and don't stay in one place for too long, which is why they are not registered with us. But they are in need, and that is why we visit them. We hope they can become self-sufficient, and then maybe they will, in turn, become parishioners."

Sean realized Mother Superior was being helpful. She did have a hardness to her, but she was not to be feared. He couldn't imagine her cracking the knuckles of a lefty, but he could imagine her setting down rules that needed to be followed...or else.

"I see. Can I take a look at this list, Reverend Mother?"

"Yes," she said, "this is for you." She handed him what looked like xeroxed copies taken from a notebook. There were addresses written in by hand. Some were scratched out with dates next to them, and some looked as if they had been entered in, scratched out, and entered in again.

"This is some interesting bookkeeping," he said sarcastically, raising an eyebrow as he scanned the pages. There seemed to be no rhyme or reason to it all.

"Yes, well, with Sister being away we did the best we could to get you what you were asking for." She seemed a bit annoyed with the criticism.

"Sorry, Reverend Mother. I appreciate anything you can give me. What do the dates mean?"

"The dates are most likely the time when service was either started or cancelled."

As Sean scanned the lists on each page, something caught his attention and made his heart flutter a bit. On the third page, somewhere near the bottom, was a familiar street: Beechbaum. He read further and spotted the name *Glen Lake Apartments*. However, it was one of the addresses crossed off of the list.

"Do you have any questions, Detective?"

"What does it mean again when the address is crossed out?" he asked.

"Well, it means that particular location is no longer on the list for Sister to visit. The tenant may not be living there any longer, or they have chosen to cancel service. Most likely the former."

"And what do the dates mean?"

"The dates are when service began and/or ended."

Sean could see the date for the cancellation at Glen Lake Apartments was the year prior. His heart sank a bit knowing Sister Mary Vincenza was most likely not visiting Sophie.

"This street here," he said pointing to the paperwork, "and this building, Glen Lake Apartments, this is the building Sophie lived in," said the detective, "but there is no apartment number listed."

"Well, Detective, she could have been visiting any one unit or a number of units. I am sure Sister Mary Vincenza has a more detailed record of which apartments she was visiting."

"Do you think she will also have names?"

"If there are names, only Sister would have that information. I want you to know that we here at Immaculate Conception and St. Catherine's are not about giving away personal information on any of our standing parishioners, nor future parishioners. But if this aids you in identifying your young woman or helps to find her family, then God be with you. I hope Sister can help you."

"I completely understand, Reverend Mother, and I wouldn't ask you for such private information if it was not for the nature of this case and the manner in which she died. We just want to find her family. I guess I will have to speak to Sister Mary Vincenza then, to see if any of this leads us to identifying our girl."

"God bless her soul, the poor thing," she replied. "May I ask you how she died?"

"She took her own life," he answered.

"Oh." The reverend mother's face grew dark; she seemed to be lost in thought. She was far away for a moment, but quickly regained her composure. "I understand she must have been in a very low place to go ahead and take her own life. It can be very hard to come back from the depths of despair. If Sister did know her, I only wish her counseling would have helped her find an alternative. Certainly she will be devastated to hear such news."

"So, how can I get in touch with Sister Mary Vincenza?"

"Well, you remember I told you it is nearly impossible to get a word to the sisters on retreat by phone, don't you?" she reminded the detective.

"That you did."

"So, the only way you can speak to her is by going there in person. I have the address for you." She reached over her desk and handed him a paper with the pertinent information. "Once you arrive at Our Lady of Fatima, you can ask for her."

"Ok, thank you," he said, retrieving the paper. "Is there anything more you can tell me?" He tucked the piece of paper and the list of addresses into his journal.

"No, I'm sorry detective. I think speaking to Sister would be your best bet for any further information. Our paperwork seems to be flawed. We are surely missing details, but we have been so busy getting ready for the official event celebrating the appointment of our new bishop. It has been years in the making and is an honor to actually have someone of our own parish being ordained. All of our attention and energies have been put elsewhere."

"Yes, I saw them sprucing up St. Catherine's the first time we met. It must be very exciting for all of you," he replied, forcing a smile, wishing people would get their priorities straight.

"Oh yes, well, that project is finally finished, thank the dear Lord," she replied. "Is there anything else I can do for you detective?"

"One more thing. Maybe I can stop by during the next dinner and speak to the people there. See if they knew Sophie."

"Oh, they are on hold for now, until the bishop's appointment. They won't commence again until next year."

"Oh," Sean was disappointed, "I guess we can just touch base after I visit with Sister Mary Vincenza."

"Very well, let me see you out." She rose from her chair.

"That would be nice," said the detective, also rising from his seat. "You've got some pretty amazing books on these shelves." He gestured to the antique Bibles on his way to the door.

"Oh yes," she said, excited to share the collection. "Some of these Bibles date back to medieval times!"

"Are they yours?"

"Not any of these—most have been donated to the church itself by the parishioners or other visiting clergy. I get to enjoy them since they are housed in my office."

"Ah, so you don't pick these up at your local garage sales or antique shops?"

"No, Detective. We are not encouraged to own anything personally. Everything here belongs to the church, and all donations must be shown to a superior before it is deemed acceptable. This ensures that we keep our hearts fixed on Heaven rather than on earthly possessions."

"I see. Well, are you allowed to have a favorite one?"

"Of course! My favorite one is a small black Bible, and I can actually call this one my own." She turned back toward her desk and pulled a weary black book from the top drawer. "It's the same one given to all the sisters here at Immaculate Conception Convent." The pages of the old book appeared to be buckled by water damage, its cover worn from obvious use over the years.

"You see, you can tell by this small golden insignia of a cherry blossom on the spine that it belongs to this particular convent in this diocese."

Sean noticed the little gold insignia. "Ah yes, that makes sense. I did admire all of the cherry blossom trees on my way in."

"Nowadays, the sisters have their initials embossed under the logo. Mine is not that fancy, but, to me, this is the most beautiful of all of the Bibles in this office. It is modest, but it means the most to me because it marked a turning point in my life."

'Well, sometimes the best things in life are the things that nobody else would deem valuable," he said.

"You're right, Detective," she replied. Suddenly she looked very sad. "It is so easy for people to throw away the very thing they should love the most." She seemed to get lost in her own thoughts once again.

"Yes, like the babies down the hall." *Where did that come from?* He surprised himself with his own statement and at how insensitive it sounded. "I just don't understand how a mother can give up her child." He thought back to the fact he was adopted. It was a closed adoption so he could never know who or where his birth parents were. He loved his adoptive parents very much and had a great life, but it still did not stop him from wondering about where he really came from.

"Well, sometimes the mothers don't have a choice, Detective." She seemed exhausted at his remark. Sad. Then suddenly back to the stern Mother Superior he first met that day back at St. Catherine's. She snapped the Bible closed, causing him to jump a bit, and placed it on her desk. "That'll be all, I will see you out now."

As the detective descended the stairs of the stately convent, something didn't sit right with him, yet he couldn't quite put his finger on it. While passing the impeccably manicured bushes and walking through the lovely path lined with aromatic cherry blossoms, he heard the familiar tune of the songbirds that sang upon his arrival. Only this time their notes were sour, out of tune just the slightest bit, creating an eerily warped song. Suddenly, everything there seemed a little too pristine. A little too perfect. As if the stage had been set. It was a production of magnanimous proportions, and to Detective Sean McGovern, anything that utopian made the hairs on his arms stand at attention. His fingertips were tingling and his gut was telling him to look beyond the obvious beauty that surrounded him. If there was a hidden seedy underbelly lurking among this paradise, he was the man who was going to find it.

25

MAKING PLANS

Sean pushed through the station doors like a kid rushing in to buy their favorite candy at the five and dime after a long day at school.

"Where's the fire, Detective"?

Hearing Joann's voice, he looked to his right to see the tiny woman standing atop what appeared to be an overturned apple crate, feeding papers into the copier. The light from each pass of the machine reflected onto her face, like the rotating beacon of a lighthouse, illuminating the pressed powder dusted across her nose and cheeks, giving her the eerie quality of a camp counselor telling ghost stories with a flashlight propped under her chin.

"What are you doing standing on that box?" he said, puzzled at the sight.

"Well, sweetie, I'll be damned if I didn't shrink two inches overnight," she said, exasperated. "I couldn't reach the copy button."

As Sean scanned the room, he could see chuckling detectives and officers with file folders in hand, raised to hide their faces, concealing their guilty looks. He knew someone must have wedged some shims underneath the cabinet, making it higher than usual. Kids at heart, they loved playing pranks on the woman they thought of as their mother hen. It was their way to ease the stresses of a difficult job.

"Whad'ya know," he said, matter-of-factly. "Just like that, huh? Well when you hop off that thing, can you meet me in my office? I've got an update on the Sophie case."

"Sure, honey, be there in a minute. There's a mountain of papers on your desk. Some new procedures to catch up on, too. That new portable DNA contraption was delivered this week, and there are protocols to learn and follow. Oh! I also left that Bible I called you about on your desk."

"Okay, thanks. I'll just grab the whole pile and take it with me and go through it at home. I have to take a road trip this afternoon. Where's Bags? I thought I might see if he'd like to ride along."

"He's on traffic duty today, hon. We've got lights out in all directions on Main due to an accident. He'll probably be out until dusk. It's going to take the city guys a while to get it fixed."

"Ah, okay. Maybe next time. See you in my office."

"Righty-oh!" she said as another flash illuminated her face.

Sean entered his office and was welcomed with a desktop piled with paperwork. "Fuck," he whispered to himself, looking at the over-abundance of reading he had to catch up on. He knew it was no one's fault but his own for letting things get away from him—he was just preoccupied. Most of the work he had to do was as easy as compiling case summary notes and reading up on new procedures. Even though it wouldn't take him much time, he knew he was going to push it off, yet again, because he had more important things to do. This case was his top priority, and he wasn't going to rest until he found what he was looking for, whatever that was.

Taking a seat behind his desk, he pushed his paperwork aside and positioned himself in front of his computer. He pulled out his journal and removed the page of information handed to him by Mother Superior. He opened the folded sheet and read to himself. Our Lady of Fatima, 16 Dalton Way, Summit Ridge, ask for Sister Mary Vincenza. He plugged the address into his computer and pulled up the directions. It would take him over an hour to get to the location, but that would give him enough time to rehearse the line of questioning he had for the nun. He printed off the directions, added them to his journal, and set them on the Bible Joann had placed atop his stack of work.

"I've got one more for you detective," said Joann, scribbling something in pencil onto one more file and adding it to his mountain of responsibility.

"You've got to be kidding me," he lamented.

"Ain't life grand, sweetie?" she answered without empathy, lifting the Bible and his journal, then placing the file on top of his stack of documents. "This should keep you out of trouble. So what's this news you have on your Sophie case?" she asked, peering over her readers while tucking her pencil into the cotton-candy-like swirl of hair piled on top of her head—the pencil almost disappeared.

"Uh..." said Sean, watching her magic trick and wondering what else she hid in there. "Well, I went over to Immaculate Conception Convent today and met with the Mother Superior. She confirmed the nun who was in charge of the church dinners makes house calls, too. One of the buildings on the list matches the location of Sophie's place."

"Really?"

"Yep, Glen Lake Apartments on Beechbaum. Unfortunately there's no apartment number. It seems last year was the last time she may have visited that address."

"Hmmm, any names on that list?"

"Nope. Is it ever that easy?"

"Honey, if it was, we wouldn't be in business. What about the landlord? What was his name? Martin? Maybe he would remember the nun."

"Yeah, I'll follow up with him. He's a shady one, though. Not a bundle of information. He couldn't even give me a last name. Some bullshit about not being able to find his paperwork. How in the world do you do business like that?"

"Well, you asked me what I could find out about him. That file I just put on the stack is about all I've got. A few lawsuits over personal property, disorderly conduct, and some traffic violations. There is one stalking case, an old girlfriend, but it seems to have been dismissed. If he's as shady as you say, I'd guess if someone showed up with a handful of cash, especially a pretty young woman, I'm assuming it'd be all the basis he'd need to rent the place. Doesn't seem like he'd want any paper trails."

"True," Sean conceded.

"Are you even sure he's got the first name right?"

"Yeah," said the detective, "I'm pretty sure he's right about that one." He wasn't going to tell Joann about hearing the name Sophie whispered to him, even before the landlord had confirmed it. She would think he was crazy. He was going to keep that to himself.

"Well," said Joann, "what's your next step?"

"I'm taking a drive up to Summit Ridge. Some religious retreat. I'm going to try to speak to the nun in person. A Sister Mary Vincenza. Hopefully, I'll get some answers."

"Are you headed up to Fatima?" She evidently knew of the place.

"Yup." He started gathering his things.

"You'd better get a move on then—it's going to take you a while to drive up there."

"Yeah," said Sean, hoisting up his pile of work. "I'll take this mess home and go over it when I get back from my road trip. See you tomorrow."

"Godspeed, Detective."

"Hey, Joann?"

"Yeah, honey?"

"One last thing? Can you set up a meeting with Silas Martin for me for tomorrow? I want to meet him at his office. Help him find his missing paperwork."

"You got it!"

26

OUR LADY IS MISSING

The mountain of paperwork previously stacked on the detective's desk was now splayed out across the entire back seat of his car, inching itself further and further apart with every bump and turn. Unfortunately, re-sorting the intermingled papers was going to double his work time. He didn't notice.

His mind was fixed on other things.

The long, lonely drive to Our Lady of Fatima allowed him time to think. He planned to rehearse the questions he was going to ask Sister Mary Vincenza. *When did you first meet Sophie? How long have you been visiting her? What did she look like? Can you spell her last name? How I can contact her next of kin?* It was routine for him to go over questions in his head and then visualize the answers that may come back to him. He knew the first question would lead to a second and then to a third. But as he proposed his imaginary questions, he kept getting stuck. As soon as his mind would quietly ask, "When did you first meet Sophie?" his thoughts would fixate on her name and repeat it over and over again. He was sidetracked. Daydreaming. Putting himself right back into that godforsaken closet on the fated day when he was introduced to the ethereal corpse with the ruby red lips. He couldn't get her out of his mind. In a way, he felt protective of her. Was it her barely lived-in apartment, with no personal objects to make it a home, that tugged at his heart? He felt a sadness in the place, an emptiness. Something gnawed at him, telling him it was not where she was meant to live, or die for that matter. Why the lipstick? Was it some sort of war paint? A sign of some kind? And why in the hell did her landlord not know anything about her? Yes, he was a greedy fuck who probably loved the cash, but wouldn't he at least remember her last name? He was definitely the type to put on the pressure if she fell behind in her rent. Wouldn't that information be pertinent to him? Someone to chase after if she bolted in the middle of the night? Unless, maybe, she didn't want him to know her details. Maybe she needed to be invisible. Maybe that's why the place had no personality, why it lacked a lived-in feel. But if she was on the run, what or who was she running from?

Suddenly, a deer appeared out of nowhere. "Jesus Fucking Christ!" he shrieked as he slammed on the brakes, causing his car to skid along, hurtling all of the files in the back seat onto the floor when the vehicle finally came to a stop just inches away from the beautiful animal. It stood there, frozen in time, this literal deer in the headlights, its innocent, orbed eyes staring directly at him. Sean's heart pounded against his ribcage, electrified adrenaline pulsed through his veins as he yelled "WHAT?" at the doe. "GET OUT OF THE GODDAMNED ROAD! ARE YOU TRYING TO KILL YOURSELF?" and then again, in a softer tone, "Why would you want to do that, Sophie?"

As quickly as she appeared, in one graceful leap the doe disappeared back into the trees. The detective rested his forehead on the backs of his hands, still clenched tightly onto the steering wheel. He closed his eyes and took a deep breath, then exhaled slowly to try to calm his racing heart. He looked up again to make sure the coast was clear before he let his foot, that still had the brake jammed into the floor, rise slowly to set the car in motion once again. He could smell burnt rubber from the tires melting tracks onto the roadway. That's when he saw it. The sign read Our Lady of Fatima. The damned deer had crossed right in front of the entrance to the very place he was traveling to visit. He rolled forward a few more feet and, with his shaking hand, flipped down the blinker to signal a left turn into the wooded entrance.

The car's tires crackled and popped along the gravel road as they rolled through the forested approach, encompassed by pine trees soaring a hundred feet high. He watched in his rear view mirror as the street disappeared behind him; foliage engulfed him as he traveled along the arborous path.

After about a half mile drive, he began to see an opening, a clearing of sorts. Within minutes, the tunnel of trees gave way to a postcard view of a lush green lawn stippled with sunlight. Golden fingers reached through leaves of chestnut and oak trees to dot the land. The gravel path transitioned to a cobblestone roadway with mossy mounded flower beds gracing either side. Butterflies bespeckled the beds bursting with emerging hostas, hydrangeas, and maidenhair ferns. Beyond him, past what appeared to be herb gardens, upon a small hill, stood a handsome building. Stone and brick ivied walls were topped with a mansard roof. It looked more like a French country estate than a religious property. The only giveaway was the smattering of holy statues, sculpted in high relief, nestled here and there within the berms and vegetation. He parked his car in the small area designated for visitors. Three spaces for visitor parking and they were all available. Sean wondered if they were always available at this place hidden deep within the woods. As he made his way up the elevated path toward the building, he stopped to notice an inscription chiseled onto the base of one of the statues. *I will give you a new heart, and place a new spirit within you, says the Lord—Ezekiel 36:26*

"Ezekiel 36:26," announced a confident male voice. The detective turned to see a priest standing before him, a tall man with salt and pepper hair, probably in his late fifties, his face like that of an aged Roman emperor, dressed all in black except for his white clerical collar.

"I'm not familiar with Ezekiel," answered Sean, knowing full well he wasn't quite familiar with any of the saints.

"Ahh..." replied the priest. Sean felt a parochial lesson coming on. "Ezekiel is not one of the more popular saints. He was a prophet of sorts, having messages of both judgment and restoration; inviting his hearers to turn away from their sins and embrace God's covenant."

"Sounds like an interesting guy. Interesting quote anyway." Sean stuck out his hand. "Hi, Father, Detective Sean McGovern."

"How can I be of service to you, my son?" the priest replied, extending his hand to reach the detective's. Sean felt uncomfortable with the priest's soft grip and hand position. It was almost as if he wanted the detective to kiss it. Ending the awkward shake right there, Sean said, "I'm looking to speak with one of your nuns. I was hoping she could help me identify a woman who is part of a case I'm working on."

"Of course," said the priest, smiling. It was the kind of smile where the mouth did all the work and the eyes had no part in it. "Let's take a walk to the house and we can summon her for you, Detective. Hopefully, she can be of assistance to you." The priest turned around and started walking toward the building as Sean followed suit.

"Who are we looking to speak to detective?" the clergyman asked, Sean still trailing behind him.

"Sister Mary Vincenza," answered Sean. The priest stiffened a bit, as if someone had pulled his shoulder blades back. A slight hesitation. He kept walking.

"Yes…yes," said the priest, lingering on the *S* at the end of each word, producing a hissing sound. "Sister Mary Vincenza." His tone was slightly flat.

"Is everything okay, Father?" Sean asked, pulling his journal from his coat pocket and scribbling.

"Of course, my son, everything is just fine," the priest said, turning his head over his shoulder just far enough so Sean could see the profile of his Cheshire cat smile. The hair on the back of Sean's neck stood at attention.

"HERE WE ARE," announced the priest as they made their way to the double front doors. The massive doors looked much taller up close.

The priest opened both the doors, as if he were a host of *Lifestyles of the Rich and Religious*, leading the men in and over the threshold. "Make yourself at home, and I will summon sister for you."

Sean stepped through the doors and into an experience like no other. Immediately, incense stung his nose as he became dwarfed by a grand foyer with ceilings soaring two stories high. Plaster walls, stained a creamy oatmeal, were adorned with dramatic oil paintings, of what Sean guessed were a multitude of saints and angels, looking as if they were painted by the likes of Michelangelo and Caravaggio themselves. Framed by ornate gilded wood, the lifelike characters appeared as if they could step out from their canvases at any moment. A tapestry hung on a far wall, as wide and as tall as the wall itself, depicting The Victory of St. Michael by Raphael, in which Archangel Michael is vanquishing Satan.

To his right there was another carved statue, akin to the ones outside on the grounds. This one, he deduced, was the Lady of Fatima herself, standing five feet tall, housed in an alcove built into the wall. In front of him, he could count at least twenty polished stone stairs, ten feet wide, leading away and up to a landing punctuated with a fifteen foot tall window, domed at the top and consisting of hundreds of leaded panes of glass. Even more impressive than that, the stairway took a sharp turn and there were twenty more stairs coming back toward and up in the opposite direction, leading to the second floor.

The floors of this grand manor were the same polished stone as the stairs but set in a diagonal pattern, creating a vastness to the space. The furniture looked rich. Chairs turned from intricately hewn woods ended in clawed feet perched on balls, their seats swathed with velvet. These were not the donated hand-me-downs he saw in the convent. Nor did this place reflect the vows of poverty taken by Catholic clergy. In addition to the incense that bit his nostrils, it smelled of old leather, cigars, and money.

The most ominous thing of all stood to Sean's left. A massive stone fireplace. Not mortar set stone, but smooth, slabbed, carved stone, a bit darker than, but almost matching, the oatmeal walls. It stood taller than he did, hand-chiseled with floral swags and shields, and flanked by two giant lions, one on either side of its arched opening. Sean touched the mane of one of the lions; it stood the height of his shoulder. He felt the coolness of the stone. The coolness of the place, of the priest. There was an aura of stateliness, pomp and power. This place was not what he expected, though he wasn't sure what he had expected.

"Impressive isn't it?" asked the priest, watching the detective admire the fireplace. The detective nodded, not knowing how long the holy man had been standing behind him. The clergyman continued, "One lion symbolizes Mark the Evangelist, the author of the second gospel, and the other lion represents Jesus's Resurrection as Christ the King."

"Very impressive," replied the detective. "This is not a building I would expect the Catholic diocese to own."

"We actually don't own it, Detective. It is loaned to us, from an anonymous donor family, and as long as we take care of the estate and the grounds, we can have it for as long as we like, and it can be used to best serve the mission of our diocese. It has been with us for over seventy years. This week it hosts a holy retreat before the ordination."

"Yes, so I've been told." And with that, Sean was snapped back to the purpose of his visit. "Sister Mary Vincenza ?"

"Well, Detective, I'm so sorry to tell you, it appears Sister Mary Vincenza is not here at the moment."

"Not here?" Sean was incensed. "What do you mean she is not here? I was told she was here."

"Yes, my son. I am very sorry. She was sent with another sister on a short road trip, to procure the other three bishops who will officiate the ordination this weekend. She is en route to pick them up. I can have her contact you as soon as she returns in a few days."

"A few days! That's unacceptable, Father. I need to speak to her right now."

"I understand, therefore I have brought for you someone who may be able to help you in the meantime. This is Sister Ave Margaret, she is an assistant to Sister Mary Vincenza and helps her with her duties when needed. I am sure she can help to give you some guidance."

Out of the shadows stepped a timid looking nun, eyes cast downward and hands clasped in front of her as if bowed in prayer. She seemed to be in her twenties and reminded him a lot of Mary Teresa, the sprite of a nun he met when he first visited St. Catherine's. However, this nun's energy was much different than that of his eager-beaver junior detective. This young girl was timid. Nervous. The freckles on her nose spilled over into the sea of flush covering her cheeks, flaming red tendrils peeked out from her simple habit framing her wide blue eyes. Eyes that seemed a little bit pink around the edges as if she had been crying.

"Hello, Sister, nice to meet you—uh, are you okay?" Sean said, extending his hand to shake hers. She flinched just the tiniest bit. It was so small a movement only his trained eye would notice. She reached out to shake in return as the priest answered for her. "She might be a little bit nervous. I told her the reason for your visit, Detective."

"I won't bite. I only came to ask a few questions," he said, addressing the tiny nun while ignoring the priest, "Have you been crying, Sister?"

"No," she finally squeaked out. "I have allergies. There are so many flowers on the property, and I seem to be allergic to all of them," she sniffled.

"I understand. Can we sit and talk?" the detective asked.

"The two of you can sit right here," the priest said, gesturing to two antique mohair chairs situated in front of the fireplace. The detective and the diminutive nun sat opposite each other as the looming stone lions watched over them. The priest chose to take a place standing behind Sister Ave Margaret.

"That'll be all father," said Sean, looking the priest square in the eye.

The priest placed his hand onto the tiny shoulder of the girl in the mohair chair, who now looked much younger than her years. Sean saw her flinch again. "Very well," the priest said. "Peace be with you both." She closed her eyes and barely whispered, "Same to you, Father Giuseppe." And with that, he left the room to let the two of them talk.

Sean took out his journal and wrote, *Father Giuseppe—what's his story*—and then turned his attention to the nun, who was looking at him with eyes bigger than the doe he almost hit a short time ago. He smiled at her to try to ease her nerves.

"So Sister, I won't take much of your time. You help Sister Mary Vincenza with her duties, correct?"

"Uhm, yes, once in a while," she answered.

"Do you remember going with her to visit any apartment buildings on Beechbaum Street?"

"Uhm, yes, on Beechbaum, I remember visiting one apartment building with Sister. It was a kind of run down place, right?" she asked him, looking for verification.

"Is this it here?" He said, handing her a photo of the dilapidated building barely taken care of by Silas Martin.

"Yes, Detective, this is the one, Glen Lake Apartments. There was one unit we would visit, it was on the fourth floor. We would bring food, pray with the tenant, and then see if there was anything else they needed."

Sean became excited. "Was it a woman named Sophie? Unit 403? Auburn hair? Maybe thirty or so?"

"Uhm, no, I don't remember a woman by that name. The tenant in 403 was a very old man. Uhm, a Mr. Riley, I believe."

"Are you sure about that?" he said, confused. "Can you take a look at this?" He showed her the log given to him by Mother Superior.

"I'm positive. As a matter of fact, he passed on over a year ago, now. We never went back to that unit." She scanned the log presented to her. "See right here?" She pointed to a date. "This is the date Sister will have marked as discontinuation of visita—" She paused for a moment. "Hmmm…that's odd?"

"What is it sister?" He asked.

"This date is recent. I know for a fact, the man died over a year ago."

"Could she have visited another tenant in the building after the man, Mr. Riley, had passed?"

"I guess so. But if she did visit someone else there, I was not with her. Sister usually keeps very detailed notes in her log book. We really don't have a great computer system for the diocese." She shrugged her shoulders. "It's a little antiquated."

"I've heard that once before, when I visited St. Catherine's. A young nun about your age was helping them update the system. Her name is Sister Mary Teresa."

For the first time he saw a twinkle in the young nun's bloodshot eyes and she sat up a little straighter.

"I know Mary Teresa!" She perked up. "She's a friend of mine. We studied together when we first came to the convent. It's no surprise she is helping. She's great with computers."

"Sweet girl," he said. "Seemed a little spooked by Mother Superior, though." He noticed her eyes darken a bit at the mere mention of Mother Superior. He wondered if the Reverend Mother had that effect on all of the young nuns. He changed the subject. "Well, I guess I'll have to wait for Sister Mary Vincenza's return. You've been very helpful, Sister. Thank you." Sean handed Sister Ave two business cards. "Call me if you can think of anything else, and can you please give the other card to Sister Mary Vincenza when she gets back?"

"Detective…I don't." She started to say something and, as if on cue, the priest returned from the shadows. The girl with the fragile spirit quickly took the cards and tucked them into her sleeve. She looked worried all over again, eyes cast to the ground, shoulders rounded just a little bit more.

"Sister?" Sean asked. Something was not right.

"Yes, Detective, I will," she answered, addressing his shoes. "Bless you." She bowed her head and scurried off, not acknowledging the priest.

ON THE DRIVE back into town Sean felt uneasy about his meetings at Our Lady of Fatima. He'd left with more questions than answers. What was it about the priest with the Cheshire Cat smile who seemed to silently appear at will? The man who limply shook his hand once again before he left. And why did Sister Ave Margaret seem so upset and jumpy? *Allergies, my ass.* She seemed almost afraid in her surroundings. He felt that she was telling the truth about Sister Mary Vincenza not visiting Sophie. But how could there be no record of Sophie, when there was clearly evidence pointing to the church, like the flier for the spaghetti dinner in her garbage can and the candles? She seemed connected and disconnected to the church all at the same time.

His phone rang. "McGovern."

"Hiya, Detective, it's Joann," She announced herself without her byline.

"Joann who?" he teased.

"Joann from the sta—" She caught herself and laugh-snorted. "Ah, honey, you're such a character!"

"What's up?" he asked, chuckling.

"I just got off the phone with forensics. Have some updates on your Sophie case. Official report is that it was a suicide, honey. No foul play."

"Seriously? Are you sure?"

"Yep. No foreign DNA under the nails. No bruises anywhere on the body, other than the ligature marks on the neck from the belt. There were no additional marks, and toxicology came back clean."

"Wow." Sean was puzzled. "I just don't get it, Jo. I was sure they'd find something. Her face. It was unharmed, like she was sleeping. It reeked of being staged." *Like there was something still alive in her, even in death.*

"Well, I don't know what to tell ya, honey. I'll mark up the file and you can look at it when you come in. Maybe now you can just focus your efforts on finding her next of kin."

"Pshhh…" he lamented. "Needle in a haystack."

"Yeah. But if anyone can find them, it's you, Sean."

"Thanks, Jo. Talk soon."

"Hey wait! Before you hang up?"

"Yeah?"

"Did you happen to take any photos of the scene?"

"Yeah, I took a few with my phone. Why?"

"Those damn yonkos down in forensics don't have a one!"

"What do you mean? They don't even have one? I let them in myself. Saw them documenting the whole scene!"

"Yeah, but not a one came out properly. They mustn't know how to use their own damned equipment. Every photo was blown out white. Overexposed, they said."

"You've got to be fucking kidding me." Sean was mystified and more than a little pissed. "I'll check to see what I have and get them to you."

"Thanks, hon! You're a peach!"

The detective drove directly home knowing he had hours of work to finish. He parked his car along the curb and opened the back door to remove his files from the backseat.

"Fuck!" he growled through clenched jaw as he saw the jumble of papers and files on the floor of the car. He squatted down to fish everything up. Papers were all mixed in a mess. He stacked everything in his arms and as he grabbed for the last few loose sheets, he noticed something. A little glint of gold from underneath the seat. He reached in and found the small black Bible, the one Joey had given to Joann. The one from Sophie's apartment. It must have slid beneath the front seat from the backseat when he slammed on his breaks. He pulled the Bible out, revealing a gold cherry blossom insignia on the spine. The same exact insignia as the one in Mother Superior's office, and underneath the insignia on Sophie's Bible were the initials MV."

This is it! This is the proof that Sister Mary Vincenza visited Sophie. It was imperative he speak to the nun herself, to get to the bottom of things. He was pissed he drove all the way out to Fatima only to find out she was sent on a road trip. He was going to have to speak to the Reverend Mother again. He also needed to speak to Silas Martin.

Sean got up from his squat, both knees crackling, and slammed the car door shut. He walked up the stairs to his brownstone and unlocked the door. When he entered, he was surprised to hear the faint hum of the television set, aglow once again. He knew for a fact he had turned it off when he left. He set his work down on the kitchen counter along with his keys, badge, and gun. He grabbed the Bible from the top of the pile and walked over to the television set.

"What the fuck is wrong with this thing?" he asked as he pulled the plug from the outlet, shutting the TV off once and for all, then plopped down on his sofa. On the opposite wall stood Sophie's dressing table, staring at him. "I am going to get to the bottom of this," he said out loud to the table. He leaned over to click on the lamp that sat on the end table. Nothing happened. He noticed the darkened bulb.

You've got to be kidding me. Sean proceeded to examine the Bible in hand in the dimly lit room. It looked almost exactly like the one belonging to the Reverend Mother with its gold cherry blossom insignia on the spine, except this Bible was in much better shape. Newer. He remembered how the Reverend Mother's had crinkly pages —water damage—and a well-used look, as compared to this Bible with an almost pristine cover. He kicked off his shoes and grabbed the throw blanket tossed over the edge of his sofa, draping it over his body to shoo away the chill that hung in the air. He opened the Bible and began to fan the pages, and as he did, one of them fell out. Upon inspection, he found the inside of the book was not reflective of its perfect outside. Indeed, Joann was right, a whole section of the Bible was missing, torn out, toward the end of the book. It appeared as if the last chapter was completely gone. Sean continued to examine the book, reading bits and pieces, before he laid it on his chest and closed his eyes.

27

THE SLEEPING MAN

Watching the sleeping man from deep within her mirrored limbo, Sophie knew she was never going to get used to her new surroundings. It already felt like a lifetime, living in a cloudy fish bowl, trying to break away from her tragic reality. She was free of her physical body, however, her mind and soul were still imprisoned. And the worst part—it was by her own foolish and cowardly hands. Sophie did not like it, this new fate of hers. She was an actual reflection of herself. Imprisoned within a mirror. Entangled within others' stories of the past. Stains in the glass. Shadows of the lives of people whom she never knew and would never come to know. She had no acquaintances in this distorted realm, only herself, her thoughts, and the screaming fabric tucked inside the drawer for safekeeping. Its now-familiar voice was embedded within the wood, embedded within her being, within her very essence, in the confines of this secret place.

She yearned for it to be quiet. To shut up. To stop telling the tale of what happened to her. She knew what happened to her. She lived it. But the fabric would not hush. It retold the events over and over as it enshrouded her, inhabiting her mind. It was driving her crazy.

Sophie had plenty of time to think while being stuffed away. All she did was think. Think about how stupid she was. What a short-sighted fool she was to have sinned in such a horrific manner. The nonstop introspection was driving her mad. So much so, that when she became agitated, things started to happen. Things in the physical world. She was a ball of energy. A buzzing ball of energy. And when her soul became overwrought with emotion, when it would finally build to a point it could no longer be contained, occurrences happened, taking place outside of the space she inhabited.

On one recent occasion, when Sophie was in a particularly prolific rage, when she could no longer hold on to the mounting pressure, when it slipped from her grasp, she saw the television in the outside world turn itself on. She then experienced a rare moment of peace. It was strange. This uncontrollable energy seemed to explode from her being, causing a power surge in the outside world. She was fascinated as the screen burned brightly, knowing it was switched on by the release of her pent up energy. Sophie tried to make sense of it all, until the familiar man emerged from behind the closed door. He noticed the television was on, and he turned it off again, only to exit the space. Deserting her. Leaving her in deafening silence once again. However, it was a small bit of comfort to know she may have some type of control over her existence. Maybe, with a little practice, there was some way for her to be found out. Some way to be released from her prison.

There were trials and failures as Sophie attempted to recreate this energy transfer, alone in the empty space, without the man. Her attempts were unsuccessful when she focused on frustration and anger. Sure, she felt awful, but there was no power in those negative emotions. It was when she faced the truth, the truth of where she was, of what happened to her when she was among the living, that things started to happen. As in life, when one faces the truth, they harness the power to change their circumstance. All at once, Sophie succeeded in switching the dormant television back on again, and it cast its luminosity into the once-darkened space. A metaphor to the truth enlightening her darkened soul.

Sophie quickly found that once switched on, she could not turn it off. The energy she harnessed was a quick surge and then it was gone. If a light was on, she could make it flicker. If a light was off, she could flash it on, but it would quickly fritz out, causing a tiny cloud of smoke to emanate from the broken filament inside the glass, its black haze clinging to the glass walls of the orb. Not much of a feat, but something was better than nothing.

It was during this time of experimentation that the familiar man came back once again into the physical space he inhabited. She watched him throw a pile of papers onto the countertop and walk over to the television to address the white noise she initiated. This was a good sign, him noticing. Surely he would start to investigate why the television was turning on at random. But to her dismay, he unplugged the cord, frustrated, thus disconnecting any chance she had to signal the outside world. Sophie was devastated.

However, as he turned around she saw something in his hand, something familiar to her. The Bible! He sat, took his shoes off, curled himself up under a blanket, and fanned through the pages. One of the pages fell out, making him notice the back end of the book and how the last chapter was missing. She took note of the look on his face, his deliberate introspection. At that moment she knew he was questioning why the book would be in such a state. She knew he was contemplating the reason behind the missing pages. Sophie knew, instinctively, the man would look further, and he would find the answers. Answers that would lead him to her. At least she hoped for that to be true.

For the first time in her eternal limbo, an unfamiliar feeling came over Sophie. For a brief second, she had a knowing. That even as the man placed the Bible on his chest and fell into a deep sleep, she knew he would dream of her. She knew he would glean some answers in his subconscious, and she only hoped he was astute enough to follow his intuition to wherever it would lead. For if he did, it would certainly lead him to her, and to the answers to the questions he would not otherwise think to ask.

As she sat in silence watching the sleeping man, pictures ran through her mind, flashbacks of looking at her own face in the mirror, and of times before that, of who she was and of what was done to her. The things she hoped to forget by tucking her secrets into a mahogany box guarded by an ethereal butterfly, by ending her life, were somehow now more vivid and in the forefront of her mind. The truth was not to be ignored. She knew that now.

Sophie no longer tried to push them out, or make them stop. The contents of the drawer. The screaming fabric. The crystal rosary with its crucifix tinged the slightest of red. The pages of the Bible repurposed into a letter of sorts, folded and stuffed into an envelope. All waiting to be found. Waiting to tell her story.

28

DREAMS

Sean was jolted awake from a dream he couldn't quite remember. The Bible once resting on his chest was thrown to the floor, and his cell phone vibrated on the end table displaying a message from Officer Caputo—or Joey Bags as it was entered in his contacts.

Where ya been? the message asked. *Meet me at O'Doyle's.*

Sean rubbed his eyes and focused on the time. It was 9:17 in the evening. He'd been asleep for hours, dreaming turbulent dreams he couldn't quite remember. *Be there in ten*, he typed out. He knew he needed to get out of the house or else he would not be able to sleep through the night after taking such a long nap.

In the car ride over to meet the officer, he called the Reverend Mother, leaving a voicemail. "Uh, yeah, this message is for the Reverend Mother. Hi, Reverend Mother, this is Detective McGovern. I know it's late but can you give me a call in the morning? I wanted to let you know I drove up to Fatima today and Sister Mary Vincenza was not there. I was wondering if you knew any—" Beep. The machine cut him off. "Shit!" he said and clicked off of the call.

When he arrived at the bar, it was like arriving at a relative's house —a familiar place with familiar faces was always the scene at

O'Doyle's. Quiet on this late weeknight, only a few people inhabited the place. A lone patron sat at a corner table swirling ice cubes in an amber colored liquid with one hand, while clenching an unlit cigar in the other, simultaneously picking flecks of cigar leaves off of the tip of his tongue. The man watched as four others played shuffleboard off to the side, still in their soiled work clothes, hooting and hollering as their weighted disks slid across the board and clicked their opponent's game pieces off of the edge, leaving their own pieces on a better score. The detective spotted Joey sitting at the bar, in the usual spot, shooting the breeze with Jimmy.

"There he is," cried Officer Caputo, standing to shake his friend's hand while giving him a simultaneous guy hug.

"Hey Bags, great to see ya. Hey, Jimmy," he replied, sliding onto the stool next to the officer.

"What'll you have, Sean?" asked Jimmy.

"Jack and coke, hold the coke, and make it a double, Jimmy."

"Whoa," teased Joey, "Rough day, Gov?"

"Frustrating day, Bags. I drove all the way up to Summit Ridge to stop by Fatima only to find that my contact was not there."

The bartender slid the drink in front of the detective and the two men watched as Sean took a long sip, then continued, "Amazing place up there. Beautiful property, HUGE building."

"I've never been—guess I've never had a reason. I heard it's tucked deep in the woods," said Officer Caputo. "Jimmy, can I get a sausage and pepper sandwich and a beer?"

"Sure thing, Joe," answered Jimmy, removing the pencil from behind his ear and scribbling on a lined green pad. "What about you, Sean?"

"Yeah." he answered, his grumbling stomach reminding him he had not eaten since breakfast. "That sounds great, Jimmy."

The bartender disappeared into the small kitchen behind the bar. Sean returned to the previous conversation with his friend. "It is tucked in the woods. I almost clocked a deer on the way there."

"Whoa. What were you doing up at Fatima?" asked Officer Caputo.

"I had a bit of a lead on Sophie's case. I was on my way up there to speak to a nun who may have counseled her, and I wanted to try to get some more information. Like a last name, or if she has any relatives in the area, anything at all. But when I got there, the nun was not there. Just some cagey priest who shuffled some other nun off on me."

"Aw man, that sucks," his friend commiserated. "So, her prints didn't return anything at all?"

"Nope. And now I'm probably going to have to take another trip back up there at some point. Waste of time," he huffed, and took another sip.

Jimmy laid two plates, accompanied by two bottles of beer, in front of the men. Both officers closed their eyes and inhaled the aromatic steam rising from the juicy sausage links smothered with fried onions and green peppers, all stuffed inside a crusty roll. Mouths watering, they dug in to their dishes.

"I've been up to Fatima," Jimmy said as he watched the men devour their sandwiches, mouths too full to speak. "I used to go up on church retreats with my youth group when I was a kid. It really is beautiful up there."

"Yeah," Sean mumbled, his cheek stuffed with food like a harvesting squirrel. "I can't believe the building on that property! It's like a mega mansion from the middle ages." He took a swig of beer, washing down the tasty meal.

"Totally," Jimmy concurred. "I hear the mob owns the property."

"The mob?" Joey choked slightly on his beer.

"Yep. They've loaned it to the church for years for the tax write-offs. Plus, I hear they always have priests embedded within the church. I used to hear stories when I was a kid, and now that I'm a bartender," Jimmy shrugged. "Well, I hear everything."

The officers looked at each other. For as long as they'd know good old Jimmy the bartender, they'd never heard this much information coming from him. Jimmy lowered his voice a bit, "Those guys are connected. Secret meetings within the confessional booths, smuggling hooch through the back doors. Gambling in the basement. No one is suspect a holy man of foul play. Plus, the church is never going to tell because they get huge donations from these guys."

"Wow, Jimmy, that's quite a tale!" exclaimed Joey.

"It's true! Just ask Aunt Joann!"

Their dear Joann had been a part of the police force longer than both of the officers combined.

"I heard you say the priest was cagey. What's his name?" asked Jimmy.

Sean thought for a moment. "Father Giuseppe. Not sure he gave me his last name." Sean did recall the hair on the back of his neck standing up.

"Huh, well I'd be curious, especially up at that place. You know, my sister's kid is an altar boy at St. Catherine's. He's serving at both masses this weekend; he probably knows the priest," Jimmy said, removing the empty plates from in front of the satiated men. "The next round of drinks is on me. Would you like another?"

"Sure, I'll have one more," replied Sean.

"Me, too, thanks," replied Joey. The three men talked well into the night as Jimmy shared stories, keeping them all entertained.

29

RESTLESSNESS

S ean tossed and turned all night. He had dreams of Sophie, her face, her red lips, her hanging there. He saw himself, with her, in her closet just before she took her own life. He saw her stepping up on the chair and wrapping the belt around her neck. He was there with her as she moved to step off of the chair, and he ran toward her in slow motion to try to prevent her from committing the act. "NOOOOO!" he tried to scream, but no voice came out. He attempted to grab her legs, to hoist her up, but her body exploded into a million little butterflies, he was too late. She was gone.

The same scenario played over and over in his mind, along with other events he could make no rhyme or reason of. In one instance she was locked on the other side of a dirty glass wall, pounding on it, screaming to be let out, begging for him to help her. In another she was sitting on the floor, encircled by red church candles, hugging her legs tightly to her chest rocking back and forth, forehead to knees, crying, while torn pieces of Bible pages floated down all around her.

Sean wanted to reach out to Sophie, to touch her shoulder, to help her up and to tell her everything was going to be alright. But when he drew near, when he extended his hand out to her, it passed right through her and she dissipated into mist. The mist became fog. Fog he found himself driving through as his headlights reflected off it, glaring back at him, making it even more difficult to see what was beyond. In his dream, he drove faster into the obscurity, not knowing what lay ahead of him, but he sensed a definite danger. He slammed on the brakes, which did not hold. They easily gave way to the floor. They would not grip the tires no matter how hard he stomped. The car picked up momentum as it sped faster and faster through the dense air, his hands gripping the wheel, holding on for dear life. Suddenly, in a flash, a deer appeared, and he became transfixed on its eyes as the car careened toward it, closer and closer, faster and faster, as his foot smashed through the floorboard, his leg now caught in the hole. He barreled toward the frightened animal which morphed into Sophie and then into Father Giuseppe. A thunderous impact!

In a panic, Sean awakened from his nightmare as thunder and lightning filled the dark morning sky. Drenched in sweat, his night clothes clung to his body and his heart was beating out of his chest. The sound of the storm outside, combined with the all too realistic dream, had him spooked.

He peeled his damp clothes off, dropped them onto the floor, and hopped into the shower. No time to waste, he had a busy day ahead of him. Once out of the shower, a towel wrapped around his waist, he stood in front of his steamy mirror, lathering his stubbled face with shaving cream, but it was all for naught. The storm outside cut the power, and now he couldn't see a damned thing. Shaving would have to wait until the storm subsided, so he wiped off the cream and hurriedly got dressed. He poured black coffee from the day before into a travel cup, grabbed his things, and headed out of his darkened brownstone.

As Sean shut the locked door and descended the stairs, he did not look back. If he had, he would have noticed the lights in his townhouse had turned themselves on again. Instead, he was distracted by his ringing phone, "McGovern."

"Hello, Detective, it's Reverend Mother. I received your message this morning, and I am very confused. I know for certain Sister Mary

Vincenza is at Our Lady of Fatima. I personally chose the nuns that would attend the retreat. There must be some mistake."

"Thanks for getting back to me so quickly, Reverend Mother. Yeah, well, the priest up there told me she and a few others were sent on a road trip to pick up others who were coming in as part of the ceremony to appoint the new bishop?"

There was a slight hesitation on the other end. "A road trip?" she asked, sounding baffled. "Who told you that?"

"Father Giuseppe," answered the detective.

Sean heard a pause on the line, then, "Uh, oh, uhm," the Reverend mother stuttered. "I will speak with Father Giuseppe myself and get back to you, Detective."

"Okay, I'd appreciate that," he replied. "Is everything okay, Reverend Mother?"

"Yes, yes," she replied. "I'll speak with Father and call you back."

"Time is of the essence, Mother…" he heard her click off on the other end. "Sheesh," he whispered aloud, "What the fuck is going on?"

When Sean got to the station, he hurried to his desk as if no one else existed. He pulled out his journal and started making notes for himself, notes about his strange visit to Our Lady of Fatima, notes about his dreams, notes about his curious call with the confused Mother Superior. His gut told him there was something more happening behind the scenes. As he saw Joann approach his office, he also remembered the jumbled files and paperwork still sitting at his place. Work he did not finish. This case was consuming his thoughts and taking time away from his other duties. As she entered, he felt like a schoolboy who forgot to finish his homework.

"Everything okay, honey?" she asked. He was immediately relieved. "Aw, Joann, I forgot the files at my place," he said apologetically. "I slammed on my brakes yesterday and they fell onto the floor of my car and got all messed up. I promise I will grab 'em this afternoon and bring 'em back to you, all organized and updated."

"I heard. Jimmy, told me you almost hit a deer yesterday. Just glad you are okay. That could have been a tragedy."

"Yeah! The damned thing jumped right outta nowhere," he exclaimed.

"As they always do," she replied. "How was your visit at Fatima?"

"Weird. I'm more confused than ever now. The nun I went up there to talk to wasn't there. Then a priest, named Father Giuseppe, introduces me to some other nun, a young one, and she really didn't have anything for me. She was nervous and jumpy about something. I think it was a waste of time, if you ask me."

"Well, you may just have met the man who is going to be the next bishop," she proclaimed. "Father Giuseppe, from St. Catherine's, is the one who is going to be ordained."

Sean was not surprised Joann knew that information; she and her family attended services at St. Catherine's. Most of the town did.

"Really? So he's the one all that sprucing up and hubbub is about? Maybe that's why I got the chills when I met the guy. He's the 'Great and Powerful Oz,'" Sean said sarcastically.

"Ha," she laughed politely at his joke. Then she turned to close the door to his office. Once closed, she approached his desk and lowered her voice a bit. "He will be powerful in the church once he is the bishop." Joann then laid another file on his desk.

"Oh no, not more work," he whined.

"You want to read this one, hon. But it's for your eyes only. I pulled it when Jimmy told me about your meeting with Father Giuseppe. I knew you were going up to Fatima and I know this case was important to you."

"This case is important me," he stressed.

"Chief's taking you off, hon. Since it's been deemed a suicide, there's nothing more to investigate."

"WHAT? What about who the fuck she is? Her next of kin? Who's going to claim her? Bury her?"

"Look, I'm not the chief, so until you speak to him, do what you want. I'm not stopping ya, honey. I'm helping. Read the file. I'm not sure how or if this ties in with your girl, but I didn't put two and two together until Jimmy said that you met Father Giuseppe. My great-nephew is an altar boy in the church."

"Yeah, Jimmy told me." He paused. "Sorry for getting excited, Jo."

"Don't you worry yourself about getting excited. You didn't hurt my feelings, hon. And, you may not have gotten chills because he is powerful. You may be on to something big, honey. Just be careful."

Joann turned, leaving Sean alone with the file. He took a closer look and saw it was a cold case, something her late husband Mickey must have worked on back when the police chief was still an investigator. The case was unsolved, just waiting for a breath of fresh evidence to have it reopened. In reading the file, Sean found it was somewhat of a local history lesson, picking up and continuing the stories Jimmy hinted at the night before at O'Doyle's. This time there were names and details. Old Mickey must have shared stories with his nephew but in a very general way, merely brushing on the tip of the iceberg. For within the folder Joann had laid in front of Sean were the chronicles of a powerful, local family, using the church as one of many covers for their clandestine meetings and backdoor dealings.

There was talk of money laundering, hushed through large donations, hidden deep within the sanctions of the church. There were messages shared from mobster to priest, to mobster again, safe within the confines of a confessional box. There were even quiet rumblings of unspeakable acts between grown men in black and altar boys. But none of it was proven, so it lost momentum and never picked up any publicity. Soon it was stuffed and stapled and jammed into the back of a tin file drawer. The one thing Sean took away from reading was the mob had its ties deeply imbedded in the church. The chosen priest was to keep an eye out, listen for the latest business dealings, relay messages, and, ultimately, be the cover for illicit happenings.

The last priest of note was a Father Salvatore Riccio. He was in line to be the next bishop, but died suddenly. The coroner's report gave the cause of death as a heart attack, however, foul play was eventually suspected. Residue of an anthracycline drug was found on a glass he drank from. He'd had a history of heart disease, and such a drug could induce heart failure. Unfortunately, the glass in question turned up missing from the evidence locker, and the priest was buried before a second toxicology could be performed. No one spoke of it again.

Sean wasn't exactly sure why Joann gave him the file. He planned to ask her, but if his time was running out, if it was true the chief was going to take him off the case, he needed to rush over to Silas Martin's office to get the information he needed before it was too late.

SEAN PICKED his way through the basement of the Beechbaum building. It was dark and musty, and smelled like mold as moisture seeped from the cracks in the underground cement walls. Exposed lead pipe pinged and popped above his head as steam forced its way through the system, the noise chasing away scurrying mice in search for more peaceful tenements. *You cannot make this shit up.* The setting seemed an appropriate place to house Silas Martin's office. He knocked on the peeling, overpainted door.

"WHAT?" a cantankerous voice yelled from the other side of the dirty door.

"Mr. Martin, it's Detective McGovern. Can I have a word?"

Sean heard the rustling of papers and drawers opening and closing as Silas's flustered voice called out, "Oh, er, uh, yeah, Detective, give me a minute."

"Bullshit," Sean whispered to himself. He did not wait. He turned the knob on the door. "I'm coming in, Mr. Martin."

"Yeah, uh, ok, sure, Detective come on in."

Sean entered the man's unkempt office just in time to see him swiping a pile of crumpled money into the top drawer of his desk with his forearm, while simultaneously attempting to kick a bottom drawer closed with his foot. The room looked like a disaster zone. As if an old-timey cartoon character had pressed the T-bar on top of a TNT canister, exploding paperwork all over the place. Dirty files, yellowed newspapers and magazines were piled everywhere: on top of file cabinets, crammed into bulging drawers that were stuffed to the brim and unable to be closed. Mounds of papers were also spread across a lone sofa, upholstery chewed with moth holes.

Box upon box littered the floor, piled with more papers and books, and everything was covered in a thick layer of dust, as if it had been there for decades. On Silas's desk were more mounds of papers, empty cups, and half-eaten bags of chips, all covering a calendar blotter from years gone by. It, too, was coffee and food stained. Sean wrinkled his nose at the odor of rancid Chinese food. As the clock on the wall announced the incorrect time, the man behind the messy desk scrambled to look busy.

Silas Martin was clothed in a yellowing wife-beater and filthy work pants. His hair was disheveled, and he looked as if he hadn't showered in days. Sean could barely keep from shaking his head in disgust. Silas tried to smooth his hair as he stood to greet the detective, but it sprung back up in greasy defiance. Silas held out his hand, and Sean reluctantly shook it, which caused the slumlord's unbuckled belt to jangle, reminding the unkempt man to secure it.

"Haha...oh," the man said with nervous laughter as he buckled his belt. "I ain't as fit as I used to be, I gotta unbuckle my pants while I'm workin' at my desk." He then scurried over to a chair in front of his desk, removing more piles of stuff and throwing them onto the already blanketed couch. "Here, here, Detective, have a seat. I'm just tryna catch up on a shitload a paperwork."

"I can see that," the detective said, surreptitiously wiping his hands on his pants, while scanning the room as he sat in the chair offered to him. "Looks like you've got your work cut out for you."

"You wouldn't believe it detective, but I know just where everything is in this mess."

"Great," replied Sean. "Then you'll know just where your paperwork on Sophie is."

"Uh...yeah...right," replied Silas, who then proceeded to open and close all of the drawers connected to his desk—except for the top one containing the money—returning nothing. Raising a finger, he said, "Hold on, it's gotta be here somewhere."

"Mr. Martin."

"No, no, really Detective, I got a file on 'er." The man stood up and walked over to the file cabinet with the stuck drawers. "It's in here somewheres." He began to fish through each one of them, returning nothing as precious time passed on the incorrect clock.

"Mr. Martin."

"Wait, wait." Finger in the air. The landlord then moved over to a plastic wastebasket and bent over to begin rummaging through it, digging through shredded papers and the previous week's lunches. But it was the crack of his hairy ass sticking out above his now-belted pants that sent Sean over the edge.

"MISTER MARTIN!"

"Here… here, here it is!" The nervous man spun around waving a crumpled paper in the air. "Here's her paperwork! Rae! Her name is Sophie Rae!"

30

MOTHER AND FATHER

Mother Superior rapped on the door of Father Giuseppe's office. She took a deep breath and straightened herself as she waited for an answer.

"Enter," he said, "and close the door behind you."

She'd heard he had come back to the seminary earlier that morning, and she wanted to talk to him about why Sister Mary Vincenza had not been at retreat. She opened the door and entered. His darkened office always smelled a little woodsy, as if it had been newly smoked with frankincense. An incense normally used at mass as a symbol of purification. A symbol of the faithful rising to heaven. However, in his presence, it always felt the opposite. It was a feeling she could not shake.

"Father, thank you for seeing me," she said as she bowed her head slightly. "I need to speak to you about something."

"Yes, Reverend Mother. I don't have much time. How can I help you?" His arrogance was palpable.

"I was wondering why Sister Mary Vincenza was not to be found at Fatima when I sent Detective McGovern to speak with her?"

"YOU were the one who sent that detective to disrupt our retreat?" he said, clearly agitated. "Why in the world does he need to speak with Sister Mary Vincenza?"

"Yes, Father, I sent him," she replied, unmoved by his annoyance. "He is working on a case. He came to visit the rectory because an unidentified woman has died. She may have been part of our congregation, and Sister may have been the last person to see her."

"Who is the woman who died?"

"Well, the detective doesn't know. That's why he is looking for Sister Mary Vincenza, to see if she can help with identification. He only has a first name of Sophie."

"So this Sophie could be anyone. I don't recognize the name. Do you? Why in the world does he think this Sophie woman is connected to our congregation?" He stood from behind his desk and walked toward the Mother Superior.

What happened to you? She wanted to ask as he sauntered toward her. *Is your appointment to bishop going to your head even before you are sworn in, you pompous ass?* She wondered how he was going to act once he actually became the bishop? She was getting annoyed.

"Father, a woman is dead," she sternly persisted, knowing she could be just as strong as he was. "And where is Sister Mary Vincenza? I appointed her to the retreat myself. If anyone should be alerted to her change of assignment, it should be me."

"I sent her off to pick up the bishops, so they can settle in before the service this weekend, and I answer to no one." He raised an arrogant brow.

She frowned. "It is not her responsibility to pick up the bishops. We have priests for that. The sisters are to prepare the events following the service."

"There are plenty of sisters there to plan, MOTHER."

"That is not the point, FATHER. I am the Reverend Mother Superior. I am in charge of the nuns, and I need to be consulted regarding any decisions made concerning them."

"In this instance you were NOT consulted," he snapped at her.

"Well, I should have been, JOSEPH!" She caught them both by surprise, calling the priest by the name he once used when she loved him all those years ago.

"You can leave now, AILENE." They both knew that was coming.

She turned away from him, face ruddy with an emotion she refused to reveal to him. The tears welling in her eyes were not from sadness. No, she would never be that weak again. She was angry—angry and bitter.

It had been forty years since Joseph Riccio had followed the trail to find her and their baby at Immaculate Conception Convent. She was shocked he had actually shown up to claim the two of them all those years ago. She had no idea he would come to find her. She remembered the day when her father had thrown her newly pregnant self into the car and driven her away from her only love. She had watched out of the back window of the car as Joseph just stood there, his silhouette fading to a sliver in the sunlight. She had wondered why he was not running after them. At that moment, she resigned herself to the fact he would never come to find her.

Soon after that, she removed her father from her life, and she decided Joseph was gone as well. She once thought he had whisked by her as she sat on a bench in the cherry blossom courtyard, but she played it off as her wishful imagination. She was shocked when many months later, while praying alone in the small chapel on campus, he appeared out of nowhere. Like a specter on the altar. Young Ailene had to wipe away her cloudy tears and blink hard to realize she was not seeing things.

"Joseph?" she asked the apparition.

"Yes, it's me," he said.

She ran into his arms and squeezed him tight. "Joseph, my Joseph, what are you doing here?"

"I have come to take you and the baby. We don't have much time. My Uncle Salvatore is the priest here. He is the one who has been communicating with you. We need to leave now." They were still holding each other tight. She was so happy to finally have at least one person in her life to love. Then the realization of what he said set in.

"Your Uncle? Father Salvatore? I don't even know who that is. He has not been in touch with me."

"What are you talking about? He's been coming to see you on

behalf of me. He is the one who is reuniting me with you and the baby."

"Oh Joseph," she said sadly, searching his chestnut eyes. "I'm broken. We don't have a baby."

He loosened his embrace and pulled away from her, holding her at arm's length by her small shoulders. "What do you mean we don't have a baby?"

"Our baby died," she cried, tears streaming down her face. "It was stillborn. I'm so sorry." She tried to lean into him for support.

Instead of being sad about their child, instead of being empathetic and consoling the poor young mother who was clearly devastated, Joseph grew angry. Ailene saw his eyes change from warm brown to almost black. "Good God, girl!" he reprimanded, slightly confused, pushing her away. "Can't you do anything right? You're a liar!"

"Joseph, please!" she said, trying to reach out to him, gulping for air as her sobs caught her breath. "It wasn't my fault! I loved our little baby!"

"Get away from me," he said swatting her hand away. A look of disgust distorted his face. "We have no baby, we have no we! All you have is your pathetic self!"

"Joseph, no!" she wailed, falling to her knees as she watched him walk out of the chapel, leaving her there on the floor, sobbing at the altar. She cried for hours, mourning the death of their baby all over again. Mourning the death of them.

She thought she would never see him again, but, to her bewilderment, he had enrolled in seminary under the tutelage of his uncle, the man she never met. Father Riccio groomed him to be the next powerful priest to represent the connected Riccio family within the church. Salvatore Riccio planned on becoming a bishop and moving to Rome, leaving his local legacy to his nephew, who would continue his dealings hidden deep under the cover of a holy front.

Eventually Joseph became Father Giuseppe Riccio, and with each accomplishment, with each success, his ego grew larger and larger. He was the polar opposite of a gracious holy man. He was a conceited, perverse, egomaniacal man. When his uncle died, Father Giuseppe

Riccio became the most powerful priest in the church. And just like any flawed, toxic, codependent relationship would have it, Ailene would also remain in the church, becoming a nun in the same congregation, rising up the ranks with a guarded heart, until she became the Reverend Mother Superior.

They would never have a romantic or physical relationship again, but they would coexist, codependent on one another in the same tainted world, under the guise of being the most holy upon high. They appeared to be the gold standard to others, and yet, in reality, they were two of the most flawed human beings on earth.

No, she would never shed a tear in sadness for that man again, and this day was no exception. She would also no longer cover for his misogynistic tendencies. As she left his office, she decided she would speak to Sister Mary Vincenza herself before the bishop's mass. She would arrange for Sister Mary Vincenza and herself to meet with Detective McGovern in the rectory after the service. She was tired of women always falling by the wayside while the men flourished in their wake. She would help the detective get to the bottom of his case, if it was the last thing she did. She wanted to finally do something right.

31

HOLIER THAN THOU

F ather Giuseppe Riccio's apathetic eyes followed Mother Superior out as she turned and left his office, slamming the door behind her. He dare not let himself remember her as Ailene Aherne.

"Stupid woman," he spat.

He waited for her to leave, then turned to face the armoire where his majestic silken garment lay hidden inside. It was buried deep behind other mundane attire, the bland black pants and shirts worn by regular priests. He opened the doors and dug through fabric until his hands came upon the grand fibers of the stolen, golden-threaded robe, dangling on a padded hanger in hushed secrecy. He didn't remove the robe, he didn't dare expose it to the light, he just stroked it, grabbing a fist full of the vestment's fabric. Not unlike a madman, he closed his eyes and took a deep breath, trying to calm himself from the trauma of her visit.

The priest wouldn't dare let himself feel any of the weak emotions he associated with his youth. He would not give in to feelings of melancholia, for they were for the fragile, for the faint of heart, for those who did not advance in life. He was powerful and strong, and he would be ordained in just a few days. After that, he would leave the country, residing in Rome as a regal bishop. Studying under the Pope himself, learning how to become the next one.

Father Riccio's mind kept going back to his confrontation with Mother Superior as flashes of Ailene's young face replaced those of the now-matured woman. Trying to shake it off, he squeezed the robe tighter, a security blanket of sorts, reminding him of his connections to strength and power. But Mother Superior's presence brought him right back to the past, when he first came to the seminary to find her and the child, all those years ago. He was sure he arrived with his own best intentions, intentions to ascend. He never really came to rescue the girl who loved him. He only came to claim his property. The child. His own flesh and blood. And when he found out about the baby, when Ailene told him of its death, he pushed her aside just as he intended to do all along. She was so weak. It was easy for him. Women were a dime a dozen. He never had it in his angry heart to love a woman. Eventually, he wanted only to condemn them for their sins. For what woman ever nurtured him? Even his own mother abandoned him, leaving him to be raised by men without morals.

As a matter of fact, the only one worth loving was himself. Even his uncle, his own flesh and blood, failed him.

It bought him back forty years, when as young Joseph, he turned to his uncle for help. When Father Salvatore Riccio said he would contact Ailene on behalf of young Joseph, he believed his elder. Joseph obeyed his uncle's suggestion to lie low, so no one would know he was there. He did the jobs for the family his uncle sent him out to do. Jobs he had to grow the stomach to execute. He thought, in time, his uncle would reward him, arrange for his reunion with Ailene and their baby.

Unfortunately, the old priest had other plans. Salvatore blatantly lied to his nephew. He had no intentions of contacting the girl. He knew the baby was no longer there, for Father Salvatore Riccio was the head of the ring, hidden deep within the church, that stole babies from their unwed teen mothers, telling them their babies had died, and then selling them to other families.

The priest didn't want Joseph to be bogged down with a child and a foolish girl. Instead, he groomed Joseph, calling him by his Italian name, Giuseppe, molding him into a functional member of the family. Lying to his nephew about the girl, telling him the time was not right, sending the young man out on jobs to keep him busy, jobs for the family, knowing Giuseppe would grow accustomed to the work over time. First there were simple jobs, relaying communications or making deliveries of mysterious packages. Then, they became more intense— stealing artifacts, embezzling money, riding along on hits made to send a message. Over time, Giuseppe became anesthetized to the horrors, and the more he got away with, the more egocentric he became. Giuseppe was untouchable. He was invincible.

When his uncle arranged for the paperwork to fast track Giuseppe into the priesthood, Giuseppe loved the idea, for it gave him cover in plain sight. No one would ever suspect a holy man of such atrocities. However, his uncle was too successful in his quest to groom his nephew. It was easy to help Giuseppe rise to power, for over time, it was power and control that drove him. Giuseppe's heart hardened, and although he pretended to be a holy man, he lived the life of a sinner. One of his sins came the day he actually had a weak human emotion, the day he decided to disobey his uncle and try to speak to Ailene himself. It was the day she told him his uncle never went to visit her. That she had no idea who the old priest was. That their baby had died.

Soon after his conversation with Ailene, Father GiuseppeRiccio and Father Salvatore Riccio sat in front of the massive stone fireplace in the mansion owned by their family at Our Lady of Fatima. Two larger-than-life, carved, stone lions loomed over them, listening to their conversation.

"Uncle, there is something I need to tell you." He rose from his seat in front of the fireplace and walked over to the table displaying a bottle of brandy and two glasses.

"Yes, Nephew. I'm listening."

"I went to see Ailene today." Giuseppestarted pouring a brandy for each of them, his back to his uncle. Not turning around, he raised his head slightly, awaiting reply.

"You did?" The old priest shifted in his seat. "Tell me about it."

"She told me you never went to speak to her. She doesn't even know who you are. She also told me our baby died at birth."

"You are right, Nephew. I never went to speak to her. There was no need. The baby was already gone."

"Why couldn't you just tell me yourself, Uncle? That the baby had died?"

"Because the baby was not dead, my son." The old man watched as his nephew spun to face him. "It was not dead, but adopted out to another family. There was no need in you fretting about it."

"But why, Uncle? That was my flesh and blood."

"I'm sorry, Nephew. You are both too young. You needed to grow up. Besides, this is your place now. There is no room for a child in the life of a priest, in the life of this family. There is a business to run. You must focus."

"But this child would have been family," Giuseppe replied, trying to conceal his fury. He turned back to the glasses of brandy and removed the vial hidden in his sleeve.

"That child was conceived in sin," his uncle replied coldly.

Secret adoptions were the unspoken, underground protocol of the church as it unwittingly became for any unwed mother who dared to enter. According to the church, it was a sin to have sexual relations before marriage. According to Father Salvatore Riccio, any child conceived in sin would be given away in a closed adoption, that neither the church, nor the receiving family, would ever speak of again. A substantial donation to the church would soon follow the adoption.

Giuseppe silently poured the contents of the vial into his uncle's cup. "Then let's drink to family," Giuseppe said, turning, handing his uncle the tainted cup. He raised his own glass toward his uncle's. "To family."

"Alla famiglia," his uncle replied, drinking his drink, laced with a concoction that would be innocuous to anyone with a healthy heart, but fatal to an old man with a bad one.

The next day, the old priest was found dead, and the young priest took his place within the church. Father Giuseppe Riccio became a stone-cold version of his uncle—an egotistical man without empathy, without remorse. He never told the young girl Ailene their baby was alive and, to this day, as the Reverend Mother Mary Runa, she was still unknowing. Her suffering brought him joy. This secret was the one thing he had over her.

Still grasping his garment of silk, he basked in knowledge he'd soon become bishop.

32

COLD CASE

"Where's Joann?" the detective questioned one of the officers whose desk was closest to hers.

"I think she said somethin' about headin' over to O'Doyle's," the officer answered. Sean looked at his watch. It was four o'clock on Thursday afternoon—he couldn't believe how quickly time had flown. "A little early for happy hour, don't ya think?"

The officer chuckled. "It's happy hour somewhere! Hey, by the way, Chief's lookin' for ya."

"Yeah, if you see him, tell him I'm at O'Doyle's." Sean exited the station, file in hand. He wasn't going to make himself available for the chief. He didn't want to be told Sophie's case was officially closed.

Entering O'Doyle's, he shook the rain from his overcoat. The strongest part of the storm had passed, yet only Joann and Jimmy sat at the bar. This time Jimmy was on a stool next to his aunt.

"Hey, Sean," Jimmy said as Sean sat to join them.

"Hiya, honey," said Joann.

"I didn't realize it was happy hour already. Where was my invite?" said Sean. They all chuckled. "This is some file you handed me, Jo. You think it's connected to Sophie?" he asked.

Jimmy got up and walked to the door, locking it as he flipped the open sign to a notice that read "back in ten." He pulled a draft and placed it in front of the detective, then pulled one for himself. Joann sipped on what looked to be a Tom Collins.

"You know, Sean," said Joann, "Jimmy and I were just discussing this. I'm not sure if it is relevant to your Sophie, but it's definitely relevant to Father Giuseppe. His last name is Riccio, honey, and his uncle was Father Salvatore Riccio of THE Riccio crime family. The family is definitely doing business under the cover of the church. Has been for years. When the elder priest died, things got quiet within the church, and Mickey used to always tell me that when things get quiet, they get dangerous." She swirled the cherry in her drink by its stem, "Mickey was on to something. Something about the death of the old man possibly being foul play." She sighed and took a sip of her drink. "But nothing ever came of it. The case went cold and then he died. It broke my heart to see him go before it was solved."

"Do you think Father Giuseppe Riccio killed his uncle?" asked the detective.

"There were rumblings. He did take his uncle's place right after. But now you've got a case where a girl has died and it's leading right back to this guy. I thought long and hard about pulling the file and blowing off the dust, but if it helps you crack down on something, anything, then so be it. It is just good information for you to have in the back of your mind while dealing with these people. An educated detective is a good one. But be careful."

"Will do, Jo. And, thanks," he said, reassuring her he would be careful, knowing full well no one was ever really in control of any situation. "To Mickey!" he said, raising his glass. They all clinked a toast to the late chief. Sean chugged his whole beer. "I'm going to run back home and get that paperwork done like I promised. I'll have it ready for you tomorrow."

"Great!" Joann said. "Oh, by the way, Chief keeps asking me to close the file. I've got you at least one more day because I told him the photos from forensics were bad and you were going to send me yours."

"Oh yeah, I forgot to get those to you," He took out his phone and opened his photos. As he scrolled through the pictures from Sophie's apartment, he saw they were all overexposed. "What the fuck?" he said, scrolling through the lot of them, each one filled with a bright white orb, washing out the scene behind it. "Lemme look through my phone when I get home—there's got to be a few good ones in here. When I find them, I'll email them to you." Sean stood, his head feeling a little light from the afternoon drink.

Jimmy unlocked the door for the detective and flipped the sign back to open. As Jimmy opened the door a small butterfly flew in and flittered around Sean's head as he unsuccessfully tried to swat it away. "Ha! Little guy's lookin' for some shelter from the storm. See ya later, Detective."

Arriving back home, Sean entered to find every light in his place was on. He drew his gun and searched every room, finding no intruders. "What. The. Fuck." he said out loud. "I am losing my mind!" He tried to remember if he'd turned off all of the lights before he left, but then remembered the storm was messing with the electricity. He rubbed the stubble on his itchy face as he flicked off each light, one by one, leaving only one of them on. He was thinking about Sophie. She was always at the forefront of his mind, especially when he was in the silence of his own home. It was as if he felt her presence, hanging heavy in the chilly air. He grabbed all of the files and paperwork he'd promised to finish for Joann, including the one she had just given him, and spread them out on his kitchen table. It took him hours to reorganize them, distribute them into their coordinating folders, and jot down his own notes on each.

When he completed his work, he neatly piled it up and walked it over to Sophie's dressing table, the closest piece of furniture to the front door. He placed the files on top so he would not forget to grab them in the morning. He walked back into his kitchen and picked up his cell phone to, once again, scroll through the photos he took at Sophie's apartment. None of them were clear enough to send to Joann. Each one was overexposed, blown out white. Except for the accidental selfie he snapped in the mirror, in her closet.

As he zoomed in to the photo of himself standing in front of the mirror, the flash from his camera reflected in the glass, there was something else he noticed over his shoulder in the photo. A face. Someone behind him, staring into the same mirror. Tiny hairs all over his body stood on end as he threw his phone onto the table. *What the fuck is wrong with you?* He scolded himself, rubbing his tired eyes and shaking his head. Enough. He took a chair from his kitchen table and sat in it in front of the old dressing table. He leaned forward on his forearms and stared into the mirror.

"What are you not telling me?" he asked. "What is it I need to know that I am not seeing?" He rested his forehead in his hands, to concentrate. He dozed off.

The next thing he knew, he was waking up, slumped over the dressing table, drooling from his sleepy mouth onto the stack of newly organized files. As he straightened up, he caught a glimpse of himself in the mottled mirror. Standing behind him, both of her hands placed on his shoulders, was Sophie. He gasped, heart in throat, and spun around to confront the apparition, trying to draw the gun he didn't have, knocking his newly organized files onto the floor, scattering them around once again. There was nothing there. No Sophie.

"Jesus Christ!" His racing heart pulsed adrenaline through his veins. His face felt hot. Then he noticed the jumble of files on the floor. "Fuck that!" he said, and made his way back to the kitchen. He was done for the day. He threw in a microwaveable dinner and washed it down with a good bottle of Scotch. He made sure he drank enough to help him sleep through the night.

33

CLOUDY THOUGHTS

F rom his pillow, Sean watched with one groggy eye as his cell phone vibrated violently, almost walking itself off the end table. As he reached for the phone, he groaned from the pressure in his head, a rubber-banded hangover from the scotch he drank with dinner.

"M'Govern…" he mumbled, closing his eyes so as not to let in any more light.

"Hello, Detective? Are you there?" said a hushed voice on the other end.

"Um-hum," he mumbled again, not wanting to expend any more energy than was necessary.

"Detective, this is Sister Mary Teresa, do you remember me?" The detective squinted his already closed eyes even tighter as he tried to think. The voice continued, "From St. Catherine's?"

"Yup, I remember. Hang on a second," Sean knew he was going to have to get up eventually, so, with a grunt and a moan, he pushed himself to an upright position on the edge of his bed. His head throbbed like a bass drum as he remembered his eager-beaver junior detective who'd made a quick exit at the sight of Mother Superior. He put the phone back up to his ear. "Yes, Sister, how are you?"

"I'm okay, thank you. Uhm, I wanted to talk to you about Sister Ave Margaret. Well, she wanted me to talk to you," the nun was almost whispering, and due to the pounding in his head, he didn't mind it one bit.

"Yes, the young nun I met at Fatima. The one who worked alongside Sister Mary Vincenza," he stated, remembering how something was a bit off about her.

"That's her. She is actually here with me. The retreat is over now, and she wanted me to call you."

"Not a problem," he said. "And not that I mind, but why are you whispering?"

"I can't talk long detective," She didn't answer his question. "Sister Ave is very upset. She wants to let you know she is sorry. She didn't quite tell you the whole truth when you spoke with her at Fatima."

"She didn't?" he asked. His mouth felt full of cotton.

"No, she wanted me to let you know, Sister Mary Vincenza never showed up at retreat."

"She didn't?" he repeated, not having the wherewithal to form any other words .

"No, but she wants me to let you know everything else she told you was true, about accompanying Sister on her visits, and the paperwork and all that."

"Why didn't she tell me about Sister Mary Vincenza not being there?" He felt bile rising in the back of his throat. He really regretted the scotch.

"Because Father told her not to," she said. He then heard her cover the phone with her hand and say something to her friend, that was all muffled, but sounded like "You need to tell him." Her voice became clear again.

"What is it, Sister? Is there something you need to tell me?" he asked, swallowing harder.

"Detective, uhm, there is something else you need to know, uhm," she started to cry. "Oh God, there is something awful that you need to know…"

"Is it about Sister Mary Vincenza?" he asked, trying not to throw up.

"No," she whispered hard, "It's about Father..." He heard her catch her breath and thought he also heard someone else crying the background. "Oh! Someone's coming, Detective! We've got to go!" *Click.* She hung up.

"Sister? What is it about Father that I need to know?"

She was no longer on the line, and it didn't matter. He couldn't wait any longer. He ran to the toilet and threw up. The microwave dinner, the Scotch, the beer from O'Doyle's and the image of Father Giuseppe Riccio all swirled together into the bowl and down the drain with one flush.

He fell back onto bed and pulled the covers over his head, determined to sleep his fog off—until his phone buzzed again.

"Sister?" he answered.

"Yes, how did you know?" It was the Reverend Mother on the line.

"Oh, uhm, how are you, Reverend Mother?"

"Better than you sound. Detective, I wanted to call you to let you know that I spoke to Father Giuseppe about Sister Mary Vincenza."

"And?" He wasn't going to let the Reverend Mother know about the information he had just received from Sister Mary Teresa.

"I wanted you to know that I was never consulted about Sister Mary Vincenza being sent to pick up the bishops, and I am not happy about it. Retreat is now over and I am going to be speaking to Sister myself."

"Are you sure she even went to retreat?" he asked, confused as to how it was not reported back to her, the one in charge, that Sister Mary Vincenza had never even shown up.

"Of course I am sure. I am the one who ordered her to go. Why do you ask?"

"Have you spoken to her since she has been back?" he inquired.

"Well, no. They all went straight to St. Catherine's. Father is there with the visiting bishops and so are the sisters. I will be heading there soon."

"Would you like me to meet you there, at St. Catherine's?" he asked.

"It's a busy week, Detective, and it will be a busy weekend. Can it wait until Sunday, at least? We can meet after the anointing of the bishop."

"Sunday?" Sean felt foggy.

"Yes," the nun replied. "I'm not sure how we can make it any sooner. Tomorrow, Father will be performing Saturday mass, eight thirty in the morning. We have a luncheon with the bishops immediately after and meetings all day, and then the next morning is his ordination at ten o'clock. After that, there will be plenty of time to visit with Sister Mary Vincenza. You can meet us in the rectory after Sunday's ordination mass. Actually, why don't you just come to mass on Sunday? It should be quite a spectacle."

Sean felt too shitty to argue, so he just agreed to attend the Sunday's mass. He hung up the phone, turned it off, and pulled the covers over his head.

It was six in the evening before he felt well enough to surface from his bedroom. The scotch he drank the night before had helped him sleep nightmare-free, but he despised the hangover left in its wake. He dragged himself to the kitchen and opened a window to let in some air. His stomach was hungry, but his head still felt as if he were submerged under water. He made himself some black coffee, scrambled eggs, fried ham, and dry toast. As he sat at the kitchen table staring at the plate of food, he caught a glimpse of the files in the other room, still strewn across the floor by Sophie's dressing table.

"Ugh," he moaned, knowing he was going to have to re-sort the jumbled mess once again. He dipped his dry toast into his coffee and took a bite as he made notations into his leather journal. *Sister Mary Vincenza (No Show.) Mother Superior (In the dark?) Young nuns (Afraid. What's their story?) Father Giuseppe Riccio (Mobster?)*

The toast seemed to be all he had the stomach for, so he washed a handful of ibuprofen down with a swig of antacid, hoping the chalky concoction would cure what ailed him. Leaving the rest of his meal sitting on the table, he made his way over to the mess of papers and didn't even bother to pick them up. Instead, he sat on the floor and organized them right there. He wrapped them all tightly together with large rubber bands, longways and crossways, like a package, insuring they would not move at all, even if he threw them across the room. Once he was done, he lay down on the floor, right there where he was. It felt good, his head resting on the cool slate. He was starting to feel a bit better. Five more minutes in this position would do the trick.

As he lay there, he had a unique view of Sophie's dressing table. He had always focused mainly on the mirror, its storied blemishes seducing him, drawing him in. In his current position, he had a different perspective of the old piece of furniture. It was quite something. His eyes followed.the lines of the beautiful antique; it was small and delicate, with curving cabriole legs carved with flowers and padded feet. The craftsmanship was impeccable.

As he mindlessly stared at the old wooden piece, he pictured Sophie sitting there and an overwhelming sadness came over him. She must have felt so alone, so helpless, to do something so radical to end her pain. Why did she suffer so? He was lost in thought when something caught his eye. A small butterfly flittered around Sophie's dressing table. *What the hell?* The butterfly danced around the table's legs. *How did you get in here?* The butterfly then flew underneath the table top and seemed to disappear. *Hey!* Sean did not see where it went. From his vantage point, something else didn't make sense. There were seams underneath the table top where the wood did not meet—as if there was another drawer built into the old piece of furniture. But there was no drawer in that specific place, not as far as the eye could see. There were other obvious drawers, but he knew they were empty, probably scavenged by Silas Martin, the greedy crook.

He got up from his position on the floor and approached the table. He ran his hands along the underside and felt the lines. Yes, there was definitely a separation in the wood, but as he felt along the front of the piece, there were no obvious seams. Before he got a chance to investigate any further, there was a knock at his door. He opened it to see Officer Caputo standing there.

"Where you been, Gov? I have been trying to call you all day," said the large officer, dressed in his uniform.

"Ah, Joey, I had a battle with a bottle of scotch, and the scotch won. Sorry. I had to turn my phone off so I could sleep it off. Come on in. You want a cuppa coffee?"

The officer followed Sean into the kitchen. Sean poured him a cup of coffee and set it on the table next to the food he could not eat. Joey Bag-a-Donuts, who never met a meal he didn't like, asked, "You gonna finish this?"

"Nope, it's all yours," said Sean, gesturing for his friend to sit. The wail of an ambulance rushed by the open kitchen window. *That's how you got in.* He closed the window and poured himself another coffee. "What's up?"

"You're never gonna believe it," said the officer, slicing a piece of the fried ham and popping it into his mouth. "We got a call today about a shooting over on Beechbaum."

Sean knew right away it had to do with Silas Martin. "Don't tell me —Silas Martin is involved," said the detective. "What did he do now?"

"He got himself murdered, that's what he did," answered the officer, stabbing a few piles of the scrambled eggs, lodging them onto the fork.

"Murdered?"

"Yup," he continued, sliding the eggs into his mouth. "It seems that one of his cash paying tenants, some big dude with a snake tattooed on his neck and a bunch of priors, was away for a few weeks and old Silas thought he'd split town." He washed the eggs down with a swig of coffee. "Well, when the guy returns he finds out Martin sold all of his possessions on the sidewalk, just like he did when we found him selling Sophie's stuff. All the guy's stuff is gone, and he's pissed!"

Sean nodded, "I bet."

"Witnesses say they got into an argument over the missing stuff and then over money, and the perp jammed a wad full of cash into Silas Martin's mouth, making him choke on it, before the guy shot him dead."

"Did you catch the guy?"

"Yup, and the best thing is, he is connected to another murder across town. That's probably where he was when he was away. It reeks of a mob hit, the other murder." The officer continued to finish the rest of the meal. "He was in the basement on Beechbaum, trying to torch the building when we apprehended him."

"Wow," said Sean. "Seems that old Silas hadn't learned his lesson. Sooner or later, you're gonna steal from the wrong person. That sucks though." He shook his head. "Not that he ever gave me any pertinent information on Sophie."

The satiated officer cleaned his plate and patted his mouth with a napkin. "Well, IRS confiscated all of the files out of Martin's office, something about money laundering. Maybe information will eventually turn up on Sophie. Probably take months, maybe years, though. How's that going? Your Sophie case?"

The detective let out a long sigh. "Chief wants it closed. Coroner's deemed it a suicide. But, I don't know, Joey, something reeks. At this point, I just want to find out who she is, you know? She's still in a drawer, in an icebox, until I do. I'm not giving up. I have no leads. Nothing has come in through missing persons that fits her description. No one can seem to pin down the nun that may have known her. I've got Mother Superior, who insists she sent Sister Mary Vincenza to retreat, and then I've got a young nun who said she never saw her there, and a priest who told her to lie about it. Plus, they're not going to give me any more time to work on this case. So I guess it's all just going to shit."

"What are you going to do? Wait a minute, why would a priest tell her to lie? Can you bring him in for questioning?"

"His family's connected, and he is going to become the bishop in a few days, can you believe that?" Sean asked his friend. "I've decided I'm going to show up at his masses tomorrow morning and Sunday."

"Well, call me and I'll go with you. I'm always up for the doughnuts! Thanks for the snack." said the officer.

"Hey, are you stopping by the station?" Sean asked as they walked toward the door. He picked up the stack of files from the old dressing table. "Would you drop these off to Joann for me?" He handed the officer the stack, keeping the old file on the Riccio family for himself. He wanted to study it before showing up at mass tomorrow.

"Sure thing, Gov. Be happy to." The officer took the package and left.

Sean turned on his phone to call Joann, and dialed her number.

"Joann here."

"Jo, it's Sean. Joey is bringing the files for you. Did you hear about Silas Martin?"

"Yeah, honey, we figured you were the last one to know. Where ya been?"

"I had a disagreement with a bottle of scotch. Can you do me a favor?"

"Sure thing, honey."

"The last information I got out of Mr. Martin was Sophie's last name being Rae. R.A.E. Can you run a search for me? Run it blind?"

"Will do, get back to you, ASAP."

"Thanks, you're the best."

As Sean hung up, his phone pinged a few times, alerting him to the multitude of messages he missed while it was turned off. One of them was a voicemail from Silas Martin. He pressed to listen as the man's voice spoke from beyond. "Uh, yeah, Detective, it's Silas Martin." The man sounded flustered. "I, uh…I wanted to see if I can talk to ya about Sophie Rae. There's somethin' I just realized, and I ain't got a lotta time. I gotta pack real quick and go on a vacay, 'cause someone's not happy with me. These fuckin' holier-than-thou assholes. They think they can get away with anything. Well they ain't gonna scare me. I ain't afraid of no mobsters! I'll tell all about their bullshit. I'll tell everyone! Fuckin' priests runnin' around with their bullshit collars on. They ain't no better than the rest of us. Call me, ok?"

34

A HIGHER CALLING

Father Giuseppe Riccio, soon to be bishop, couldn't be any further from holy as he sat at his desk and picked up the phone. He dialed the number of the landlord leasing an apartment to someone he had been looking for.

"Yeah?" asked the voice on the other end.

"Mr. Martin?"

"Yeah, who wants t' know?

"Mr. Martin, this is Father Giuseppe Riccio, from St. Catherine's Church. I'm calling because I was told one of our sisters is renting from you."

"Uh, yeah, Father, I think you got the wrong place. There ain't no nuns here."

"Well, one of my associates told me that, in fact, there was a nun there, renting apartment 403." The priest was agitated with the man's ineptness.

"Did you say apartment 403, Father?" the man asked, surprised.

"That's what I said, Mr. Martin." The priest rolled his eyes, picking up the pencil on his desk, tapping the lead point on the wood.

"Uh, Father, the woman in 403 is dead."

The priest stopped tapping the pencil. "Did you say dead, Mr. Martin?"

"Yeah, that's what I said. Dead."

Lead still pointed on the desktop, the priest started turning the pencil in his fingers. "How did she die, Mr. Martin?"

"She hung herself, Father."

"Impossible," the priest blurted out, believing a nun would not break her vows by taking her own life. It was a mortal sin.

"What'd ya say, Father?"

"I said, what was her name, Mr. Martin?" He grew angry.

"Look, I ain't gonna tell ya no name. She wasn't no nun."

The priest snapped the lead of the pencil into the desktop and threw it across the room. He'd snapped, as well. Spit flew from his mouth with each word he screamed into the phone. "WHAT DO YOU MEAN YOU ARE NOT GOING TO TELL ME HER NAME? DO YOU KNOW WHO I AM?"

"Yeah, I know who you are," the man dared answer back. "Yous guys have been skimmin' money from guys like me for too long. And I ain't gonna take it no more. I'm tired a payin' you money off the toppa what I get for this shit hole. I ain't gonna tell you nobody's name," he taunted, then added, "You can pay ME, and then I'll give you a goddamned name."

Father Riccio threw the phone across his desk, almost hitting the man who sat in the chair in front of it. The man with a serpent tattooed on his neck.

"Finish him!" the priest ordered the man, who nodded in agreement.

On the other end, Silas Martin scavenged his desk to find the card of Detective Sean McGovern. He dialed the number with shaking hand. There was something he needed to tell him about Sophie.

SEAN COULDN'T BELIEVE the voicemail. Silas Martin, finally speaking to him about information he had on Sophie. Information he would never get to learn, now that the man was dead. And what was that about priests and the mob? This was no coincidence. He opened the Riccio file Joann had given to him, and for the rest of the evening he poured over every detail. He spread it out on his table so as not to miss a single word. Also sitting atop the table was the Bible with the little golden cherry blossom insignia and the initials MV, sorely missing its last chapter, which had been ripped out, leaving the reader wondering about how it was to end. Next to the Bible stood Sophie's gold tube of lipstick. Talismans, assembled to bear witness to his study of the case, to help give him some intuitive insight.

As he read the file depicting the long line of Riccios, it told of suspected money laundering, racketeering, and other crimes, including gun battles, arson, thievery, beatings and extortion. Unlike other families, they considered themselves above involvement in waste management. They opted to steal valuable relics and counterfeit art and diamonds. They also invested in real estate. There were witness statements of suspicions surrounding the church and its backdoor dealings. Innocent, unsuspecting, altar boys used as the couriers, loading multitudes of crates of "altar wine" in and out. But nothing had ever been proven. The death of one of their own, Father Salvatore Riccio, was suspicious, but—again—never proven because there was never a suspect to arrest. So the case went cold.

Was Sophie's death somehow connected to the church? What about Silas Martin's? Did the old, run-down apartment building really belong to him? Or to someone else? Was he killed by a disgruntled tenant, or was it a hired hitman? Did Mother Superior have any knowledge of the goings on, or were they all taking place behind her back? And what about Sister Mary Vincenza? How did she fit in to all of this?

The icing on the cake was Father Giuseppe Riccio, soon to be the next bishop. The man who gave Sean the chills with the flash of a sadistic grin that hid something more. What was Sister Mary Teresa trying to say before she was interrupted and hung up so quickly? What was the something about Father Riccio she needed to relay? The detective needed to talk to her, to her and to her friend Sister Ave. He also wanted to talk to Mother Superior and Father Giuseppe Riccio, and he wasn't going to wait until after Sunday's mass.

Sean studied the case file until he could no longer see straight. He placed the old Bible on his nightstand and went to bed with thoughts swirling in his mind. Thoughts of Sophie, of Silas Martin, of the priest and the Riccio family, of Mother Superior and the frightened young nuns. The last person he thought of was Sister Mary Vincenza. He fell asleep formulating the questions he was going to ask her when he finally got a chance to talk to her. He was eager to meet with her; surely she would shed some light on his case.

35

PRAYING THE ROSARY

S ean dreamt of Sister Mary Vincenza. Her face obscure, shrouded by a sheer black veil. Her thoughts, plain as day.

He was a voyeur, watching the nun as she sat in darkness, in her modest room at the convent. It was her ritual every night. Her solace. Her time to recollect what she had accomplished during the day. She closed her Bible and lit a candle. She thought of all of the people she had blessed that day, making a mental note to say a prayer for each one of them.

She reflected on her time at St. Catherine's and gave thanks for her job there. She loved what she did; being in charge of feeding and clothing the homeless and making sure they had a bed at the local shelter. She took pride in visiting shut-ins, praying with them and ministering to them. She enjoyed her duties so much.

It was important to her empathetic heart that every needy soul she encountered was fed and clothed and kept warm and dry. It was important to her that people stayed safe.

She thought how more often than not, some of those she helped get back onto their feet would become members of the congregation of St. Catherine's and give back in return. She thought it a beautiful circle of compassion and charity. It felt sacred to her, reminding her of the Sacred Heart of Jesus, one of the most widely practiced and well-known Roman Catholic devotions, founded by St. Madeleine Sophie Barat.

"Sophie." Sister Mary Vincenza spoke the name aloud as she lifted the veil away from her face, exposing her ruby red lips.

She reflected on the name as she picked up her crystal rosary from the small end table next to her bed. She loved that name. She wished Mother Superior had let her choose the name Sister Sophie Rae when she became a nun. Taking a new name was symbolic in the Catholic religion—it meant one was in a new place in one's life. She wanted to take Sophie for St. Sophie and Rae, a feminine version of the first name of her father, Ray, a name scribbled on the back of a fading photograph. But, instead, Mother Superior chose a name for her. She had to settle on Vincenza, after St. Vincent, the patron saint of charitable societies. She accepted the strong handed recommendation from Mother Superior and knew she could not win that argument. She thought Sister Sophie would have been a much better name. However, it was not up to her, and she had come to accept it.

THAT was easy to accept. She knew firsthand there were other, more sinister things at Immaculate Conception Convent she could never accept. Purely evil things, things she documented, things she wished she had the power to change, if only she knew how. If only she had been strong enough.

"Enough!" She scolded herself as she knelt beside her bed; it was not the time to dwell on negativity. She clutched her rosary between folded hands and let out a cleansing breath. Now was the time for prayer. There would be a day when she would be able to change things, and that day would come sooner rather than later. She closed her eyes to start her vigil. She took the first faceted stone of her rosary and rolled it in between her fingertips, feeling the texture of the cut stone. The pattern of the undulating facets soothed and lulled her into a meditation of prayer, observing each prayerful devotion as they slipped as whispers through her lips. She alternated between the Our Father and the Hail Mary, depending on which bead was in her grasp. Hours felt like minutes and there was a peace inside her bubble of devotion. She willed her prayers to cast a protective force field around her.

Unfortunately, her peace would not last for long, and she felt her stomach begin to sour as she became startlingly aware that her protective shell was only imaginary. An all too familiar scent began to permeate her bubble. The odor of frankincense, originating in the hallway outside of her room slithered and snaked its way into her space like a predatory serpent, hissing its tongue and exposing its fangs, tickling her nostrils and bursting her protective bubble. It sent a chill up her spine, causing her to shiver with an animal instinct, warning her something was not right.

She opened her eyes for a brief moment, resting her gaze on the crack of golden light illuminating through the bottom of her closed door. As the pungent musk grew stronger she saw a shadow break the glowing plane. An intruder on the other side. She closed her eyes once again, and her heart jumped in time with the rap on the door, a knock that came with no polite inquiry to enter. She kept as quiet as a mouse, clasping the last crystal bead in the strand, feeling terror as she began to pray.

"Hail, Mary full of grace," she mouthed, no sound coming out. Her heart began racing, pounding so loudly it drowned out the words in her head.

A jiggle of the knob divulged to the uninvited the door was not locked…a slow turn of brass…

"The Lord is with thee…"she silently prayed, letting go of the bead, her trembling fingers fumbled for the crucifix instead. The cross that bore her beloved Jesus, the savior of all souls.

"Blessed art thou among women…" with eyes still closed, she traced along the cross's outline, each end rounded and smooth…save for one. As she felt the bottom of the cross, she gingerly tapped its pointed end so as not to prick her finger.

"And blessed is the fruit of thy womb, Jesus." An end she deliberately took the time to sharpen.

The door creaked open, projecting a triangle of light onto the floor of the darkened room. As the intruder entered, he heard her say aloud.

"Holy Mary, mother of God, pray for us sinners...

36

FINDING TREASURE

I t was 6:30 A.M as the buzzing phone awakened Sean from his lucid dream. He wanted to lie there, remembering the details. He knew that as soon as he answered the call they would all evaporate.

"McGovern."

"Sean, it's Joann."

"Hey Jo, you're up early. What's the good word?"

"Yep! Me and the roosters! So…I ran your Sophie Rae, with R-A-E and R-A-Y and, well, there's none."

"What do you mean there's none?"

"There is no Sophie Rae, honey. It's a fake name."

"Ugh. Damn that Silas Martin. If he wasn't dead already I'd kill him."

"Sorry, honey."

"Thanks, Jo. I'll see you soon."

The detective was disappointed as he placed the phone back on his bedside table. He saw Sister Mary Vincenza's Bible lying there. He picked it up and fanned it open, lingering on the back of the book where the last chapter was missing. He rested it, open and face down, on his chest and closed his eyes. He ran his finger along the spine of the book feeling the indentation of the cherry blossom insignia, feeling the indentation of the gilded *M* and *V* signifying it was indeed Sister Mary Vincenza's Bible. The Bible that, in his dream, she closed before lighting a candle. Sister Mary Vincenza who was nowhere to be found. Wouldn't her Bible be with her?

Sean's eyes shot open with a thumping in his chest. He hopped out of bed, Bible in hand, and ran to Sophie's dressing table, placing the book on top. He opened the visible, empty drawers. He then felt underneath at the place where the seams existed. To his knowledge, there was no drawer to be found in that particular spot, for he did not see one. Could there be a hidden compartment? He shook the table, willing some secret chamber to open, but it was to no avail.

Once again he ran his hands along the underside of the dresser, this time closer to the front ledge when, to his surprise, his finger felt a wooden button. He caught his breath, closed his eyes, and pressed the button. Nothing. He opened his eyes and peered underneath the table to get a good look. There was definitely a button there. He pressed it again. Nothing. Over and over, he pressed the button, but his efforts were futile. No magical compartment revealed itself. He grew frustrated thinking of how every lead he'd had brought him to a dead end. Even Silas Martin was dead.

He grew frustrated thinking of Sophie in all her despair, and how he wanted to do her the respect of finding her family. He needed something. Anything. He was beginning to think it was never going to happen. While his finger was still on the button, he shook the table in anger, lifted it up, and banged it back down. *What the hell are you doing, McGovern?* He didn't want to harm one of the only valuables Sophie had left in the world. He put his elbows on the dresser and held his head in his hands in despair, closing his eyes. He just sat there, defeated.

"I'm so sorry Sophie." Feelings of failure overwhelmed him.

From out of nowhere, one word. *Look.*

The detective opened his eyes, head still resting in his hands, looking straight down to the edge of the dressing table where a small sliver of molding had dislodged itself from the rest. Slowly, he reached underneath the molding and tried to pull on it. It was stuck. And there it was. The illusive hidden drawer built into the front center of the dressing table. Something seemed to be lodged inside, preventing it from opening fully. Sean pulled harder, but whatever was in there must have jammed the drawer when he banged the table in frustration. He ran to the kitchen and rummaged around, finding a flat head screwdriver, a pair of latex gloves, and some small plastic bags. He continued his exploration of the crime scene that had changed his life just over a week before. A crime scene he apparently purchased for twenty dollars.

A piece of furniture, left behind, haunted just enough to inspire intuitive dreams. He knew to listen to what the universe was telling him. He put on the gloves and slid the screwdriver into the top of the drawer, gingerly pressing down on the contents inside while he pulled the drawer from the bottom. After a few tries, the old drawer popped open. He just sat, staring.

Inside the newly discovered drawer lay someone's hidden treasures. A gold wedding band, a fading photograph of a man from long ago, a wadded piece of stained fabric, and a beautiful wooden box, adorned with a delicate butterfly. Time stood still for a moment. He took a deep breath, and the smell of mahogany permeated his nostrils. As he looked into the mirror, he felt it watching his every move.

All the mementos stashed inside the hidden drawer should have been unfamiliar to him. Most of them were. Except for one. Inside the fabric. He knew exactly what he was looking at as he removed it from the drawer and slowly unfurled the crumpled swatch. As the fabric, stiff with dried blood opened, he saw the crystal rosary from his dream the night before. The exact one Sister Mary Vincenza was praying with, the one with the sharpened end. Sean was raw with the realization his dream was, somehow, someone else's reality.

The crucifix and the silken shroud protecting it were stained with dried blood. He was careful not to over handle the contents, and he set both the fabric and the rosary into plastic bags. He did the same with the wedding band and the photograph, noticing the name Ray scribbled on the back in fading ink. The last thing nestled inside of the secret drawer was the lovely butterfly treasure box. He lifted it out of the drawer and placed it on top of the dressing table next to the Bible. He opened the top of the box to find an envelope. Inside the envelope was a grouping of Bible pages, torn from their book, scribbled on, folded in half, and tucked away for safekeeping.

Sean smoothed the Bible pages and compared them to Sister Mary Vincenza's Bible. The orphaned pages matched the chapter torn from the back of her book, but they had been altered with what appeared to be a letter that began with *To the girl I wish I knew...* He began to read.

It was a love letter, of sorts, from a broken girl to herself, chronicling everything she had been through up to a certain point, finding herself in a place she could no longer bear to be. Originally starting a life of virtue she thought would bring love to the world, but quickly finding out those she was supposed to trust the most were the ones who would lie to, misuse, and abuse her. She was a fragile soul, betrayed by the barbarians around her, and she could no longer manage the pain. Tears welled in his eyes as got to the end of the letter signed *Love, Sophie.*

Sean peered into the mirror. Through swirling mercury and misty eyes, he thought he could see Sophie staring back at him. He reached out to touch the glass, to touch her face. He nodded, as if to say it's all going to be OK.

Sean placed all the contents of the secret drawer into plastic bags and then into one large paper bag. It was already eight o'clock on Saturday morning, and he knew exactly where he needed to be. He made a quick call to Joann, then to Officer Caputo, telling him to meet him at the station. They were going to make a visit to St. Catherine's Cathedral. He was going to do right by Sophie if it was the last thing he ever did.

SOPHIE'S HAND touched the mirror as she peered out at the man she had come to recognize. He'd sat in focused contemplation, in his own world, on the other side of the nebulous glass, intent on discovering her hidden drawer of secrets. Sophie was relieved and elated when she saw him remove her precious butterfly box from inside the old drawer.

As the man read her letter, she heard the screaming fabric once again. It was the first time she didn't wish for it to hush; she knew it would tell her story to the man in a way she could not. It was brutal. It was honest. It was terrifying. Her heart went out to him as she witnessed deep emotion wash over his body. At the same time, something else happened. The anxious energy that used to fill her soul, the electrified buzzing in herself that haunted her from within her oblivion, seemed to dissipate as she saw him realize what had happened to her. She felt a profound tranquility wash over her. Suddenly, she no longer felt guilty for taking her own life. There was a reason she could not deal with living, and it was not her fault. It was never her fault. Sophie finally forgave herself.

She watched the man, as he stared at her, reached out to her. She knew everything was going to be OK. She felt peace fill her soul. White light filled her being. For the first time, she felt weightless, freed from her burdens. She wanted to thank him, but before she knew it, he was gone.

37

THE BLOOD OF CHRIST

D etective Sean McGovern and Officer Joseph Caputo sat in the last pew of St. Catherine's Cathedral as Father Giuseppe Riccio offered Saturday morning mass. Sean had not been to a church service in years and was having a full blown anxiety attack. The cellular memory of being a child and sitting next to his praying mother, while trying to drown out the voices in his head, was clear as day. The last pew seemed a safe place to sit, as it was closest to the exit.

It took him some time to remember the rituals of a Catholic mass, when to sit, when to stand, and when to kneel. He was just following Officer Caputo's lead; Joey was a regular at morning mass. Well, he was a regular eater-of-donuts after morning mass, as he wasn't able to resist the soft, warm rings. Sean was willing to bet Joey's mind was already on the sweet endings.

Sean's intense focus was on Father Giuseppe Riccio, who was theatrically addressing his congregation. It was apparent the priest was basking in the fact that all eyes were upon him. It was time for communion, a time for the faithful to receive the body and blood of Jesus Christ. Blessed by and presented to them by none other than the man who would be the next new bishop in twenty-four hours. A man who, Sean knew, was unfit to hold that title.

Sean watched as Father Riccio stood at the altar, flanked by his altar boys, who were there to assist with the preparation of the bread and the wine. Anxiety looming, the thought of alcohol made Sean's stomach turn. He tried to ignore the knot forming in his stomach. He could see the motions of the priest, but only fragments of sentences were coming through. He thought he heard a ringing in his ears.

"Take this, all of you, and eat it. This is my body, which will be given up for you."

Sean heard the words as Father Riccio held the round wafer up to the heavens. Looking around the congregation, he wondered how many people the priest had taken advantage of. Sean thought he heard whispering and looked behind him. No one was there. The priest picked up the golden chalice of wine.

"Take this, all of you, and drink from it. This is my blood. The blood of the new and everlasting covenant. It will be shed for you, and for all, so that sins may be forgiven. Do this in memory of me."

All Sean could see was Sophie's face, her memory burned into his mind. Then the blood on the crucifix, reminding him of what the priest had done.

After a few more muffled prayers, the officers watched the priest ingest the wafer and take a sip from the chalice of wine.

Sean leaned over to Officer Caputo, "Meet me outside in ten."

The priest placed the wine chalice back down and approached his congregation with altar boy number one to serve communion wafers to his parishioners. Altar boy number two stayed behind to pick up the chalice by the stem, being careful to use the sleeves of his robe, leaving another chalice in its place. He walked it back into the Sacristy. In the Sacristy, the altar boy dumped the wine from the chalice and placed the chalice into a plastic bag. He zipped the top of the bag and made his way to the back exit. He opened the door and handed the evidence over to Detective McGovern. Sean gave him a wink and the boy went back into the church to help finish the mass.

Sean walked around to the front of the church where Joey was waiting, three donuts in hand. "You want a donut?" he asked.

"Nah, they're all yours. I've got to get to the station. No time to waste." He nodded at the church. "Wait here, grab the priest after mass, and bring him in. I want to ask him a few questions."

38

GET IT DONE

S ean's car screeched to the curb in front of the station, and he
bounded up the stairs faster than ever, straight to Joann's desk
where she was waiting with the DNA lab tech. He had called
her on his way to mass that morning and asked her to come in to the
office. He trusted only her with the responsibility of finding a tech to
handle the evidence. He was hoping their new portable DNA system,
the one everyone had to read up on, could scan the items within
twenty-four hours. Hopefully, to retrieve at least preliminary results. It
was just a question of having the right tech there to do it, and Detective
McGovern did not have the time to waste, so Joann was the exact
person to get the job done.

"Is this it?" she asked as he rushed toward her with the large brown
bag, complete with the items from Sophie's dressing table, plus the
chalice he just obtained from mass. Jimmy's nephew had done a great
job procuring it without being noticed.

"Yes," he said, addressing Joann while handing the bag to the technician. "I am going to need proof as soon as humanly possible. I'm not
going to be able to hold this bastard without DNA evidence."

"We'll do our best, honey. Who are we looking at?" While on the phone, Sean had not told her the details—he just asked her to show up. "Is this for your Sophie case?"

"Yes," he replied flatly. "And you're never going to believe it." Right on cue, the doors to the station opened and in walked Officer Joseph Caputo along with Father Giuseppe Riccio.

Joann was taken aback. "Uhm. We'll get this handled," she said, nodding to the technician, who then turned and walked toward the elevator. Joann looked at the priest who loomed over her tiny frame and addressed him, "Father." He nodded at her and turned to the detective as Joann walked off to follow the technician.

"Great! Thanks, Jo," Sean called to her as she was stepping in the elevator. "We'll be in room two if you have any updates on the progress." She stared at him in bewilderment as the elevator doors closed.

"What is this all about detective? Why have you summoned me here? This is not the best timing. I'm supposed to be at a luncheon. I am a very busy man."

"Father," Sean said, shaking the priest's hand while patting him on the shoulder. "Thank you so much for taking time out of your busy schedule to accompany Officer Caputo and myself." Goosebumps chilled Sean's skin as Sophie's face flashed before his eyes. He brushed it off. "I know you have a big day coming up tomorrow. This won't take very long. We just wanted to ask you a few questions, if that is okay with you? Can we just have a few minutes of your time, please?" He forced a smile.

"Well, yes, I guess," the priest answered, "but I cannot stay very long."

"Great. Let's just step into this room where we can have some privacy," the detective said, leading the man into one of the interrogation rooms. One away from any semblance of a police department, to make him feel as comfortable as possible "You can leave any time you'd like. Can we get you some water? Coffee, perhaps?"

"No, thank you, I'm fine."

"Officer Caputo, can you grab me a coffee, and bring a bottle of water for Father, just in case he gets thirsty?"

"Sure, Detective. Be right back."

Detective McGovern motioned for the priest to sit on an armless chair and took a seat next to a small writing table. There was no barrier between them. Just two guys talking to one another. Sean pulled out his journal and his phone and sent a text to Joann. *Jo, if you get any results while he is here, pop your head in, let me know.*

"That was a great mass today, Father."

"You were there?" The priest looked surprised. "I haven't seen you at mass before."

"When I was a kid, my parents were big church goers. We went to St Jude's just across town."

"Ah, I know it well, my son. You don't attend mass now?"

"Nah, but I'm thinking about maybe turning over a new leaf. Maybe going to mass once in a while. Congratulations on your upcoming ordination."

"Thank you, it should be a wonderful ceremony."

"You must be honored by this momentous occasion." *Too bad your uncle had to be murdered for you to get there.*

"Yes, I am. You know, my uncle was actually to become bishop of this diocese years ago, but, unfortunately, he passed of a massive heart attack before he was appointed."

"You don't say?" *You fucking asshole, don't get too comfortable.*

"Such a tragedy, losing him. But I am so happy to be able to keep the family tradition going," replied the smooth-talking, holy man.

"Of course. So...how long have you had a relationship with Sister Mary Vincenza?"

The priest shifted in his seat. "What? We don't have a relationship."

"I'm sorry, that was a poor choice of words." *Or a fucking perfect one. I saw you squirming in your seat.* "I mean, how long have you known each other?"

"Oh." Collecting his composure, he said, "I've known her for quite a few years. For as long as she has been here at St. Catherine's."

"And how long do you think that is, Father? Ballpark."

"Let's see, she entered when she was just shy of twenty, and she is probably in her early thirties, so I would say over ten years."

"So, for quite a while, then?" *She suffered at your hands, you bastard.*

"And where is she now?"

"I suppose she is preparing for tomorrow's mass."

"Father, can you remind me, one more time, where she was when I came to Fatima to look for her?"

"She went to pick up the bishops, but I already told you that, Detective. Why all of the questions about Sister Mary Vincenza? Why don't you just ask her yourself?"

Because she's dead you fucking idiot, and it's all your fault! Sean prayed the priest couldn't read his thoughts. He could feel himself getting angrier and angrier, but he didn't want to blow it. He needed to control his emotions. Especially now, when he needed to wait for the DNA evidence to come back. He did not want Father Giuseppe Riccio skipping town. He had one more day until the priest was out of the country for good. The smug bastard. He felt the urge to just reach out and choke the life out of the guy. Make him suffer the same brutal consequences Sophie suffered at the end of her life. He flashed back to just hours before, when he read the little bundle of Bible pages upon which Sophie detailed what he had done to her.

The detective was still presenting questions to the priest, but the scene started to shrink. He felt his soul leave his body to watch himself, to watch them both, as the interrogation continued. He found it harder and harder to focus as both of their voices became muffled to him, drowned out by the noise in his head; a different voice, screaming at him, telling him what Sophie suffered at the hands of this monster.

39

THE EVENT

I t's me again, in all my glory, and I am here to tell you I saw it all, them all, each and every hideous instance, and there were many. I was a part of them. Of course not willingly participating, but witnessing. Horrified. With a front and center seat to watch the heinous acts of a madman.

On those dreadful nights, his ritual would begin by pulling me out of my hiding spot, where I was nestled behind garments woven of lesser fabrics, all aligned in the dark mahogany armoire, which stood like a somber statesman in the recesses of his chamber. He would hang me on the front of the door and admire my silken threads, bathed in the divine candlelight once again. A holy vestment, in all my glorious splendor.

This malevolent man would then pick up his brass thurible by its chains. As the smoke of its burning frankincense wafted through the holes cut into its ornate lid, he would swing it in a pendulum-like motion, anointing the entire room, including the bed, the half-drunk bottle of brandy he removed from the stash under the floorboard, and me, a glorious robe of kingdoms past. The white tuft of smoke would envelop me, and I would absorb its licorice scent as it encircled and clung to my delicate fibers.

He would then slip me over his naked body, aroused by the way my silken threads slid over his erection, camouflaging his perversion. He would admire us in the mirror. He believed I enhanced his being. He believed I made him more powerful, allowing him to do as he pleased. And do as he pleased he would. However, he did not need me to feed his immorality, for his heart was already black. He did not need my fibers to perpetuate his sexual deviation, for it was already woven into the very fibers of his soul. I refused to enhance this mad man's delusions. With all my might, I refused to let one ounce of my being help him in any way. The only power he held was that which fueled his dirty mind. I was the cloak that covered his physical form, yet he had a bigger shroud than I, and his invisibility was perpetuated by the one who kept his secrets.

Unfortunately, for me, there were no secrets. I saw everything. Witnessed every heinous act he committed in the name of religion. He stole power from the innocent, leaving terror in his wake. He was a madman donning a bishop's robe; however, he was not a bishop yet. In his warped and twisted mind, he was worthy. In reality, it was just a matter of months before the official indoctrination would bring him to the next level of power he so desperately desired. Someone needed to stop him, for every act he committed became more twisted than the next. He had many victims, but one in particular was the prey he sought the most, and this evening was no exception.

With his all-encompassing ego in hand, and an aura of preeminence, we exited his chamber in the darkest hour of night, slipping silently down the hall and around a corner that led to nowhere, or so it seemed. The old door that hid behind the dusty, heavy tapestry was known to but a select corrupt few. Making sure no one was in his presence, he lifted the tapestry and slipped behind it, slid his skeleton key into the lock, and quickly entered, revealing an abandoned stone stairwell, leading to a tunnel connecting seminary to convent. How convenient. An underground passageway for evil doings, a passageway that bore the same burdens as I, in that it also witnessed the shrouded happenings of the past. If the damp limestone could talk, it would tell stories of secret rendezvous between degenerate priests and naughty nuns. Of secret babies taken from their unwed mothers, misguided treasure hunts of stolen art, and stashed, sacred vessels. Tonight, if the walls could talk, they would tell of the trespass through their corridor of a self-serving demon on his way to violate a helpless lamb, while cloaked in the glorious stolen shroud of a selfless God.

As we exited the tunnel at the other end, our emergence was just as clandestine. A short wooden makeshift ladder led up to a trap door in the floor of the broom closet, forgotten in the back of the tiny chapel room in the Immaculate Conception Convent. It was quite a route to a final destination, but one that had to be taken so as not to be discovered. He was a stealthy predator, and I, his unwilling accomplice, a lustrous adornment abducted for the hideous journey.

I could feel the heat emanating from his body as my fibers tried to wick the droplets of sweat forming on his skin. I could feel the patter of his pulse racing from the adrenaline rushing through his veins, fueled by the perverse excitement he garnered from his malicious doings. At this point, I knew his thoughts, burning like fire, would conveniently blind his sight from witnessing his own dirty deeds. It was as if he willed himself to become destitute of vision and betrothed onto me the responsibility of recording every awful account. Before I knew it, we were standing in front of her door, the same door he had visited many times before as an unwanted, unsolicited intruder of the worst kind. A nightmare that never went away. More frightening in the light of day than in the dreams of the godforsaken.

Why he bothered knocking, I was not sure. Knocking was something a visitor did when they were politely waiting for the hostess to answer. There was nothing polite about this savage. He was not going to ask permission to be let in, he was going to take what he wanted.

As if on cue to my thoughts, he reached down and turned the doorknob. It was not locked, it served as no barrier between assailant and victim. We would enter the room, together. I was now sticking to his body like an extra layer of flesh. My beautiful luxurious fabric pasted onto him by his venomous sweat. No barrier between me and him. The stain of his soul being imprinted into my very being.

It was disgusting. I was humiliated by the depths of his depravity, but there was nothing I could do about it. I just hung there, an accessory, witness to a crime about to be committed.

Just a few feet away she sat quietly in prayer, kneeling with her back to the door. She was clothed in a humble black dress, made of a fabric lesser than mine, one saved for servants, not lords. But it didn't make her less of a person, for she was grand. Her goodness emanated beyond appearances. Even when she wore the black veil that was now draped on the chair next to her, her loveliness could not be hidden. But here she was, secluded in a sanctuary that existed under false pretenses. Her bare feet made her seem even more innocent, if that was possible. I wanted to scream at her, *Turn around! Fight! Run! Do whatever you can to get away from this monster!* But I was choking from the combination of the incense and sweat that drenched my being. Could she smell it? For it was ghastly.

As she knelt in silence, we approached and I felt sick to have a part in this play. I watched as he reached out his hand, rested it atop her head, and began stroking her auburn hair. She stayed frozen, like a fawn in the headlights, nary a twitch, praying he would just go away. But she knew better.

"Ahh, my child." I heard him say as he slowly and deliberately petted the hair on the top of her head. "Are you ready to atone for your sins?"

Still no movement, no acknowledgement of our presence.

"I have come here to absolve you from all of your transgressions," he fabricated, now patting harder on her hair, his tone changing as I felt his heartbeat start to pound in his chest.

"You know that you are in violation of all that is sacred and holy," he lied as he grabbed a handful of all the hair he could fit in his clenched fist.

She let out a small gasp. He pulled her head back by her hair, forcing her to look at us. Forcing me to look at her. As her head was tilted back, tears ran from the outer corners of her frightened eyes, back toward her ears. Still grabbing her hair with his right hand he took her face in his left hand, squeezing her cheeks so hard it made her mouth pucker. His face was inches away from hers

"You are a dirty harlot with lust and desire oozing out of every pore!" His brandy-tainted breath punctuated every word. "You are lucky I am here to exorcise you of your demons," he hissed, like the serpent he was. He lifted me above his waist, exposing himself, and shoved himself into her mouth. She gagged as he thrust himself into her face. "You will be absolved of your sins. I am the one with the power and the glory. I am the one who will forgive you of your trespass. You are too lascivious for your own good, whore!"

He pulled himself away from her and pushed her to the floor, lifting up her dress to expose her panties. It was then I saw her still clutching her rosary, with a grip so tight, her knuckles were white; she was not intending to let it go. But where was her God now? How could he help her?

"I will gain access to your carnal soul," he whispered loud into her face as he tore her panties from her body. The corner of her mouth was bloodied from the force of his previous aggressions. I felt so dirty. My beautiful vestment remained crushed between his putrid sweat and her fragile body. She closed her eyes tight, seemingly willing herself to disappear so as not to have to experience the raping of her very existence. He forced himself into her, letting out an animalistic moan. "Aargh, repent for your sins. Repent for your sins. Repent for your sins," he repeated over and over as her face was buried deep into my soaked fibers.

I wanted to comfort her. I wanted to help her escape this torture. I wished I could suffocate her so she would not exist in this space anymore. But I had no power. I was ruined, dirtied, changed from a royal vestment to a corrupt and contaminated rag.

"Repent for your sins. Repent for your sins. Rep—YEOHH!" He screamed in pain.

I felt the force of the pointed tip rip straight through my textile and into his skin. She had taken the rosary she held so tightly, the crucifix filed to a sharp point, and plunged it deep into his chest. Not deep enough to kill him, unfortunately. But deep enough to rip into his flesh, cutting into him. He reeled back in pain, looking down at the rosary still hanging from his body. He just stared at it, shocked that his sacrifi-

cial lamb had fought back. She stood to face him, face us, with a defiance in her eyes brought on by an animal instinct, possessing her in
order for her to escape the corner she was backed into.

She lunged toward him, blood clotting on the side of her mouth,
blood dripping down her legs, a fire burning in her eyes. Eyes set on
that crucifix. I knew she wanted to plunge it deeper into his chest, to
strike the empty cavern where his heart should be. He knew it too. As
she grabbed the rosary he pulled away and ran for the door like the true
coward he was. If only she had known his cowardice all along, all the
times he had allowed himself into her room and stole her innocence. If
I could have shoved that crucifix deep into his heart myself, I would
have. I clung to that crucifix with all my might. My fabric tendrils
wrapped tightly around the very symbol of love and forgiveness.
Wrapped so tightly that when she caught the rosary in her hand, and he
ran toward the door, it pulled away a tattered piece of me. My silken,
dirty, tainted, bloodied shard of fabric was ripped from me and left
hanging on the crucifix, to stay with her for the rest of her days. Saved,
to tell her story to the one who was gifted enough to hear it.

She ran to the door and slammed it shut; she wedged the back of a
chair underneath the doorknob to prevent re-entry. She fell to the floor,
curled into a ball and sobbed, holding her dear sweet Jesus and me up
to her face as she did. Tears falling on us, washing away our mortal
sins.

SEAN HAD to let Father Giuseppe Riccio leave the station for the time
being. There was no DNA evidence ready that would pin him to
Sophie's abuse. Abuse that lead her to end her life. It took Joann quite
a while to find a technician skilled enough to use the new apparatus,
and it was going to take more time than expected to yield some results.
Especially results that would match the blood on the crucifix and the
tattered swatch of fabric. The one good thing they did have was the
chalice Jimmy's nephew grabbed during mass, right after Father Riccio
drank out of it. That was brilliant. The kid did an amazing job. If it was

his DNA on Sophie's evidence, they would be able to match it perfectly. But time was not on their side. For right after Sunday's mass, the newly ordained Bishop Riccio was booked on a plane to Rome, Italy. The monster would be blessed by the Pope at the Vatican, and once he was out of the country, he would be gone forever.

40

EVIL INCARNATE

"Where have you been?" she asked, looking less like the Reverend Mother Superior and more like Ailene Aherne as she barged into Father Riccio's room without knocking, interrupting his packing.

"What are you doing here?" He spun around. She had startled him. "Don't you know how to knock, woman? Did anyone see you coming in here?"

"No! No one saw me coming. Do you think you're the only one who knows how to travel between these buildings unseen?"

Ah yes! When the Reverend Mother was still a young Sister Mary Runa, she took the name Runa because it meant secret love. For a little while, she held a candle for her beloved Giuseppe Riccio. So pathetic. She would follow him, seemingly undetected, as he made his way through secret passageways and tunnels. Watching as Father Riccio, to all who knew him, held clandestine meetups with willing participants. It made her jealous. It hardened her heart, and that was his intention. He wanted to squash her stupid schoolgirl crush, once and for all. And squash it, he did. She stopped caring, after a while, and she stopped following him.

Eventually, his sexual encounters also stopped being consensual.

As his power grew, he started taking what he wanted, when he wanted. Sister Mary Runa did not know the details of his abuses and, as Mother Superior, she did not care to see them.

"Where were you?" she asked again.

"I was at the police station with your new friend, Detective McGovern. Apparently, he needed to speak to me."

"What did he want?"

"He was asking questions about Sister Mary Vincenza."

"Where is she?"

"I don't know where she is, you dolt! But she'd better show up soon or she is going to have holy hell to pay." He shook his head and straightened his shoulders. It was still too easy for her to ruffle his feathers.

"You told both of us you sent her to pick up the bishops. But now I know that's not true. She is nowhere to be found. The detective wants to speak to her tomorrow after your ordination. I told him we would meet him in the rectory after mass, but I cannot seem to locate her."

"Well that's your problem," he scoffed. "I will be on a plane out of the country when the mass is over. I will be meeting with the Pope in Rome, while you are still trying to find that bitch. That is your mess to clean up, not mine."

Her eyes narrowed, and through tight, bloodless lips, she ground out, "MY mess? You think this is MY mess? I've been cleaning up YOUR messes for years. Covering up your dalliances. Making excuses for your absences. Getting rid of all the evidence of your family's business dealings. Who do you think has protected you for the past four damn decades?"

He began to clap slowly. "Oh BRA-vo! Let's hear it for the Martyr Superior. I never asked you to clean up anything for me. Do you know what I had to put up with? Watching your pathetic existence. You following me around like a lost puppy dog, begging for my attention? You should get on your knees and thank God, every day, that you can actually have contact with me. You should be honored that I even give you the time of day, you whore!" *I am a glorious, fucking asshole!*

Mother Superior stopped. Just stood there. She just stared at him, loathing written on her face, her eyes as hard as stone. She turned and walked out. Without saying a word. It scared the shit out of him.

41

DON'T CROSS MOTHER

It was nine forty-five Sunday morning by the time Detective McGovern reached St. Catherine's Cathedral. He had stopped by the station to check on any initial DNA results. There was nothing yet. As he approached the cathedral, parishioners flowed up the vast expanse of stairs and in through the massive double doors of the recently sanitized church, to bear witness to the ordination of Father Giuseppe Riccio as their new bishop. Little did they know their beloved priest was not divine at all, but evil incarnate.

Sean merged in with the flock. Ascending the cement stairs one by one, he could feel the vibrations of the church bell's peal, echoing through his own chest as it was rung to summon one and all to the impending spectacle. Upon entering the doors of the cathedral, memories of his childhood anxiety weighed on him. A sea of candles surrounded the entire perimeter of the vestibule. Glowing invocations. They were lined up in staggered, ascending rows, fiery wicks flickering through red glass. Most likely lit by the innocent, offering their devotional prayers to the heavens. Seeing the flames, he started to perspire. They were the same candles. The candles he saw in Sophie's lonely apartment. Was she ever lucky enough to be able to light a wick in gratitude? Or, were her prayers silent pleas to her God to end her suffering at the hands of the monster who abused her? The monster who was about to be the next bishop of this unwitting congregation. His heart started to pound. His breathing became strained. His stomach knotted as trusting churchgoers dipped their fingertips into pristine bowls of holy water, perched atop marble pedestals, on either side of the aisle. They blessed themselves to leave behind the secular and enter into the sacred world of the church. If only they knew their elder's life was a mockery of all they held sacred.

The pious genuflected toward the altar before they piled into pews, one by one, making room for each other, so each pew was packed from end to end with the devoted. Like sardines at a sermon, they sat shoulder to shoulder in awe of the majesty of the cathedral. The room began to close in on Sean. He failed to notice the details of the handsome basilica. Its Gothic architecture punctuated by grand chandeliers. Chiseled saints, set within the recesses of the walls, keeping watch over the prayerful, unsuspecting congregation, while stained glass windows rose from floor to soaring ceiling, its plaster walls painted with idyllic, cherubic frescoes.

The altar was draped in silken fabrics of shimmering gold and amaranth red. Feeling faint, Sean tried to focus on the two ornate baroque candelabras that flanked the altar. The heavy brass fixtures were almost as tall as the detective himself. He had seen a matching pair outside the front doors of the church.

The first few rows, right in front of the altar, were awash in a sea of black—a gaggle of nuns. Those he did not know and a few he recognized. He saw Sister Mary Teresa and Sister Ave Margaret, both sitting next to each other, dressed in their habits and looking much younger than their years. He also saw the Reverend Mother Superior, looking more stern than ever, sitting in the front row, rosary in hand, praying. Every once in a while, she glanced around as if looking for someone. Sister Mary Vincenza, perhaps? It made his blood boil knowing that Sophie, Sister Mary Vincenza, was not here in the church she loved. She would never be there again. Because of the monster who was to be celebrated in a few minutes.

The organist started to play, signaling the congregation to rise to its feet and turn to the back of the church to witness the procession of the visiting clergy. The old priests and bishops had just arrived and were gathering in the vestibule. As the congregation turned, Sean saw all eyes were on him. He was standing in the center of the aisle, at the back of the church, blocking the procession. Did they all recognize a grown man having an anxiety attack? He did not move, until he heard a gentle voice behind him. "Excuse me, son, can you take a seat so that we may proceed?" He turned and saw a kindly old priest smiling at him, peeking past the altar boy leading the procession, wielding an oversized crucifix. Sean smiled. This priest seemed like one of the good guys, but who knew anymore?

As Sean stepped to the side, he saw Officer Joseph Caputo enter the church. Sean signaled to him to watch the doors. "Don't let anyone out," he mouthed to his friend, who in turn signaled to the other officers waiting on standby outside, to stake out the rear and sides of the church.

With hymnal music blaring and the congregation singing along, the procession had started and slowly made its way down the aisle. Sean, seeing no end to the line of clergymen, decided to cut through.

"I'm sorry, Fathers," he addressed the ordained as he walked forward and down the aisle, hurrying to take a seat. His cotton mouth made it hard for him to swallow. Sisters Mary Teresa and Ave Margaret recognized him and whispered into each other's ears as the other nuns looked confused, seeing the detective disrupt the holy event. Mother Superior looked appalled as he took a seat right next to her. He gave her a lopsided smile. Suddenly, and without warning, his anxiety subsided. A calm washed over him and he was focused once more.

"Best seat in the house," he said to her.

She shushed him and looked forward toward the altar. The detective was surprised by the formality of the mass for the ordination. It had been a long time, and even then, he'd never witnessed such a thing. Songs were sung as another procession of clergy made up of local and visiting priests walked forward, bowed to the cross and made their way to the right of the altar. Next, very dramatic organ music set the mood for another seemingly endless line of clergy. This time bishops from all over the world entered the cathedral, parading in and filling up the other side of the altar. Having not been to church his entire adult life and brazenly seated next to the Reverend Mother, Sean had a moment of unease, feeling unworthy of his front row seat. His boldness held in check by divine intervention. The last members of the procession looked like the Knights of the Templar, wielding swords and sporting marabou feathered hats. Sean was almost moved by the service. But then HE entered. The one that all the fuss was about, and once again the semblance of a circus returned. There he was. The last in line. The devil himself. Father Giuseppe Riccio made his way up the aisle, appearing to bask in the fawning adoration of the congregation. Shrouding his repugnance in a shimmering robe. Sean grit his teeth. If only his loyal parishioners saw the ugly, malevolent beast hidden behind the regalia.

As Father Giuseppe Riccio passed the crowd, they cooed and whispered hushed prayers, feeling blessed to be in his presence. He passed the gaggle of nuns. Some smiled, some prayed with eyes closed. All clung to their rosaries, counting prayers and beads. Sean noted that few cried with devotion, and a handful seemed to squirm in their pews. Sisters Mary Teresa and Ave Margaret were holding each other up, clinging to each other for dear life. As Father Riccio approached, he locked eyes with the detective, and Sean saw a hitch in his step. Just a very slight hesitation. Sean smirked.

As the priest passed the detective, Sean got a closer glimpse of his robe. A small patch was sewn into the chest area to repair what must have been a hole. A hole, that Sean would bet, matched the piece of fabric tucked safely away in Sophie's drawer.

Sean checked his phone, and Mother Superior gave him a reprimanding side eye. There was no message from Joann yet. She was to text him as soon as she got the DNA results back from the lab. All the detective could think of was Sophie. He saw her in the flickering wicks of the pure white candles melting onto the brass of the heavy golden candelabras. He saw her in the faces of the cherubs painted into the ceiling frescoes, tears in their eyes as they touched the feet of their sweet Jesus dying on the cross. He saw her on the cross itself, crucified for being too innocent and pure. This filled his heart with rage, and he was growing more impatient by the minute. Through every sermon and every song, he waited for the message from Joann, telling him to proceed with the arrest. To stop the promotion of a madman parading as a priest. *Hurry up, Jo! We've gotta get him before he boards that plane.*

Father Giuseppe Riccio knelt on the altar, in front of his whole congregation, looking for all the world as if he were a saint. Sean's gorge began to rise. This madman was not a saint—he wasn't even a good man! He was a failure of a human being. As each bishop took turns touching the top of Father Riccio's head, blessing him, Sean half expected the demon to burst into flames. The idea of that visual consumed him. He didn't notice Joann slide into the pew right next to him until she whispered "Well, well, I never thought I'd see you in the first row at church."

"Joann! I thought you were going to text me," he whispered back. Mother Superior was now glaring at both of them, like naughty children.

"There was no phone service in the lab." Joann added, "Plus, I wouldn't miss this for the life of me."

"The ordination?" Sean asked.

"No, you nailing his ass." She paused for a second. "It's a match." She squeezed Sean's hand. Sean felt his heart leap into his throat.

"The DNA is a match?" he asked, needing to confirm what he'd just heard. "The DNA from Sophie's items is a match to the DNA on the chalice?" he whispered loudly, drawing another shush from the Reverend Mother.

"Yes!" replied Joann. "What are you waiting for?" She handed him the paperwork.

Detective McGovern turned around to see Officer Caputo standing in the back of the Cathedral, and as the Archbishop reached to anoint Father Giuseppe Riccio with holy oil, Sean stood. "Stop right there!"

Mother Superior grabbed him by the arm, 'What are you doing?" she reprimanded. The organist stopped playing and all eyes were on Detective McGovern, once again.

"My son," said the Archbishop, "I beg your pardon. Why are you interrupting a holy ceremony?" Still on bended knee, Father Riccio turned around and glared at Sean.

"You cannot ordain this man. He is a criminal." The whole of the congregation gasped as Sean walked toward the altar.

Father Riccio now stood to face the detective. "You must be mad! What are you talking about?"

"You want to do this here, or do you want to come with me?" Sean maintained eye contact as he swept his arm out toward the congregation. "Your choice, Riccio."

"I am not coming with you—you can wait five minutes." Father Riccio defiantly knelt back down. "Continue, Archbishop!" he demanded. All of the other bishops and clergy were standing, dumbstruck.

The archbishop looked at the expectant priest and did nothing. He looked at Sean, then back at Father Riccio. "What is he talking about, Father Riccio?" he asked. "Have you sinned?" Sean crossed his arms; Riccio's indignation was amusing him.

"Just anoint me, Archbishop!" he spat, trying to grab the holy oil from the Archbishop's hand. The Archbishop pulled away as the criminal continued, "It's fine! This man doesn't know what he is talking about! Anoint me!"

Sean uncrossed his arms, wielding the paperwork Joann had handed him. Paperwork in hand, he spoke gently to the confused Archbishop. "Your Holiness, we have DNA evidence proving Father Riccio raped a young woman." He stepped closer and put out a precautionary arm as the color drained from the elderly priest's face. "He is unfit to be a priest, let alone a bishop," Sean grabbed the rapist's arm. "Father Giuseppe Anthony Riccio, you are under arrest for the sexual assault and battery of Sophie Rae."

Another gasp, louder this time, from the gaggle of nuns. Mother Superior rose. "Detective!" she scolded, "What are you talking about?"

Sean turned and answered her. "He has raped a woman, repeatedly, over the course of many years, and she has taken her own life due to the unbearable shame and pain of it all."

The archbishop moved away from Father Riccio. The visiting clergy all looked on in bewilderment as they whispered to each other.

Father Riccio rose. "I don't even know a Sophie Rae! You are a lying fool!" he laughed.

"Oh, that's right," Sean said. "You know her as Sister Mary Vincenza." The crowd, still seated, gasped in horror. Sean imagined that Sister Mary Vincenza's work in the community was known by many of those attending. He glanced at the gaggle of nuns and saw tears, shock, outrage, and the shattered visage of other possible victims. "Turn around and place your hands behind your back," he ordered the priest.

"You don't know what you are doing, Detective. You don't know who I am. You will be sorry!" the priest seethed. "You can't keep me locked up! You have no proof!"

"I have all the proof I need," Sean replied as he clicked on the handcuffs and started to lead the priest away from the altar and down to the aisle.

Mother Superior stepped in front of them and confronted Father Riccio, "What have you done?"

"What do you care what I've done? It's none of your business what I've done!" he hissed at her, then he addressed the congregation. "It's none of anyone's business what I have done! You are all sinners and whores!" The audience gasped. The fallen priest turned back to Mother Superior. "You're the biggest whore of all! If you weren't such a failure, life would be different for the both of us! It's all your fault my life ended up this way!"

"I couldn't help it our baby died!" she blurted out. "That was in God's hands."

The congregation was silent, mouths agape. Confusion contorted the mass of startled faces.

"HA!" He laughed like a madman, eyes wild with fury, "You idiot! The baby didn't die! The baby was given away, because you were a stupid pregnant girl, raised by a stupid Mick. They took the baby away from you, Ailene. They gave it away!"

Sean could not believe what he was seeing and hearing. Mother

Superior's face went dead white, and she began to sway. She reached back to try to find something to hold on to as she stumbled back into the pew. A few of the other nuns started to tend to her. Sean wasn't exactly sure what Riccio had said to her, but whatever it was, it was too much for her to bear.

"C'mon," Sean said, yanking on Riccio's arm, "that's enough from you!"

One could have heard a hummingbird's wing beat as Sean lead Riccio past the sea of black. Slowly nuns began to stand, one here, one there, staring vehemently at the outed rapist. Sister Ave Margaret rose as well and stepped out into the aisle. She spat into the priest's face.

"I hope you rot in hell, you son of a bitch." She turned to Sean, tears in her eyes. "Sister Mary Vincenza was not the only one."

Sean's heart constricted as he watched her return to her seat, ever grateful Sister Mary Teresa was there for her as they both cried and comforted each other.

Looking back at Riccio, Sean clenched the priest's arm until he winced, then, with deliberate and slow steps, he walked the fallen priest down the center aisle of St. Catherine's Cathedral. It was a long walk of shame for the fallen Father Giuseppe Riccio. Every single person's disapproving eyes were on the corrupt holy man. They all got a good look at him as Sean led him through the vestibule and out the front doors. Sean could hear the chatter of the crowd erupt inside the cathedral as soon as he had the priest out of sight. He and Riccio were at the top of the stairs when Sean turned away from the priest toward Officer Caputo, "Can you read him his rights and put him in your squad car? I want to go back in to get a statement from Sister Ave Margaret."

"Sure," said Joey.

Suddenly, there was a loud crack. An unholy sound. Sean saw Father Riccio's knees buckle and his body torque, sending the priest plummeting down the cement stairs of the cathedral. Bone fractured upon cement. His hands cuffed behind his back, Riccio was unable to shield himself from the fall. His head and neck were defenseless against the brutal impact. Tumbling down. Stair by stair. Riccio's bruised and broken body rested in a mangled mass of bloodied silk.

Sean turned to see Mother Superior standing at the top of the stairs, a bent candelabra in her hands as wax dripped from the overturned candles, their extinguished flames replaced by the fiery rage burning in her eyes.

Someone shouted, "Call for an ambulance!"

42

KARMA

The ticking clock echoed in the eerily quiet hallway of Mercy Hospital while a slight whooshing of the respirator, the one that was doing the breathing for Father Giuseppe Riccio, could be heard through the closed door of room 926. Detective McGovern chatted with the police officer assigned to watch the door of the fallen priest.

"Wow, it sure is quiet in this place," Sean said as he handed the officer a black coffee in a Styrofoam cup. "Here, this will help keep you awake."

"Thanks, Detective." The officer took the cup and blew the steam from the top.

Sean ticked his head toward the priest's hospital door. "You gonna be alright watching over this one?"

"I'll be fine. He's paralyzed from the neck down, he ain't going nowhere."

"Yeah. Fucker! I'd like to see him try to use his dick now." Sean was not joking.

"What makes a guy do shit like that, Detective?"

"I dunno. Power, rage. Just sick in the head, I guess."

"I heard he's connected."

"Yep. That's why you're here. No visitors in or out, okay? Only cleared medical personnel."

"Got it! I heard a nun bashed him in the spine when you weren't looking." The officer took a sip of coffee, suddenly embarrassed he'd called out the detective for not keeping an eye on his suspect.

Sean let out a huff, "Yeah."

"Sorry detective I didn't mean t—"

"Don't worry about it." He shrugged. "Karma, I guess."

A few minutes passed. The clock was the only one who had anything to say.

"I got this detective. You can go," said the officer. "It'll be fine."

"Okay, Deputy. I've got a lot a shit to finish anyway. I'll see you at the station." Sean left the officer to finish his work undistracted.

The deputy watched as the detective entered the elevator, pressed the button, and gave a wave as the doors closed. Just then, the scritch of a squeaky wheel was added to the vacuous soundtrack. An orderly pushed a hospital cart toward the officer.

"It's time for his meds," said the man.

The deputy stood from his seat stationed in front of the door. "ID?"

The orderly presented his identification to the officer, who checked it against his list of approved personnel. The officer then patted him down, making sure no weapons were concealed beneath his lab coat or scrubs. He also checked around and under the metal cart. Once cleared, the orderly was allowed to enter the room. The deputy resumed his position outside the door.

THE MAN casually wheeled the squeaky cart over to Father Giuseppe Riccio's bedside as if he'd done it countless times before. He lifted a syringe from the cart and squeezed out a bubble of air, projecting a mini stream of liquid up and out of the needle. He carefully injected the man's prescribed medicine into his IV.

Next, he tucked in the priest's bed sheets and blanket, making sure the father was snug as a bug in a rug. He fluffed one of the pillows behind the patient's head and removed the other for himself. He then stood there. Holding it. He waited for the paralyzed man to open his eyes.

Eventually, it happened. Father Riccio's eyes grew wide with fear as he recognized the man standing above him at his bedside. The orderly reached out and touched the scar right below the priest's left collarbone—the freshly healed wound torn by Sophie's sharpened crucifix only months before.

"She left her mark on you, Giuseppe," he said, pressing on the pink, raised scar and lifting his hand away. "Just as you've left a black mark on the family."

The priest could not move a muscle, nor could he speak. Tears trickled from the corners of his eyes.

"In this family, we don't rape nuns."

As the man placed the pillow over the priest's face, he whispered, "Uncle Salvatore is waiting for you."

43

CATCHING UP

S ean lit the candle on Sophie's dressing table and blew out the matchstick, causing a sulfur smoke signal to spiral up to heaven. On the table in front of him was his leather journal, the one with the notes on her case. While paging through it, he realized he had hardly written anything down over the course of his investigation. Most of his clues were the intuitive; quiet voices whispered into his ear when he least expected it. Not to mention the dreams. Inside his journal, he taped the pages from her Bible, the last torn chapter she had used to write her story on. He read it over and over again, wishing there was more, if only for the conversation.

He missed feeling Sophie's presence, missed his arm hairs standing on end, the vivid dreams, the oddities with the electricity. It all went away the day he found her letter and read what Father Riccio had done to her. It was the one job she had left to do: lead the detective to find her abuser. Once her job was complete, she seemed to disappear. He hoped she was in heaven. He prayed she was happy. Her memory as Sister Mary Vincenza was honored with a mass at St. Catherine's. The cathedral was packed with parishioners from the marbled floors to the frescoed ceilings. An anonymous donor provided the funds for her service, and she was buried in the private cemetery on the Immaculate Conception Convent grounds, underneath the cherry blossom trees.

No one knows where Father Giuseppe Riccio was buried. It has been over a month since his death. The priest died in the hospital of asphyxiation when, somehow, his breathing tube had become dislodged. No one cared to ask any questions. If there were suspicions surrounding his death, Sean was not going to be the one to look into them. It turned out the monster was raping several of the nuns in the diocese, including Sister Ave Margaret.

There were fifteen lawsuits filed against the diocese for their failure to recognize his crimes. The confirmation of Father Giuseppe Riccio's DNA also uncovered the fact he had murdered his uncle, Father Salvatore Riccio, when the missing glass was found stashed in the back of Father Giuseppe Riccio's armoire. Mickey's cold case was solved, leading to further investigations into the Riccio family, ultimately proving all of the racketeering rumors were true.

Sean thought of Mother Superior, who was taken into custody for the attempted murder of Father Riccio, but released on her own recognizance. She was currently awaiting her trial. Sean hoped the judge would be lenient on her, given that Father Riccio had taunted her with his knowledge of her child being stolen and given away. What other abuses had she suffered at his hands? It was no wonder she became temporarily insane and broke his spine with the heavy candelabra. The whole congregation saw him belittle her, and there were many letters being written to the judge on her behalf. They all felt empathy for the childless woman.

It turned out, in years past one of the church's other dirty secrets was stealing newborn babies from unwed teenage mothers and adopting them out to unwitting families. All the while telling the new mothers their babies had died. Sean felt a sadness for the Reverend Mother, living all those years thinking her baby had died. Forty years alone, when she could have actually had a child to love and nurture.

If there was a positive, when Giuseppe Riccio murdered his Uncle Salvatore the baby stealing ended there, as he was the ring-leader. The investigation into Father Riccio was long and deep, and new information was being discovered every day, all thanks to Sophie. Sean gathered up his journal and wrapped a rubber band around it. He pressed and jiggled the button hidden underneath Sophie's dressing table and unlocked the secret drawer. He placed his journal into the drawer and closed it, saying a little prayer of devotion to Sophie and blowing out the red candle in gratitude. His phone buzzed, making him jump out of his seat. He picked it up, "McGovern."

"Honey, it's Joann from the station."

He walked into his kitchen and grabbed a beer from the fridge, popped it open, and took a sip. "Hey Jo, how are your sparks doing?" He could hear her laugh-snort on the other end.

"They're Spanx, honey, and they're, thankfully, holding me together! Whatcha doing?"

"Ah, just putting some things away. What's up?"

"I just wanted to thank you, Sean, for helping to solve the Riccio murder. Mickey died, frustrated, never knowing the outcome. He knew someone had murdered the old priest, but they could never confirm it. I never thought I would live to see the day."

"You don't have to call me to thank me for something like that, Jo —it's my job."

"I know." She grew quiet.

"Is everything ok, Jo?"

"You sitting down, honey?"

"Yep," he lied as he walked back into the living room.

"So," she paused, "we're getting new information, every day, from the church on all of that crazy adoption drama from all those years ago, ya know?"

"Yeah?" he replied.

"I mean, they are in so much trouble from the fallout of Father Riccio's crimes, they just want to cooperate in any way possible. They are trying to make good."

" As they should! What a cluster over there." He took another swig of beer.

"Yeah, well, they are handing over records that were previously buried when the old priest Salvatore died. Secret files, ya know? Names of doctors, and mothers, and all."

"Yup. So?"

"Within the records there's a baby boy, Sean. He jumps out from the paperwork, you know, because of who his birth parents were. He was adopted out to a local family…around forty years ago."

A flood of goosebumps washed over Sean's body as he sat himself down on his sofa. "What are you trying to tell me, Jo?" he asked, watching the droplets of sweat form on his beer.

"Well, honey, this baby was adopted by the McGoverns. By your mom and dad. This baby was you."

"Shit," he said. He loved his adopted parents no matter what. "And you know who my birth parents are."

"Yes, honey, I do."

Sean looked across the room at Sophie's dressing table. He could see his distant reflection in its mottled mirror as it peacefully watched his every move, urging him to live his truth.

"Well, go ahead then," he said. "Let's have it."

"Sean, your birth mother's name, is Ailene…Ailene Aherne."

44

O'DOYLE'S

Old neon buzzed in a hushed O'Doyle's as Sean sat at the bar staring into his drink. Joann and Joey were perched in silence on either side of him as Jimmy leaned in close to the huddled group.

Sounds of the street rushed in as the door of the bar opened, filling the room with the cacophony of traffic for just a moment and then sucked back out just as quickly as the door closed. Sean didn't notice. He was in deep, meditative thought, eyeing the patterns in his ice cubes as he replayed everything that had transpired over the past weeks. It was only when the hair on his arms stood at attention did Sean look up at Jimmy, who ticked his head toward the small table next to the front door.

There she was. Sean almost didn't recognize her as she sat at the table. She was dressed in her street clothes, with flowing raven hair barely salted with gray, set free from the confines of her veil. At that moment, she looked less like Mother Superior and more like Ailene Aherne. Vulnerable. Hands clasped on the table in front of her, the thumb of one hand trying to soothe the other.

Sean rose from his seat and walked toward her. His heart drummed his ribcage so forcefully, he was certain it was audible in the quiet room.

As Sean approached Ailene, his hazel eyes locked with hers, knowing she finally recognized herself in him as her eyes searched his face, looking for—longing for—the lifetime they never had together. She opened her mouth to speak, but no words came out—only a gasp for air and quiet sobs as forty years of tears were finally set free.

A hitch in his own breath, Sean reached out toward his birthmother's folded hands, placing his own over hers. Ailene kissed the hands of the son she never knew, and like nothing ever before in his life, a flood of warmth and knowing washed over him.

FIN.

AFTERWORD

If you or anyone you know are having thoughts about suicide, please
reach out for help.
Talk to a family member, a friend, a neighbor, a stranger…just talk to
someone. You are not alone.

National Suicide Prevention Lifeline
1-800-273-8255

ACKNOWLEDGMENTS

THANK YOU, for taking the time to read my novel. I am grateful beyond words. Without readers, our books would be orphans, our stories would go unread and our imaginations would grow stagnant. You are the reason we strive to assemble words thoughtfully and artfully.

Also, thank you so much to all who have helped me along the way, it was fun to complete this project with your time, undivided attention and input. Tex Thompson, thank you for selflessly sharing all of your wordcrafting wisdom.

Officer Maureen (Mo) Messner, thank you for your continued consult and wise suggestions, and most of all for your service. Your life's dedication to protect us has not gone unnoticed.

My Book Club Alphas - Susan, Sandy, Leann, Kris, Lori, JoAnn, Melissa, April and Amy, thank you for accepting the task of reading through the very first iteration of this novel and sharing your thoughts with me. I appreciate your overlooking my typos and grammatical errors in order to digest the story and give me your honest input.

My critique sisters, Jane and Janet, thank you for reading each week and sharing your eyes, edits and ideas, you make me a better writer. Jane you're an amazing editor! Most of all thank you both for your support, it's so much fun to be in your group.

My gifted friend Brian Guilliaux, for helping me create the exact cover I saw in my head. Your eye is amazing and your talent is beyond. You make me strive to be a better artist.

Marge, the best mom a girl could have, for reading at hyper-speed and giving me spot on advice that helped in developing my characters.

My family, Mark, Roman and Marcella - my loves my life - for forever supporting my crazy ideas and giving me the time needed to see them to fruition.

Roman and Marcella you are my heart and soul and YOUR individual gifts are endless, use them fully, nurture them, grow them, never take no for an answer, work hard and have NO FEAR. I am forever proud of you… xx

ABOUT THE AUTHOR

CHERIE FRUEHAN is an artist and writer who was born and raised in Scranton, Pennsylvania. She earned her BFA from Marywood, University and credits her education as inspiring her to dabble in all things creative. She now resides in Dallas, Texas with her husband and two dogs. A member of MENSA, her artwork has been featured on the front cover and inside pages of MENSA magazine. The Suicide of Sophie Rae is her first novel.

www.cheriefruehan.com

She is currently working on her second novel
Dinner With The Hawthornes

facebook.com/cheriefruehanofficial

twitter.com/cheriefruehan

instagram.com/cheriefruehan